Wolf Tales II

Wolf Tales II

KATE DOUGLAS

APHRODISIA

KENSINGTON PUBLISHING CORP.
http://www.kensingtonbooks.com

To paraphrase a well-known politician, it takes a village to write a book. I am so fortunate to have such a terrific village supporting me—friends who are so willing to read my rough drafts and be brutally honest in their assessment—sometimes a little too brutal, if you want the truth! My sincere thanks to Camille Anthony, Dakota Cassidy, Sheri Carucci, Ann Jacobs, Shelby Morgan, Willa Okati, Treva Harte, Cassie Walder and Karen "MT" Williams. These are just a few of the people who help me bring my Chanku to life.

APHRODISIA BOOKS are published by

Kensington Publishing Corp.
850 Third Avenue
New York, NY 10022

All Kensington Titles, Imprints, and Distributed Lines are available at special quantity discounts for bulk purchases for sales promotions, premiums, fund-raising, and educational or institutional use.

Special book excerpts or customized printings can also be created to fit specific needs. For details, write or phone the office of the Kensington special sales manager: Kensington Publishing Corp., 850 Third Avenue, New York, NY 10022, attn: Special Sales Department, Phone: 1-800-221-2647.

Aphrodisia and the A logo are trademarks of Kensington Publishing Corp.

ISBN 0-7582-1387-5

First Kensington Trade Paperback Printing: July 2006

10 9 8 7 6 5 4 3 2

Printed in the United States of America

Prologue

San Francisco, California—January 1986

A gun-metal-gray sky closed in upon the small group of mourners standing near an open grave. Ulrich Mason glanced down at the tiny hand clasped in his and wondered once again how any father went about explaining death to a six-year-old.

Mommy's gone to live with the angels? That, of course, raised the question of why Mommy loved the angels more than she loved Tia or Daddy. *God needs Mommy in heaven?* How could God possibly need Mommy more than they did? Mommy belonged here, alive and laughing, her strength a tangible support in the structure of their lives.

The small fingers wrapped in his large hand trembled. Ulrich took a deep breath and closed his eyes against the pain.

Damn you, Camille!

How the hell could she leave them like this? Damn her, she'd done things her own way, in spite of the risk.

How the hell was he going to survive without her?

And what about Tianna? Ulrich leaned down, lifted his daughter easily, and held her tightly against his shoulder.

The expected, "I'm a big girl, Daddy. Put me down," went unsaid. Instead he felt Tianna's bony little frame shudder, heard her soft, broken sigh, then lifted his chin to make room for the defeated press of her head against his throat. She tucked herself tightly under his jaw. Tianna's wild frizz of blond curls, so beautiful against her deeply bronzed skin, tickled his ear.

The minister's soft words floated in and out of Ulrich's reality. Caught in the rhythm of Tianna's warm breath against his throat, he inhaled her clean, fresh-soap, little-girl scent. He was only peripherally aware of the scuffling and quiet movements of the few mourners standing around the grave and the steady hum of traffic on a nearby freeway.

Ulrich let his memories wander back to Camille. Warm and alive, she paused just outside his consciousness, smiling that secretive, seductive smile that had caught and held him so neatly just eight short years ago.

He felt her warmth, her love, her strong, courageous nature, and, most of all, her amazing sensuality surrounding him, holding both of them close. Camille's beautiful eyes, caught somewhere between green and gold, sparkled in the sunlight. She raised her hand, her silky skin shades darker than their daughter's, and beckoned him, calling. . . .

A soft tap on his shoulder yanked Ulrich back. He blinked, noticed the minister had closed his Bible, saw the other mourners now talking quietly among themselves. Ulrich turned slowly to see who had touched him, who had dragged him away from visions of Camille.

A tall, powerfully built young man wearing Marine Corps dress blues stood beside him.

"Captain Mason?"

Ulrich shifted Tianna's slight weight in his arms. She sagged against him, asleep finally after so many sleepless nights. "Yes. I'm Ulrich Mason."

As tall as Ulrich and darkly handsome, the mourner could have been any young marine officer, though there was something about him, something Ulrich sensed beneath the clean-cut surface. A friend of Camille's? A lover? Ulrich didn't recognize him—at least, not at first.

"I . . ." The man looked away, down at his sharply polished shoes, back at Ulrich. "I am . . ."

The truth exploded in Ulrich's mind, took the breath from his lungs. Suddenly made sense in a most horrible manner. "You are the one who shot my wife." Ulrich nodded at the man's stricken look. "I thought so."

"I am so sorry, Captain Mason. It was a horrible accident, it was . . ."

"It was inevitable." Ulrich sighed and rubbed his chin against Tia's silky crown. Suddenly he felt much older than his forty-three years, and very, very tired. He stared into the younger man's amber eyes, eyes very much like his own, very much like Camille's, and knew exactly what he had to do.

"You . . . this . . . all of it makes Camille's death even more tragic, if that is at all possible." With one last glance at the dark scar in the earth, the final resting place for his beloved wife, Ulrich turned away.

The young man waited, obviously confused. Ulrich stopped. "Aren't you coming?"

"With you?"

"Of course." Impatient now, facing the path he knew his life must take, Ulrich shifted his small daughter's weight in his arms and led his wife's killer across the wet grass toward the parking lot.

Ulrich tucked the soft blanket under Tianna's chin, brushed the tangled strands back from her forehead and left a light kiss on her temple. He watched her a moment as she settled into sleep, so much like her mother in spite of her lighter brown skin and yellow hair, it made his heart ache. He backed away quietly with a prayer in his soul that somehow they would find a routine, a way to go on.

Without Camille. He'd never imagined anything like this. He'd always thought he would die first, of course . . . but not for many, many years. A slight sound from below caught Ulrich's attention, brought him back to his place here in his daughter's doorway at the head of the stairs. There was no use putting it off any longer. With a last glance toward Tianna, Ulrich went down to talk with the man who had changed all their lives with a single, well-placed gunshot.

It felt terribly awkward, waiting here in the living room, surrounded by photos, keepsakes, and the almost palpable essence of the woman whose life he'd ended. Waiting while her grieving husband put their beautiful daughter to bed, wondering why he'd agreed to come here, knowing there'd been no other choice.

Lucien Stone reached for a small portrait on the mantel and looked into the eyes of Camille Mason. He'd seen pictures of her, snapshots in color and black and white, photos the press had splashed all over the front page in the five days since she had died, but not this one. Not one of her smiling into the lens, laughter evident in the sparkling eyes, the deep dimple on her left cheek. Damn, other than Tianna's lighter coloring, their daughter was the spitting image of her mother. What was she now? Five, maybe six. . . . Tianna Mason was going to drive her father crazy someday . . . along with every little boy in the classroom.

Luc was still staring at the photo when Tianna's father entered the room.

Carefully he set the picture back on the mantel and turned toward Ulrich Mason. A rookie cop fresh out of the marines, Luc had heard of Mason, though never met him before. As big as the San Francisco Police Department was, Luc knew very few officers outside his own precinct.

The huge man stood on the last step. His broad shoulders stooped, his entire body shouted exhaustion, grief . . . the misery of a strong man brought down.

All Luc's fault. If only . . .

Ulrich straightened and was immediately the imposing, intimidating figure Luc recalled from the publicity photos, the standard shots of the young police captain whose beautiful wife had been tragically killed.

Mason's demeanor and voice commanded attention. "You're still a rookie, aren't you? New to the force?"

"Yes, but . . ."

Ulrich stepped into the room. "I want you to tell me exactly what happened last Friday, exactly what you saw."

Luc took a step back, challenged by the quiet threat in Mason's voice. He fought an unexplainable urge to grovel at Mason's feet. "It's in the reports, sir. I'm sure you've seen them."

"No. Not your official report. I've read it, the one that says you saw a naked African-American woman run out of the woods and thought she was a threat to a group of schoolkids. Tell me, Officer Stone, what really happened. Exactly the way you recall. What you saw that night. This is between you and me. It's not for the police. It's not for any court proceedings, nor any investigation. It's for me. Camille Mason's husband. I want the truth."

The truth. Did he really believe anymore? Luc stared down at his hands, remembering. When he looked up, Mason was handing him a glass of brandy. A peace offering? The crystal goblet reflected the light from the overhead chandelier and felt warm in the palms of his hands. Luc took a deep breath and almost smiled at the stupidity of his next move.

He would tell Ulrich Mason exactly what he saw before he killed the captain's wife.

First Luc took a long swallow of the brandy and blinked against his quick tears from the potent liquor. He cleared his throat and stared into the glass as he spoke.

"I was patrolling north of the park, close to the Presidio. There was an 'all points' out. Someone had spotted a wolf running near Fulton Way. It sounded absurd, but the orders were real and the dispatcher seemed serious. The caller said the animal snarled at a group of tourists and then disappeared into the bushes as though headed back into Golden Gate Park. Since I was close, I went for a quick look. I thought I heard screams coming from a wooded area near the Japanese Tea Garden. I drew my weapon and ran toward the sound."

He paused here, at the point where the truth he told Mason differed from the official story in his report. "That's when I saw it. Not a naked woman, definitely a wolf. Beautiful, alert, not at all like the pathetic creatures you see in a zoo. The animal turned and stared at me. . . . It wasn't afraid but I was stopped cold by a sense of uncanny intelligence, of almost human understanding." Luc paused, shook his head in denial, then whispered, "I had the strangest feeling, as if the wolf knew something about me, some great secret."

He turned and looked at Mason, caught in the image, the sense of wonder, of disbelief he'd felt. A wolf in Golden Gate Park! Mason stared back at him, unblinking.

"Just then a group of five or six kids came racing around the bend in the walking trail. They were screaming their heads off. I couldn't tell if they were scared or playing, but they headed right for the wolf. I shouted at them but I don't think they heard me. The wolf turned and crouched down low. I could see its teeth and I thought it might attack. It looked threatening, ready to spring. The kids were coming closer and I just reacted. I shot it. There was a moment of silence, the recoil of the gun in my hand. . . .

I'm amazed I was accurate at that distance." Again, he shook his head.

"I swear the wolf understood exactly what I'd done. It looked right at me again, and the really odd thing was, I felt almost like it was trying to talk to me, somehow to communicate. I swear, if I didn't know better, I . . ." Luc hung his head, feeling horribly sad, not a little bit foolish. He swallowed back the lump in his throat and looked up, directly into Mason's eyes. "I thought, for the briefest of moments, that the wolf forgave me, that it understood why I had to shoot it, but I know that's impossible."

He shrugged away the image—those intelligent eyes, the beautiful creature he'd killed. *If only* . . . Shaking off the sense of disbelief, Luc slowly continued. "Before I could react, the animal dropped in its tracks. The kids scattered, still screaming. By the time I reached the clearing, they were gone. Detectives were able to locate a few of them. They all heard the gunshot, but not one of them saw the wolf. They thought I was shooting at them and that's why they ran."

Ulrich Mason sipped at his brandy. His eyes were so deep-set, it was hard to tell their color. Luc had the strange sense he was gazing into his own eyes.

"What happened next?

Once again Luc stared into the brandy, wishing there were some way to change time, to return to the man he'd been before. He took a deep breath, remembering, and had to clear his throat to speak.

"I radioed for backup. I didn't say I'd shot a wolf. I mean, in Golden Gate Park? I couldn't believe it. I reported I'd fired my weapon and might have hit a large dog. Then I went to check on the wolf, to make sure it was dead. Instead of a wolf, I found a woman lying in the grass, naked. She was young, African-American, very beautiful. I checked for a pulse but couldn't find one. I'd aimed for the wolf's shoulder, hoping to hit something vital. The bullet had gone through her chest. She was dead. It wasn't until the next day I discovered the woman I killed was your wife."

Luc sat down hard on the leather couch, the brandy snifter clutched in both hands. He still had no idea how it had happened. How his bullet, intended to protect a group of children, had killed a woman. "I swear, Captain. I saw a wolf. I did not shoot at your wife. I don't know how the hell . . ."

Almost to himself, Mason whispered, "Always, you did it your way. Ah, Camille. I never dreamed . . ." Mason sighed. "Let me tell you about my wife, about Camille."

Luc felt the sofa dip as Mason sat down next to him, but he continued staring into the amber depths of his brandy.

"First, though, difficult as this is, I must thank you. You've been truthful even though your mind disbelieves what your eyes have seen."

Luc raised his head and stared at Mason. The older man looked back at him, his eyes the same odd shade of green and amber as Luc's. Why, Luc wondered, did that seem so terribly important?

"As unbelievable as it sounds, when you saw the wolf, you saw Camille, my wife." Mason looked away. He coughed, rubbed his hand across his eyes. Luc felt as if his own heart broke, mortally wounded by the fathomless pain in the other man's voice.

"She was unique in many ways, a woman of the forest. A woman destined to be my mate, the perfect match for me . . . but she was not what she seemed. Camille was not merely of African-American descent. She was a member of a unique race, a separate species, actually, long forgotten, often misunderstood. A species that gave rise to fearful legends and fantasies, almost all of them false. Still, she was impetuous, often careless, but always beloved. She was Chanku."

"What?" Luc leaned back to better see Ulrich. The man appeared lost in his own world of dreams and thought. "What do you mean . . . Chanku?"

"Chanku. A species of wolf native to the Himalayas." Ulrich turned and looked straight into Luc's eyes. "A species of wolf, but also human. Interchangeable, able to shift from one form to the other, with the intelligence of a human yet all the senses of its wild counterpart. The wolf you saw was my wife. The shift back to her human roots occurred at the time of her death. Camille, myself, our daughter . . . and, if I am not mistaken, you, Lucien Stone, are all Chanku."

Chapter 1

Oakland, California—August 2006

Luc sipped his brandy and stared out the large bay window of Ulrich Mason's Marina District home and reflected on the night's mission while he waited for his commander's return. Things had gone better than expected—the young kidnap victim was unharmed and now safe with his parents. Even better, the intelligence had been good, for a change.

Lights reflected off the bay. Traffic, even this late at night, still raced along Marina Boulevard. The rest of the pack had gone off to their respective homes for the night, all heading toward a group of apartments carved out of an old Victorian mansion in the Sunset District. The boy had been returned safely to his parents, the press kept totally out of the story, and the first, cursory debriefing was complete.

There would be time for more details later, after they'd all caught up on some badly needed sleep, but for now Luc appreciated a moment to merely sit and relax and enjoy the pleasurable feeling of a job well done.

What did he have to go home to, anyway? There was no mate waiting, no children. No life beyond the camaraderie of the pack and whatever job came next.

Since the terrorist attack on New York, the pack had worked overtime, their unique abilities in demand by the government as never before. A small band of men, all Chanku, brought together by one retired police captain who long ago had recognized his own heritage and realized he could not be the only shape-shifter in existence.

Still, Luc could count on one hand the number of Chanku recruited by Ulrich Mason over the last twenty years to work in Pack Dynamics, the cover for a force so secret even the president was unaware of its identity. Four other men, ranging in age from the newest member, barely into his midtwenties, to Luc, now forty-one. Not counting the commander, of course. Ulrich Mason was an entity unto himself.

There were other Chanku out there. Others with the unique ability to shift from human to wolf, but, just as Luc had been ignorant of his heritage, many of them remained unaware of their potential. So often they led lives of quiet misery, aware of something lacking, but never learning what.

Luc knew Ulrich had recently made contact with the leader of another pack, a group now living in Montana. Ulrich hadn't said too much about them, though Luc had sensed Ulrich's respect for their leader, a man reputed to be a powerful wizard as well as Chanku.

Now that was an interesting combination . . . a magical shape-shifter? Luc chuckled quietly to himself. Accepting the concept of shape-shifting was hard enough, but adding magic to the mix was a bit much. Still, it was heartening to know there were others out there aware of their heritage, living with their own kind.

Camille Mason had been the key for Ulrich, close enough to her Tibetan roots to retain the knowledge of the grasses the Chanku needed, the combination of vitamins and enzymes and other nutrients that enabled that small part of the brain unique to their breed to function as it was genetically intended. Ulrich had explained it all to a disbelieving Luc that long-ago night.

Luc shifted in his chair, remembering the emotions he'd experienced sitting in this same room, in the home of the woman he'd killed. He'd quit the force the day it happened, emotionally devastated by such a horrible mistake. The quiet, graveside memorial had been even worse, but he'd felt an overwhelming desire to attend. No longer a cop, he'd worn his military blues out of respect. He'd stood apart, feeling the husband's grief, sensing the man's terrible pain, Ulrich's love for his little girl, his loss.

His unimaginable loss.

What would it be like to find a mate of the same species? A woman as attuned to your every thought and need as Camille must have been to Ulrich's? Though the pack was always on the alert for female Chanku, none had been found. The only one Luc had ever known was Tia, and she was just a kid, as far as he knew completely unaware of her shape-shifting nature. The last time he'd seen her, almost ten years ago, she'd been a tall, gangly teenager with smooth, mocha skin, braces on her teeth, and freckles sprinkled liberally across her nose.

She'd inherited some of her mother's dark coloring—skin the color of coffee with cream and the most beautiful amber eyes he'd ever seen. She even had her mother's dimple in her left cheek. Her hair, though, was dark blond, just as her father's must once have been, and she'd worn it tied in a ponytail to control the wild tangles.

It was difficult to imagine her as a woman now.

As a young teen she'd had an inherent grace that hinted of sensuality to come, a natural beauty both unique and compelling. He was a young man in his prime, alone without the prospect of a mate, but a winsome and endearing teenager had been more fun to tease than consider even remotely as an object of desire.

Then Tia was gone, off to that private boarding school

with her best friend, and eventually on to college some-where back east . . . Boston? She'd been home rarely for very brief visits, though Ulrich had occasionally gone to Boston to visit her. Luc wondered what Tia would be like now, wondered if Ulrich had ever told Tia the truth about her mother, about herself?

Did Tia know how her mother died? Did she remember?

"Thanks for waiting, Luc."

Ulrich stepped into the room. He'd removed his suit coat and loosened his tie. His thick shock of white hair was a bit ruffled and out of place, but for a man in his six-ties, Ulrich still carried an air of authority no one would ever strip from him.

"No problem, boss. It feels good to sit with absolutely nothing on my mind for a change."

"You deserve to relax." Ulrich poured brandy into a crystal goblet and sat in the leather chair opposite Luc's. "Just don't get used to it."

Luc laughed. Ulrich lifted the brandy in a silent toast. "You did well tonight. The boy is safe, the press still bliss-fully unaware of our existence, and no one was injured."

"Thank you. I was concerned about the intelligence, but it was good for a change. That's important. Unfortunately, it's also rare."

Ulrich nodded. "I know. That's why I asked you to stay. The lack of good intelligence can be a real problem. We never really know exactly what to expect." He concen-trated on his glass for a moment and then raised his head and stared intently at Luc. Though they regularly commu-nicated telepathically, as was the way of the pack, Ulrich's thoughts remained blocked.

Luc waited, his curiosity growing with each beat of his heart.

Finally Ulrich shifted in his chair and leaned forward. "Tianna called. She's moving back to San Francisco."

Ulrich rolled the glass between his palms. "She plans to teach . . . a private school over in the Sunset. There's a small apartment at the school, so she'll live there."

That was the last thing Luc had expected to hear. He studied his mentor for a moment before answering. "You don't seem very happy about it. I would think you would be thrilled to have your daughter close by."

"It scares the shit out of me, having her so close. Think of what we do, what we're like." Ulrich stood up, as if his body could no longer contain his emotion. "You haven't seen Tianna in a long time, Luc. There's a reason for that. I didn't want you—not any of the pack—near my daughter. I don't think I could have handled it, watching you bastards sniff around her like the animals you are. You're male, all Chanku. You've been with a lot of women. Hell, you've probably been with just as many men. That's the nature of the beast, literally." Ulrich turned and smiled, but there was little humor in his expression. "Our sex drive is sometimes overwhelming, isn't it?"

Luc nodded, but he wondered where Ulrich was taking this, and he wasn't sure he liked the implications that he'd be unsafe around Tia. Granted, the sex drive was something he'd had a difficult time with at first, once the special diet Ulrich started him on had unlocked his Chanku spirit. The need, the urge to mate, to fuck any available woman— or man—any time he had the chance. It had taken years to achieve control over that part of his nature, to find some sort of balance that allowed him to live without constantly thinking about who he might screw next.

"We can't deny sex is a huge part of what we are, a powerful drive even before the supplements are added to the diet, impossible for many years after. I couldn't let you, of all the pack, near my daughter, not while she was growing up, not when you were the one man who knew exactly how strong the bloodline runs in her veins."

Luc's short bark of laughter barely hid the shaft of

anger slicing through him. "I'd like to think you could trust me with your only daughter, boss. I—"

"Settle down. Don't take it personally. Put yourself in my place. I've not been celibate since Camille's death, though I've never found another life mate. Not like Camille. You didn't know my wife. Her sexual drives were often beyond her control. Mine weren't much better. Neither of us was faithful during our marriage, though it was by mutual choice." Ulrich shrugged and took a sip of his brandy. "You're aware Chanku are not monogamous by nature, though we reproduce only with our life mate. The need for sexual satisfaction runs strongly in our women and they rarely hesitate to experience relations with as many men and women as possible. Sexually transmitted human diseases don't affect us and the woman has total control over conception, so there's no reason not to enjoy sexual freedom."

Ulrich flashed a self-deprecating smile at Luc. "However grand it sounds in theory, and no matter how well it works with adults, I don't think I could have handled that overt sexuality with my daughter, nor would it have been fair for me to attempt to curtail it. The preteen years were hard enough."

Luc relaxed as the tension went out of him.

Ulrich grinned. "Trust me, you have no idea how relieved I was when she and her friend Shannon decided they wanted to go to an all-girls boarding school. I felt like the gods had granted me a favor."

"She doesn't know, does she?" Luc had suspected but never asked.

Ulrich shook his head. "No. I've never told her, and Tianna has not been given the nutrients she needs to activate her Chanku nature. Until she adds the supplement to her diet, she is just another highly sexual human. She doesn't know. She hasn't got a clue who she is, what she is. I didn't . . . I couldn't . . ." He shook his head again, as though acknowledging there were no valid excuses or acceptable explanations.

"Do you think that's fair to her?"

"Hell, I don't know if it's fair or not." Ulrich fairly bristled. "Her mother and I felt it best to keep the truth from her until she was old enough to understand the need for secrecy. Then Camille was gone and I couldn't find the right time. The ability to shift emerges at puberty if the child has a steady diet of the nutrients. I kept them from Tianna on purpose. How do you tell a little girl, facing her first period without her mother there to guide her, that, oh, by the way, not only are you going to bleed every month, you now have the power to shift into a wolf? I couldn't then. Now I don't know if I even want her to know."

"Why? It's her right, don't you think?" Luc stood up and placed his hand on his friend's shoulder. "You didn't hesitate to tell me. Hell, you scared the crap out of me that night, shifting into a wolf without warning me what the fuck you were doing!"

Ulrich laughed out loud. "Got your attention, didn't I?"

"I guess you could say that. I just about shit my pants."

"Sorry, but you looked at me as if I'd lost my mind and I had to prove our existence. Besides, I didn't care a whit about you or your psyche. All I cared about was your DNA. I needed you to start my pack. I'd dreamed about a secret force of shape-shifters ever since Camille took me through my first change from man to wolf. You were the only other Chanku I'd ever found and I hated your guts. Protecting your self-esteem was the last thing on my mind."

Luc shook his head, sobered by the memories of how they'd met. "Okay. I guess I can accept that. So, tell me what you expect me to do?"

"There's a major lack of good intelligence and always the risk of discovery. I am afraid I won't have the information I need to keep my daughter safe. She's an adult. There's no way I can watch her every minute. Luc, I want you to protect her. The pack, as well as the true purpose of Pack Dynamics, is, so far, a well-kept secret, but at some point, somewhere, we will be found out. It's inevitable. I have no idea how we'll deal with that when it happens—and it will happen—but our work is too important to let fear of discovery put us out of business."

The same concerns kept Luc awake far too many nights. "I know. Can you imagine the uproar if someone gets proof of our existence? None of us would be safe."

"Agreed." Ulrich raked his fingers through his white hair. "Just last month we had that reporter writing about werewolves in some tabloid. Next thing you know, he's jumped off the Golden Gate. Might have solved our problem, except one of the cops thought he saw two wolves on the bridge, chasing the man, and he put that in his report. You get enough reports like that and someone's going to start paying attention. One good thing about the incident is that's how I discovered the existence of the Montana pack. I suspected others in the area; I'd sensed Chanku nearby on more than one occasion." Ulrich paused. "I told you I made initial contact with their alpha male, Anton Cheval. He's an amazing man with powers we can only imagine. I hope we can all meet at some point. There's much we can learn from Cheval."

Ulrich stared into the brandy for a moment, as though considering his words. Finally, he looked back at Luc. "There's something I didn't tell you at the time, that the Montana pack leader's mate is my niece. Her mother was Camille's sister."

Luc felt a chill run the length of his spine. "Your niece? Why haven't you ever mentioned her? Is the sister, her mother, still alive?"

Ulrich shook his head and set his glass down on an end table. "No. She was the victim of a hit-and-run shortly before I lost Camille. Killed near the park, in fact, not far from where Camille died. I assumed her daughter had inherited the genes, but, like an idiot, I never followed through. I'll admit I went a little crazy when Camille died. I had Tianna to worry about. I lost track of Keisha; to be honest, I never tried to keep in touch. Developing the pack consumed my life and I honestly forgot all about her."

Ulrich held his hands out, palms up, a helpless gesture Luc never would have associated with the man. "It was foolish. All these years, searching for more Chanku, and I never thought of my own damned niece. Then a few months ago I read the tabloid story about a werewolf attack, did some snooping, called in some markers, and got the identity of the rape victim. I recognized her name. It was all too coincidental, the werewolf-attack story and all. I figured, knowing Camille's genetics and their relationship, she had to be Chanku."

"How many in their pack?"

"Four. Two men, two women."

"All Chanku? Both men have mates?" Luc felt an ache deep in his gut at Ulrich's slow nod.

"My niece, Keisha, is a landscape architect. It appears she is the one who designed the memorial garden in Golden Gate Park."

There was no need to wonder which memorial Ulrich described. Every one of the pack had noticed the developing garden, drawn to it by the selection of grasses native to Tibet. Grasses every Chanku needed to help him shift.

"So it wasn't a chance selection of plants." Luc recalled the attractive African-American woman directing the workers when the garden was under construction. Shouldn't he have sensed her? Why hadn't he noticed her basic nature?

"As far as I know, my niece was unaware of her ability to shift. Keisha didn't find out until she was assaulted. She shifted and killed her attackers."

"I remember reading about a dog attack in the *Chronicle.*

The article said three men were killed by pit bulls, that it was some sort of gang retaliation."

"The paper got it wrong. The only publication that was even remotely close was the tabloid that ran the werewolf story."

Luc laughed. "You got me there. I don't read tabloids."

"Neither do I, usually. This particular headline caught my eye. I've not gotten the details from my niece, but I intend to question her next time we meet."

"I wonder how the reporter got his information? I don't know the entire story behind the guy's death, but I can't be sorry he's gone."

Ulrich scraped his hands over his face. "I'm surprised we've maintained our anonymity this long. Luc, right now Tianna is my only weak point, the only way anyone can get to me short of outright killing me. She's beautiful, she's brilliant, and she's vulnerable."

"She wouldn't be so vulnerable if she knew the truth." Luc's soft words practically echoed in the quiet room.

"That's exactly why I've asked you to stay this evening." Ulrich finished his brandy and set the glass on the mantel. He shoved his hands into his pockets. "I know you're right. I trust you, Luc. If I've learned nothing else over the years, I've learned you are an honorable man who tells the truth. As for me, I will always see Tianna as a little girl. That's wrong, and it's unfair to her but that's the way it is with fathers and daughters. Someday I hope you have a daughter of your own so you'll understand what I'm saying. Tianna's a woman now. I want you to get to know her as a woman, find out her strengths and her weaknesses. See if you think she'll be able to handle the truth. Help her accept who she is. Luc, I want you to find a way to tell her."

"You realize what you're asking, don't you?"

Ulrich nodded, but at least he was smiling. "I know. Don't make me come right out and say it. I'm her father and she will always be my little girl. I'm not ready to think of her in a sexual relationship with anyone, including you. I'd rather just pretend it's not happening. You haven't seen her for a long time, Luc. She's beautiful. She's so much like her mother, it breaks my heart, but she's an innocent."

At Luc's look of surprise, Ulrich smiled. "Hell, I don't know if she's a virgin or not. That's her business and, like I said, she's a grown woman. I mean she's innocent of her heritage, of her birthright. She's twenty-six now. She's all I've got left of her mother and I want her safe."

"Okay. Let's get this straight." Luc poured himself another snifter of brandy and took a long swallow, coughed, and sipped more cautiously the next time. Anger roiled in his gut and he fought the Chanku sense of hackles rising. "You want me to keep your daughter safe. She probably doesn't remember me, she has never heard of the pack, she doesn't have a clue that she's not even a normal human, much less what Chanku is. She thinks you're a retired cop dabbling in detective work with Pack Dynamics, not the commander of a top-secret government agency, and, on top of that, she doesn't know that I'm the man who shot and killed her mother while Camille was running around Golden Gate Park in broad daylight as a wolf. Okay. Fine. And you expect me to do this how?"

"Calm down. I know you, Lucien. You'll think of a way to get through to her. You have to make her trust you. Take your time. Get her comfortable with the idea of Chanku, let her know her connection gently. You can do it."

"Yeah. Right. Before or after I tell her about her mother?" Luc definitely felt his hackles rise this time, a strange sensation in human form and not nearly as satisfactory.

"Lucien, damnit! Calm down."

"How does she think her mother died?" Luc sat heavily on the couch. He'd known this day would eventually come. He'd never been able to get the vision of that beautiful little girl sleeping in her father's arms out of his mind. Someday she would find out exactly what part Lucien Stone had played in her mother's death.

"She believes the story we fed to the papers, that Camille was the victim of a sexual assault and in her attempt to escape she was shot and killed by her attacker."

"How the hell did you manage that?" Luc stared at the carpet beneath his feet, reliving the horror of that day almost twenty years ago as if it had occurred this morning. "The entire time after it happened is a blur to me. It wasn't until years later I realized I'd never even been questioned by my supervisor after I gave my initial report, much less any form of investigative panel. It was as if I'd never been there."

"As far as public record is concerned, you never saw my wife. I called in some markers, Luc. Leave it at that. You left the force, I retired. We made it all go away. I was a captain with twenty years' service and times were different then. It was easier to keep things under wraps. Hell, now there'd be half a dozen videos from as many angles showing how Camille died."

"Those must have been some markers, boss. Tia's going to hate me when she finds out."

"Then don't tell her." Ulrich stood up, grabbed Luc's coat, and threw it at him. "I certainly don't intend to. Go home. Get some sleep. Tomorrow my car will be unavailable and you're taking me to the airport to pick up my daughter. It will give you a chance to get reacquainted."

"Still calling in those markers, boss?"

"Do I have to?" Ulrich stared straight at Luc, one alpha wolf challenging another.

Luc shook his head. "You know you don't. What time?"

"I'll see you here at ten. Her flight's due in at SFO just after eleven."

Chapter 2

The hand cupping Tia's breast was warm and rough, both palm and fingertips callused. Her nipple rose to a painful, unbelievably sensitive peak, pinched between a blunt thumb and forefinger. Her vagina actually pulsed with each beat of her heart as a moist tongue followed a line from her breastbone to her navel, then dipped inside and swirled. She shivered, caught in that sensual state between sleep and wakefulness, her arousal growing with each gentle caress.

Lapping slowly, surely, the long, slick, and very mobile tongue now swept the crease of her buttocks then delved between her sensitive labia and licked deeply into her pussy. She caught back a cry as the fiery trail swept upward, barely teasing at her clit before sliding once more across her lower belly.

Spreading her legs even wider, slipping lower in her seat, she raised one eyelid to get a better view of her lover.

Time stood still—painfully, irrevocably still.

A wolf stared back at her, amber eyes glowing, tongue still lapping slowly at her belly, his ivory canines curved like sharpened sabers. He looked up and slowly licked his muzzle, wrapping that long, rough tongue almost all the way around.

The scream caught in her throat.

A soothing voice clicked into Tia's consciousness and shattered the image crouched between her knees.

"We've started our descent into San Francisco International Airport and are currently flying at 27,500 feet. If you're on the left side of the plane you should be able to look out your window and see Half Dome in Yosemite, sticking up like a . . ."

Tia gasped. Her lungs pumped like a bellows and her skin flushed from hot to cold. She blinked rapidly, noted that the older man next to her still snored, blissfully asleep. Quickly scooting back in her seat, Tia sat upright and smoothed her wrinkled denim skirt. Her breath escaped in a long sigh. For extra measure, she fastened her seat belt, pulled it firmly across her middle, and prayed the moisture between her legs hadn't soaked through the denim.

Damn the dreams. Until last week, she hadn't had any this explicit in almost three months. Why now? Tia glanced once more at the man sleeping next to her and flushed, her skin once again going hot and cold all over. What if he'd awakened? What if someone had seen her, sprawled out, legs spread wide, lips parted, and breasts heaving?

She cupped her forehead in the palm of her hand and shuddered. Damn, this had better be the right choice, this move back to San Francisco. Somehow she needed to understand the dreams, the explicit, sensual dreams that had finally broken the link between her and Shannon, Tia's dearest friend in the world.

Her friend and her lover. She'd been with Shannon for ten years, ever since they were teenagers heading off to boarding school together, their hormones in high gear and their need for one another overwhelming. It had been so good then, so perfect, both emotionally and physically.

Tia sighed. She missed the intensity of their teenage affair, the forbidden nature of love with another female, the heart-stopping, lung-bursting climaxes they'd managed to wring out of one another. So good at first. So fulfilling, for a time, at least; then slowly, surely, Tia had acknowledged something important was missing.

So had Shannon. The last five years their relationship had merely been a safety net for both of them. A safety net held together by friendship and, only rarely, sexual love.

Even Shannon admitted to occasional sex with a man, something Tia enjoyed as well, but it had never been enough. Not with one man, not even with multiple partners. The sense of something else, something more powerful, more sensual, lured her out of every relationship, away from any commitment.

Away from Shannon.

The dreams hadn't helped. Explicit, arousing, forbidden dreams. Always the wolf, amber eyes glowing, teeth sharp and glistening, the rough, mobile tongue lapping, licking . . . Tia blinked away the image and scrubbed at her wrists and forearms. Why, when she remembered the dreams, did her skin crawl? She hated it, the itchy, agitating sense of something just beneath the surface. Sometimes she wondered if she were losing her mind, descending into some unexplainable madness.

The plane jerked a bit as it descended. The FASTEN SEAT BELT sign blinked overhead. An attendant leaned close, awakened the man sleeping next to Tia, and asked him to fasten his belt. She smiled at Tia and moved on to the next sleeping passenger.

Tia shook off the strange sensations, and her thoughts returned to Shannon. If her father had only known how close the girls were when they'd asked to go away to boarding school together, he might have forbidden it. Obviously, he didn't have a clue. In fact, the poor man had been so relieved when Tia left, it was almost embarrassing.

It couldn't have been easy for him, raising a daughter without her mother there for guidance. Coping with hormones and emotions completely foreign to him, not to mention the issues that occasionally arose because of her biracial status. Maybe Tia and Shannon wouldn't have become lovers if they'd had mothers, but Shannon's mom had died of cancer when Shannon was only five. That shared loss had drawn the girls together.

Tia's mother had been murdered. To this day she didn't know all the details, only that her father had never even talked of remarrying. He'd loved her mother beyond all women.

He'd loved Tia as if she were a princess, put her on a pedestal. *More like a perch,* she thought, *locked securely in a gilded cage.* Rationally, she knew he'd wanted to protect her, but he'd merely driven Tia away.

What would it be like now, to live in the same city, to see her father whenever she wanted, to finally learn more about his life? She'd have a chance, maybe, to learn the details of her mother's murder. More important, she'd have the freedom her adult status now gave her to search for answers.

Tia sighed. She wished she remembered her mother more clearly, but the image she carried of Camille's smile was the face in the snapshots, the pictures both Tia and her father treasured.

Ulrich had always had presence, as far as Tia was concerned. She wondered how he did now that he was partially retired. From his letters and calls and their infrequent visits, Tia knew he was still active and involved, busy with his detective agency. He'd always had a lot of friends.

Lucien Stone's image popped into Tia's mind. *Luc.* She hadn't seen him since the summer before she and Shannon went off to Briarwood, but he and her father had always been close. He was probably married by now with a couple of kids, but he'd filled her fantasies for years. When Shannon made love to her, it was Luc's mouth tasting, licking, driving her over the edge. When Shannon had used a vibrator or dildo between Tia's legs, Tia had been filled by Luc.

She stared out the window, watching the multicolored squares in San Francisco Bay as they glided down over the salt beds, and tried to picture Lucien Stone with ten years added to his stern yet boyish good looks.

By the time the plane landed and Tia unbuckled her seat belt, she had an image in her mind of a potbellied, middle-age man with thinning hair.

When she reached for her carry-on luggage in the overhead rack, Tia added bad teeth and an earring. She was grinning as she walked down the enclosed ramp to the gate, the image of an older Lucien Stone taking on cartoon properties in her overactive imagination.

She was still smiling when she arrived at the luggage carousel. Her father waited there, just as overwhelming and handsome as when she'd last seen him, his skin ruddy from wind and sun, his hair a thick shock of white badly in need of a trim. Ulrich pulled her into a hug, his big arms and broad chest erasing every misgiving Tia had felt about coming home.

He smelled just the same as always, a combination of Dial soap and Colgate shaving cream. Tia took deep breaths, just to absorb his beloved scent.

"Sweetie, you are absolutely gorgeous."

Her father stood back for a better look, his big hands clasped tightly to her shoulders. "I've missed you. I'm glad you're home."

Tia's eyes filled with tears. She wanted nothing more than to throw herself back into her father's arms and tell him how lonely she'd been, how much she'd wanted to come home. How terribly glad she was to be back. "It's good to be here, Daddy."

"Was the trip okay?" He reached for the bag she grabbed off the carousel, set it on the floor, and then snatched another she pointed to.

"Yeah. Just long. I . . ." No. It couldn't be. Not Luc? A

chill raced along her spine, a sense of awareness that left her weak-kneed and shivering.

"Hello, Tia."

"Luc? Good lord! I haven't seen you since . . ."

"Since you were a skinny little sixteen-year-old with braces on your teeth." Smiling, Luc stepped forward and drew her into a friendly, brotherly hug.

At least, Tia assumed it was meant to be brotherly. Where her father's hug had been home and comfort, Luc's was bed and beyond. His big hands stroked her spine, the briefest of contacts that left her feeling naked and wanting. His lips brushed her cheek and she fought the urge to lean closer for more. She breathed deeply of his scent. He was spice and fresh air, deep woods and dark rivers . . . intoxicating and addictive.

When he released her—was it only seconds later?—Tia clamped her jaws together to keep her teeth from chattering. "Luc, you look . . . you haven't . . ." Her voice drifted off and she realized she was staring at him.

He grinned, obviously aware of her discomfort. His teeth were perfectly straight and very white. His nose wasn't nearly as straight, but the bump on the bridge where he'd probably broken it at some time during the past ten years only made him look stronger, more masculine.

Tia blinked. The dream she'd had earlier on the plane materialized in all its sensual detail. Damn, Lucien Stone looked exactly like that hungry wolf with his deep-set amber eyes and feral grin. It was much too easy to picture him kneeling between her thighs, his tongue lapping away at her cream.

Tia gulped, no ladylike swallow at all, but Luc ignored her faux pas and instead reached past her to pick up off the carousel the last two of her large bags. He slung one over his shoulder, gripped the other easily in his left hand, and then grabbed the two smaller ones in his right. Ulrich took Tia's carry-on bag from her and led the way to the parking garage.

Tia followed quietly, her inner thighs sliding moistly, one against the other, with each step. The two men were discussing something, but the words merely sailed past her without sense. Awareness of Luc screamed a steady beat inside her brain, echoed in the rhythmic clenching between her legs. Her chest felt tight and her skin itchy and she'd never been this aware of another human being in her life.

Tia didn't think to question how Luc had identified her mismatched set of bags out of all the others on the luggage carousel until he shoved them into the trunk and shut the lid.

Somehow he'd found them without her help. But how? Tia turned to ask, but Luc opened the door and gestured with his hand. She smiled as he seated her in the front. Ulrich stepped back on the curb when Luc moved around to the driver's side and climbed into the Mercedes.

Frowning, Tia lowered the window. "Dad? Aren't you coming with us?"

Ulrich smiled, leaned close, and kissed Tia's cheek. "I've got a meeting in Burlingame, so I'll catch a cab. Luc will get you settled and then I want him to bring you over for dinner this evening. Is that okay with you?"

Tia nodded, blinking nervously. Like she had a choice? Why did this feel planned, as though the two men followed a script? She glanced once more at her father and realized he was looking steadily at Luc. If she didn't know better, Tia would have thought Ulrich and Luc communicated without speaking. She turned to Luc, noticed his slight nod, and when she looked back at her father it was to see his broad shoulders and back as he walked purposefully out of the parking garage without another word.

A memory intruded, faint and far away, more a dream than reality. Her mother's voice, soft words of comfort whispering in Tia's mind as she fell asleep at night. Wishing her well as she worried about starting school, ordering Tia to behave when she wasn't minding. Her mother had communicated with her without audible speech.

Exactly as she imagined Luc and her father had just done. Frowning again, mind and body overwhelmed, Tia settled into the soft leather seat and fastened her safety belt. Luc was much too close for comfort. Her head ached, her heart pounded in her chest, and the skin on her forearms crawled and twitched, the feeling as unsettling as the odd interchange she'd just witnessed between Luc and her father.

Why? What had passed between the two men? Even more confusing, why did she feel the sensual clench of her womb as if an orgasm waited, just beyond reach? What was it about Lucien Stone that affected her on such an elemental level? Was it Luc's scent? Her teenage fantasies suddenly come to life? Why would this man, at least fifteen years her senior, have such a strong, physical impact on her?

Tia willed her raging libido to find peace, settled back into her seat, and concentrated on the road ahead, determined to keep a very close eye on how Luc and her father interacted.

Her gut told her something strange was going on.

Tia's heart warned her to let well enough alone and her damned brain just wanted her to get settled in her new home. Head reeling with more input than answers, Tia watched as Luc checked his rearview mirror, accelerated, and pulled away from the airport. He skillfully merged the sporty Mercedes with the heavy traffic heading north on the freeway.

From this angle he was even more attractive than she'd first thought. He wore his hair longer than she remembered. Thick and so dark it was almost black, it curled over his collar and covered his ears. He had a lean, sharp profile, dark, heavy brows over eyes hidden behind thick lashes.

There was a feral intensity about him, a perception of strength, the potential for violence. Awareness of him held Tia on edge, the feeling that she sensed more of Luc than he allowed the world to see.

Visions of her latest dream lingered in the back of Tia's consciousness, reinforced by the strong profile of the man beside her. She rubbed the crawling skin on her forearms and wondered at the powerful attraction to a man she hadn't seen in ten years.

Luc hoped like hell the woman sitting so close wouldn't notice how tightly he clenched his teeth. Damn, Tia was no more a gangly teenager than . . . well, there really was no comparison.

Not when he could smell her arousal, so close and inviting, not when he knew she was hot and wet and ready for him—even if she didn't realize it herself. He'd been hard since the first glance he'd gotten of her. She'd looked like a tall, slim, native princess, riding down the escalator with her head held high, scanning the crowd in the claims area as she searched for her father.

She still wore her unruly hair long, fastened in a clip at the base of her neck, the thick tangle of dark blond curls falling midway down her back. Her skin glowed a rich, golden brown against her turquoise blouse and casual denim skirt.

Thank goodness she'd been looking for Ulrich, not him, or Luc would have been caught staring like a horny adolescent, eyes wide, mouth open, cock hard and thrusting against his slacks. He'd almost growled when he hugged her, verging, as he was, so close to the shift from man to beast.

He checked the traffic lane to his left and then chanced

a quick glance in Tia's direction. She stared back at him, eyes wide, lips parted. Taking a chance, Luc searched her thoughts quickly.

Blocked? But how? He smiled at her.

She blinked. Her dark lashes hid her beautiful eyes for a brief instant, and then she smiled back and he knew she was waiting for him to say something.

Anything.

Conversation. Shit . . . when all he really wanted to do was rip off her clothes. Had Ulrich had any idea when he'd proposed his bloody scheme? Luc cleared his throat, swallowed . . . cleared his thoughts as well. "So, your, ah, dad gave me the address where you'll be living." He named the spot, just off Sunset Boulevard.

She looked transparently grateful that he'd said something so innocuous.

"That's right. I'll be teaching in a private school. The salary isn't much, but they provide an apartment. I haven't seen it yet. Only pictures. It's not much. . . definitely small."

"In San Francisco any kind of apartment is something." Luc glanced Tia's way once more, then turned his attention back to the highway and let out a relieved sigh.

Okay, this was easier. Talking about the high cost of rent would take any guy's mind off a beautiful, ripe, absolutely mind-blowing woman sitting just inches away.

Maybe.

"Do you still work for my father?"

Luc risked a quick look. Did Tia have any idea what Ulrich did for a living?

She answered his question. "He's never said what he does. . . . I guess I just figured it was some sort of detective agency. Pack Dynamics or something like that?"

"Something like that and, yes, to answer your question. I've been with Ulrich for twenty years now."

"Longer than some marriages." Tia smiled at him.

"I wouldn't know. I've never married." Luc glanced once more in Tia's direction. Was that a satisfied smile quirking the corner of her mouth as she turned her attention back to the road?

Once more his pants felt a bit too tight. He slowly repositioned himself in the bucket seat and took a deep breath.

Big mistake. Her scent filled the interior of the car, a rich, spicy aroma that told Luc exactly where she was in her menstrual cycle, let him know she was ripe and ready for breeding, that her body was every bit as aroused as his. He'd never been this close to a Chanku female before, even one unaware of her nature, never understood the depth of need her proximity would awaken.

For a brief moment, Luc allowed himself the luxury of absorbing the scents and sounds of Tia's body.

Bigger mistake.

Deeply aroused, body skirting the need to shift, Luc's Chanku senses locked on the equally aroused female so close beside him. He heard the rapid beat of her heart, the soft catch in her breath. Smelled the scent of her heat, more human than wolf, but with Chanku genes so strongly a part of Tia's DNA, the wolf was not that deeply buried.

He slammed on the brakes as the car in front of them slowed, and then sped up again. Damn. He really had to pay closer attention.

Tia smiled at him. "Traffic's worse here than in Boston."

"I dunno. Boston's pretty bad. Last time I was there, it was all torn up."

"That was the Big Dig. A lot of the freeways are underground now. It's better . . . some of the time."

Traffic slowed to a crawl. Tia chatted on about Boston and the Big Dig and life in the North End. Luc watched her lips move, vaguely responded to her chatter, but he felt the sensual impact of her Chanku presence all the way to his bones.

She doesn't know.

Tia didn't have a clue what she was, what she could so easily do, given the supplement. Once that small part of her brain, the tiny organ that allowed the Chanku side to take over the human response, was activated, Tia would discover an entirely new world.

She would no longer be human. Just as Luc had changed so many years ago, Tia would discover a new self, an entirely new view of the body with which she'd lived her entire life.

She would be Chanku, able to shift from woman to wolf at a moment's notice. Able to control her breeding if not her cycle . . . able to choose a mate on her own terms.

The implications practically exploded in his mind.

Luc found the address to Tia's school and followed the narrow alley between buildings to the apartment in the rear. His hands controlled the wheel, his eyes spotted the address and the tiny apartment tucked in behind the larger school building.

His mind silently repeated the same refrain, over and over again.

Choose me. Choose me. I will be your mate.

Choose me.

Tia turned and smiled at him. A question lurked beneath her dark lashes.

Luc shut down his silent plea. Tia might not be fully Chanku yet, but he had the strange feeling she had just heard every pathetic word crawling through his brain.

Chapter 3

"I never expected anything this nice." Tia swept her hand over the polished oak windowsill. No dust. The tiny apartment was not only attractively furnished, it was immaculately clean. She'd meet with the school's administrator in the morning and find out her schedule of classes, but with almost two weeks before school was scheduled to start, she had plenty of time to settle in. Maybe this hadn't been such a dumb idea after all.

Tia turned away from the window and its view of a sprawling bougainvillea on the building next door and smiled at Luc standing close behind her.

Not nearly close enough.

He held her luggage in both hands. Tia stared at the strong curve of his fingers wrapped around the handles. For a brief, heart-stopping moment, she imagined them cupping the fullness of her breasts. Blinking the image aside, Tia looked up into Luc's hooded eyes. "How did you know which bags were mine?"

"What?" He set the luggage down on the floor in the middle of the small front room, then straightened up. A thick shock of dark brown hair fell across his forehead. Luc brushed it back from his eyes and stared intently at Tia.

"My bags. You picked them off the baggage carousel

without any hesitation. How did you know they were mine?"

Luc shrugged and then grinned. Damn, his smile was dangerous. Tia felt the heat between her legs, heard the catch in her breath.

"Just good, I guess. They *are* yours, aren't they?" Luc leaned over and flicked her name tag on the closest piece of luggage. It was printed in bold, felt-tipped pen. "I can read, Tia."

Tia felt her skin go hot and cold all over. She'd forgotten about the name tags. "Well, of course, I . . ."

"S'okay." He waved one hand, as if to dismiss her. "Where do you want these?"

"Uh, right here is fine. I'll move them later."

"Why don't I put them in your bedroom? These two are pretty heavy."

Bedroom. Tia absentmindedly rubbed at her forearms. The mere thought of Luc in her bedroom made her nervous. "Um, okay. I'm not sure. . . ." She turned toward the first door to her right and opened it. The small bathroom glistened, all new blue tile and shiny white linoleum with bright yellow towels hanging on two racks.

Tia tried the next door and pushed it all the way open. A huge, four-poster bed almost filled the entire room. A shaft of afternoon sunlight cut a brilliant swath across the multicolored, satin spread. Piled high with soft pillows and a down-filled comforter folded at the foot, the bed obviously was more than big enough for two.

An image of herself and Luc, naked, their bodies tangled together amidst the pillows and slick satin, flashed into Tia's thoughts. The sunbeam showcased Luc's tightly muscled ass, the dark hair dusting his long legs, the . . .

Tia's breath caught once more as Luc nudged her aside. She felt as if she moved on legs made of wood, stepping into the room so he could fit through the door with her bags.

He set them down and turned back to her. "You okay?"

Rubbing at her arms, Tia nodded. "Just tired."

"Look, you're dealing with a long flight and a three-hour time difference. Why don't you rest for a while? I'll come back later and we can head over to your dad's for dinner."

Tia shook her head. "I think I'm too wound up to sleep. It's been a wild day."

"I could tell you a bedtime story."

She blinked, caught off guard by the laughter in Luc's voice. "I can just imagine your kind of story."

"No, really. C'mon. Take your shoes off. Lie down and get comfortable. I'll put you right to sleep."

"Said the big bad wolf to Little Red Riding Hood." Tia laughed. Luc in this kind of mood she could handle. When he was serious and quiet, she wasn't quite sure what went on behind those sexy eyes. "I don't think so. Besides, I bet you don't know the best stories."

Luc went back into the front room and retrieved the rest of Tia's luggage while she opened the first of her bags and began hanging blouses and pants in the closet. He set the smallest bag on an antique dresser tucked into one corner and leaned back against the top drawer with his arms folded across his chest. Tia noticed he'd rolled the sleeves partway up. Luc's forearms were muscled and lightly dusted with dark hair.

It looked soft as silk. Tia licked her top lip and blinked at Luc's knowing grin. Damn. He'd caught her staring again.

"Which stories are the best ones?" His voice sounded deeper, huskier.

Tia knew they weren't talking about stories at all. She turned her back on Luc and returned to hanging up her blouses. "My favorites. The amazing tales of the ancient and mystical Chanku."

"What?"

Damn, how did he do that? Tia spun around to find Luc at her elbow. "What do you mean, what?"

His eyes practically glowed with intensity. "The stories. What stories are you talking about?"

Tia blinked and fought the urge to step back, to give herself a bit of space. "Oh. The wolf stories, the ones my mom used to tell me at bedtime. I'd completely forgotten about them until just now. She used to make up stories about mythical creatures she called Chanku. They looked like people during the day but turned into wolves at night. They ran through the forest helping people and animals in need. I got a new story every night before I went to bed. I loved them. I used to dream I was a wolf."

She almost told him she still dreamed of wolves, but she didn't. The dreams that awakened her now were much too intimate to share with anyone.

"Oh. I thought. . . . Never mind." Tension seemed to melt out of him. Luc's hand came up and brushed some loose strands of hair away from her face. "I'm sorry about your mother."

Tia sucked her lips between her teeth, remembering. "Yeah. Well, it was a long time ago." She turned away. Luc was too close, her mother gone too long.

Life too unsettled.

"Do you still remember the stories?"

"Yeah, I do. Dad used to try to tell me bedtime stories, but no one could do it like my mom. I still miss her. A lot."

Luc nodded and backed away from her. She wanted to cling to him, to beg him to stay here, in her home, in her bed, but he was moving away, separating himself from her. "You try and rest. I'll come back in a while."

Tia stared at him a moment. Why did she feel as though he tried to reach her on another level? What was it about Lucien Stone that left her feeling unsettled and incomplete, filled with more questions than answers?

Without thinking of risk or consequence, she put one of

those questions to words. Tia stepped close and placed her hands on his biceps. Slowly she stroked the smooth muscles beneath his cotton sleeves and felt the strength of the man, felt his arms tense beneath her palms. She cocked her head to one side and looked up at him. As tall as she was, it was a new experience, looking up to a man.

Luc wasn't so bulky that he made her feel petite, but his size definitely made Tia feel feminine, standing this close, her hands moving slowly over his smooth muscles. A small thrill went through her and settled where every feeling she'd had since meeting Luc seemed to settle.

Right between her legs.

Gathering her courage, Tia ran her tongue across her upper lip, then quietly asked him, "What's going on, Luc? Is it just me?"

He sighed, glanced down, away from her steady gaze, and shook his head. A mere ghost of a smile touched his lips. "No, Tia. It's most definitely not just you." When he looked up, he was grinning. "Now that you've brought it up . . . I'm not quite sure what it is, but it's something I'd like to investigate a little further. With your permission."

She sucked in a breath, caught in the feral gleam in his eyes, the sense of possession hovering between them. Her fingers tightened on his biceps. Luc stood so close, mere inches away, his chest broad and muscled beneath the light chambray shirt, his arms hanging deceptively relaxed at his sides.

He must have read permission in her hopelessly besotted gaze, because he was raising his arms, his warm palms clasping her shoulders, drawing her closer still. Tia felt his biceps shift and tighten beneath her grasp. Her nipples hardened against her lacy bra at their first contact with his chest. She raised her chin, tilted her head back and lifted up on her toes, meeting Luc halfway.

His mouth found hers so easily, so naturally, his warm, mobile lips recognizing their mate in hers. He nibbled at her mouth, slipped his tongue along the seam between her lips and she parted for him, breathing him in as he tasted her.

Luc widened his stance, pulling Tia closer until her hips fit into the cradle of his strong thighs. She felt the hard ridge of his cock straining against her belly, felt the tension in his arms as he surrounded her in a sheltering embrace. His mouth, though, his mouth . . . Tia sighed with the beauty of his kiss, the deft swirl of his tongue inside her mouth. She drew him in, suckled and licked, tasted paradise on his lips.

The mattress pressed against her thighs, a welcome invitation Tia fought to ignore. This was her home now, her new life. This man was, so far, the only new friend she had. What if he was like the others? All promise, no substance? She knew nothing about Lucien, not nearly enough to risk a chance at passion, only to find, once more, something lacking.

His hands swept up her spine, fisted in her hair and held her steady for pleasure. His lips explored her mouth, her jawline, the sensitive spot behind her ear. Tia realized she had a death grip on his upper arms, as if steadying both of them against falling into something so deep neither would be able to escape.

Luc growled. She felt as much as heard the rumble deep in his chest and her body responded with a heated gush of liquid between her thighs. The skin along her forearms crawled. The same sensation rushed over her legs, up her spine. Instead of feeling irritation, Tia let her nerves pulse as they would. No matter, not when her entire body pulsed to the same rhythm.

All that mattered was Luc. His taste, his strength, his sensual touch arousing Tia beyond rational thought. His rock-hard thighs pressed close to hers, his arms, just as powerful, surrounded her, yet his touch was gentle, loving.

His growl, deep and powerful, a sound of need, of desire such as she'd never experienced, stirred Tia on a level beyond comprehension.

Searching for something more, needing more, Tia pressed her pelvis close, raising up on her toes so that her mons found his lengthening cock. She swayed against the long, hard ridge of his erection, sinuously; like a cat in heat she rubbed herself against his solid length. Blood rushed in her veins, her heart pounded, and she kissed him, frantically, passionately, wanting more, needing all of him.

His scent enveloped her, made her thoughts spin and her nostrils flare. His taste was a drug. She wanted to absorb the flavors of Luc, the sensual, invisible aura of sound and scent and taste bombarding her. Tia's senses screamed—alert, aware of everything that encompassed Lucien Stone. Her skin felt more sensitive, her needs stronger. Passion and desire somehow transferred itself to the man holding her and swept back again, to Tia.

Luc growled again. His body tightened against hers and he rubbed his cock against her belly with bruising strength, the motion frantic, out of control. His grip on her hair tightened to the point of pain. He nipped sharply at the tender skin beneath her throat, then bit again behind her ear. The sharp sting of his teeth, his hands twisting in her hair, controlling her, jerked Tia out of the sensual fog surrounding them.

No longer a gentle, questing sensual glide into arousal, this felt wrong. Something dark, something beyond Tia's understanding seemed to drive the man holding her, controlling her body with the greater strength of his.

Tia released her grasp on Luc's arms and shoved forcefully at his chest, flattening her palms against the solid muscles. She didn't say a word. She didn't have to.

Luc's body immediately stilled. He backed slowly away after a single, gentle swipe at her lips with the tip of his tongue, breathing as if he'd just run a mile. With a strangled bark of what might have been laughter, Luc leaned his forehead against Tia's. She wrapped her arms lightly around his slim waist.

It took a moment before he had his breathing under control. "Oh, my. Good lord, sweetheart. I'm so sorry. I didn't . . . I . . ." His shoulders slumped. He closed his eyes and looked up, away from Tia. "Shit. I'm glad one of us came to our senses." He hugged Tia close. She heard his heart pounding in his chest, felt the rush of his warm breath against her cheek.

"Barely. I was right there with you." She tilted up her head and made herself smile at him, searching for something light, some small comment to break the tension. "Do you always growl when you're turned on?"

"You must bring out the beast in me." Calm now, his breath no longer hissing between his teeth, Luc leaned close and kissed her on the nose. Dispassionately. As if she were no more than a mere acquaintance . . . which, Tia guessed, she was. Nothing more.

Luc backed away and stared intently at her face. "Your freckles are all gone. I remember freckles marching across your nose when you were a kid."

Tia took a deep breath, still rattled from the darkness, the sense of control rushing away. "Thank goodness that's one of the things I outgrew." Slipping her arms from around Luc's waist, Tia turned away from him. She grabbed a pale green blouse out of her suitcase with trembling fingers and shoved a hanger through the sleeves.

She couldn't look at Luc. Not with passion still simmering in her body, not with that small, niggling fear she'd felt that he might have tried to overpower her.

What the hell had just happened? Had Luc really been out of control? Of course he had, and she'd been right there with him. Only fear had stopped her. Fear of Luc?

He was strong. Stronger than any man she'd ever known, and she knew he burned for her, burned in the same way she did. Tia's body ached with need. Aroused beyond belief, her sensitive, traitorous pussy wept. Her breasts felt heavy, her nipples pressed painfully against her bra.

She moved over to the closet to hang her blouse, well aware that Luc followed her. He touched her chin lightly and turned her head so that she looked at him.

His eyes were troubled, his expression unreadable. Then he reached out with his other hand and stroked along her left cheek. "Thank goodness you didn't outgrow this."

Tia frowned. Her pussy clenched at his gentle caress. Her distended clitoris rubbed painfully against her panties. "What?"

How could such a simple touch affect her so deeply?

"Your dimple. I used to love watching that dimple when you'd smile. Always had the urge to . . ." He leaned close and ran his tongue around the small indentation.

Tia shivered and backed away. She had to force a smile. She didn't know whether she wanted to rip Luc's clothes off him and haul him to bed, or tell him to leave. "Please don't. I know where that leads."

"So do I." Luc rocked back on his heels and stuck his hands in his hip pockets. His expression looked relaxed, untroubled. He grinned, transforming himself from dark and dangerous to boyishly sweet in a heartbeat. Tia wasn't certain which one was the more attractive.

"One of these days I'm going to lead you as far as I can take you. You know it's where you really want to go."

"You think so?" Tia cocked her hip and rested her knuckles at her waist. Luc still grinned at her. Her thudding heart finally settled back into its normal cadence, and her smile felt more like the real thing. "So, you were checking out my dimple when I was just sixteen, eh? There're laws against people like you."

He wagged his finger under her nose, teasing, playful. "I just looked. Didn't touch. Rule number one: never, ever touch the boss's underage daughter. Knowing your father, that most likely would have led to a drastically shortened life span."

Tia rolled her eyes. "I know." She gave Luc a serious up-and-down look and licked her lips. She still tasted him. Still wanted him. Felt as if all her senses were full of him.

"This . . . us . . . it could get ugly. I'll always be his little girl."

"Delightfully all grown up." Luc stepped closer, once more invading her space.

Tia grinned and shoved him in the chest. "Tell that to my father." Her dry comment hung between them. She wondered if she'd just issued Luc some sort of ultimatum.

Luc's hands covered her fingers. His light grasp felt warm, strong. Comfortable. Not at all threatening.

"Maybe I will have a talk with your father. Maybe he won't be so surprised after all." Luc grinned, a lopsided smile that went straight to Tia's heart. "Get some rest." He leaned close and kissed her cheek. The soft, almost brotherly brush of his lips against her skin made Tia smile, especially after what they'd just been up to.

Luc turned away, opened the door, and stepped out on the front porch. He stuck his head back inside the partially opened door. That same lock of hair fell forward, an upside-down question mark over his left eye. "I'll be back in a couple of hours. Get some sleep. You're gonna need it." He winked, flipped the lock on the door handle, and shut the door quietly behind him.

Then he was gone.

Tia stood in the front room for a long time after Luc closed the door. She wasn't certain exactly what had happened this afternoon, had never experienced the deep, soul-shattering desire for another human being she'd felt for Luc. Somehow she sensed things were not as they seemed. No man could be so perfect, so overwhelmingly passionate.

Not so perfect. There'd been that moment of fear, as if

Luc had tossed his humanity aside and let his inner beast, a feral side she'd not recognized, free. Tia hadn't been all that far away. Was it Luc who frightened her, or Tia's own uncontrolled response?

He hadn't touched her breasts. Hadn't groped between her legs. He'd brought her close to climax with nothing more than a kiss.

But, hot damn, what a kiss!

Tia touched her lips with her fingertips, reliving the feel of Luc's mouth on hers. Then her stomach growled and she yawned. She'd missed lunch and had been up since three in order to catch her flight. She yawned again, exhausted as much from the long day as the aftermath of passion. Sleep won out over food.

Smiling, imagining Luc joining her in the big four-poster bed, Tia headed in to take a nap, undressing as she went. She left a trail of travel-worn clothes on the floor behind her.

Luc closed the car door behind him and rested his forehead on the steering wheel. *Damn.* He'd almost shifted, right there in her bedroom. He couldn't recall ever feeling so turned on, so needy. So damned out of control.

She was perfect. Everything about Tianna Mason called to him, even beyond the fact she was Chanku. Her physical beauty, her intelligence, her sense of humor. He had to bring her over, convince her to embrace her birthright. He had to do it without scaring the crap out of her.

Luc stuck the key in the ignition and pulled out onto the street. He needed a shower. He hadn't even slept with her and he still smelled like sex. For that matter, he needed to jack off and get rid of some of the tension that had kept him hard as his damned name ever since his first look at Tia.

His balls ached. His muscles hurt like he'd run a mile,

and if he hadn't been hanging on to the steering wheel like a lifeline, his hands would be shaking.

Luc laughed out loud. "You poor bastard. That little girl's got you by the balls."

So true. He should have guessed this would happen. Shit . . . he'd picked her luggage off the baggage carousel by scent alone. Thank goodness she had her name tags on the bags or he would have had a devil of a time explaining how he'd known they were hers.

He'd never even noticed the tags, not until she asked him how he'd chosen her luggage. What if he'd told her the truth? Told her both bags were rich with the scent of her heat, redolent with the essence of an alpha bitch in her prime?

After she knocked him on his ass, she probably would have called the police.

Shit.

She shouldn't be this recognizable as Chanku, not without the supplements. Her scents should still be human, her sensuality levels not nearly as powerful.

Luc glanced at the bulge in his slacks. Try telling that to his cock.

The poor fellow hadn't stayed this hard this long in years. All Luc could think of was burying his needy length in that hot, tight pussy of hers. He knew she'd been wet and ready, had smelled her sex like a dose of heavy perfume. It hung in the room, clung to him even now. He groaned aloud, shifted his butt around in the warm leather seat and then glanced at the clock on the dash. Time to get home, shower, grab a quick bite to eat, and put on some clean clothes. Time to figure out how he was going to deal with one Tianna Mason.

Damn. Ulrich's little girl was definitely all grown up.

Chapter 4

Why, when Tia saw the wolf this time, did she immediately think of Luc? Tia's chest felt tight, as if there were no room for air in her lungs. The muscles in her lower abdomen clenched and she shifted to her back, sliding softly on the slick bedspread, raising her knees in invitation, opening to him.

He stood at the end of the bed, his big paws resting on the footboard, tongue lolling, amber eyes glinting. He seemed to be trying to tell her something, but she wasn't sure what he said. All Tia could see was his upper body, the broad wolven shoulders covered in thick, black fur, the beautifully formed head, thick ruff of fur around his neck, the intelligent eyes.

Her pussy wept. She felt the cool brush of air across her damp and swollen folds, the trickle of lubricating cream as it coursed slowly over her perineum and down the crease of her ass. Her muscles clenched, begging, so needy.

She touched herself, trailing her fingers through the moisture, finding her distended, sensitive clit and shoving back its tiny, protective hood. The wolf watched, blinking slowly, its gaze penetrating, perceptive. Tia circled her clit with her fingertip, then spread her labia wide, showing him the way.

The wolf leaned closer, his sharp ears, slightly rounded at the tips, pricked forward. His eyes gleamed and his mouth opened, exposing his long, pink tongue. He swept his tongue over and around the side of his muzzle, then sat still, panting softly. The sound seemed overly loud, almost echoing in the still room.

Though her fingers were busy between her legs, Tia's concentration focused entirely on the wolf. On Luc. They'd become one and the same. Luc as wolf. The wolf, Luc.

What she did wasn't for her own pleasure, her own physical satisfaction.

This was all for Luc.

Tia stroked herself, her fingers slipping ever so slowly in and out of her slick and greedy flesh, the sounds wet and hungry, even to her own ears. Hips lifting to meet each silken thrust. Clit begging for attention, standing in the way of every outward stroke, blocking every slow, wet slide into her welcoming cunt.

Her breasts ached. Her nipples twisted, budded into tight, needy points. She rubbed her palm against them, pinched and tugged, found a rhythm that matched her other hand.

Tia felt it and welcomed it. The strange, rippling, stretching, itchy sensation across her arms, down the length of her legs. Her skin literally crawled across her bones, a feeling she linked to her impending orgasm.

This time, though, the crawling grew stronger, and, with it, the sense of something huge, something just beyond her reach. It overwhelmed the sensual pleasure of stroking herself so intimately. Cried for recognition, for acknowledgment.

The wolf yipped and stood straighter, rising up on its forelegs so that it arched over the footboard. Then, with a single leap it jumped up on the bed and sat beside her.

Watching.

Tia felt the mattress dip with the wolf's weight, sensed his tension, his massive control as he watched while she pleasured herself. She could have reached out and touched his head, stroked behind his ears, even touched his long, powerful legs, but to do so would somehow break the spell the animal seemed to have woven about her.

She turned her head in order to see his eyes. Intelligence gleamed in their amber depths. *Sentience.* Tia's limbs felt strange, disconnected. She pinched harder, faster at her swollen nipples. Her fingers flew now, circling her clit and dipping inside her slick and greedy cunt. She drew her knees up higher, raised her hips slightly off the bed to meet the thrust of her own fingers. The wet sounds of penetration were practically lost in the pounding of her heart, the rush of her quick, panting breaths.

The sound of the wolf's slow, even breathing.

So close to coming, so completely caught up in her own arousal, Tia closed her eyes, concentrated on the slide of her fingers deep inside herself, the pulsing rush of blood in her veins. She accepted the presence of the wolf and then put him away, out of her mind. She tightened her focus, became the clench of her vaginal walls, the tight ache deep in her womb, the need to touch *here*, to slide her fingers *there*.

Her breasts ached and she pinched harder at her own turgid nipples, bruising the dark tips, imagining the wolf's hot tongue sweeping across her breasts. At the moment the thought entered her mind, she felt him. Felt the animal's steamy breath, his rough tongue licking the soft curve of her left breast, felt . . . *no*. It wasn't the wolf. It was Luc beside her, leaning over the bed, taking her nipple between full lips, suckling the sensitive bit of flesh between his sharp teeth, biting . . .

Tia screamed, arched into her climax, scrabbling at the bedspread beside her with one hand while the other pressed down hard between her legs. Her entire body pulsed and clenched with the force of orgasm. She felt the hot gush of fluids between her legs, the crawling, stretching, toe-numbing sensation that made her feel as if she'd suddenly grown too big, too sensitive for her own skin.

Gasping, Tia opened her eyes and glanced quickly to her left. Of course there was no wolf, no sign of Luc. A whimper caught in her throat, a sound halfway between a laugh and a sob. Masturbation with her fantasies as active participants? Good lord, she really must be losing it. *Damn. . . .*

She lay back on the satin cover and let the final tremors of her climax recede. Waited for her heart to return to its normal beat, her breathing to resume its usual slow and easy pattern.

Why did she dream of wolves? And why, now that she knew him, had Luc become part of those dreams?

Well, the answer to the second question's easy enough. A lifetime of fantasies capped off by the real thing. Amazing how the real thing was better than any fantasy she'd ever concocted, and all they'd done was kiss.

Damn and double damn. That led to even more fantasies. What was it going to be like when they finally had sex? There was no maybe about it, no doubt in Tia's mind that it would happen, sooner or later.

Preferably sooner. Her body still thrummed with her fading orgasm, but where was the languor, the sense of completion? If anything, she felt needier, almost desperate to have Luc deep inside her.

With that thought, Tia's pussy clenched and a low, dull ache spread through her womb. She pressed her hand against her swollen labia and imagined Luc's tongue stroking her there, his large fingers probing.

His cock filling her, ever so slowly. So completely.

Moaning aloud with frustration, Tia rolled off the bed, grabbed her makeup bag, and headed for the bathroom to shower. It was almost four. Luc had seen her travel-worn and weary, yet he'd still responded to her. It might be nice to show the man that she knew how to clean up. Even nicer to see how he'd react.

* * *

Luc checked his watch. Still on time, in spite of the beer he'd stopped for at the neighborhood bar where he'd met Tinker. At least Tink appreciated the problems facing Luc . . . and Tia. No one else, except Ulrich, had a clue.

Luc knocked on the door and waited. When Tia didn't respond, he tried the handle. The door swung open. Luc was certain he'd locked it before he left, but he stuck his head through the partially opened door. "Tia? You here?"

No answer. Luc stepped into the living room. The bathroom door was closed but he heard the shower running. A trail of clothes from the living room to the bedroom told him Tia'd most likely taken her nap in the nude.

Images of Tia unclothed might be a little bit much for his overactive libido right now.

As much as he wanted her, as desperately as Luc's body needed hers, it was too much too soon. She had no idea the secrets he carried. Until he could level with her, explain her birthright as well as his role in her mother's death, Luc knew there could be no true intimacy.

Once she was fully Chanku, their minds would link, their thoughts meld. It was part of the bonding process, should he take her as mate. Luc paused in midstep. The image of himself as wolf, covering Tia's wolven body, made him hard again. As though he'd been able to lose the erection since the first time he saw Tia this morning.

He'd never taken a woman as wolf. Never experienced the intimate bond Ulrich had told him of. The concept intrigued as much as it terrified. Luc carried too many secrets in his head, and all of them would belong to Tia once they mated as wolves.

Finding out how her mother died while Luc fucked her senseless wasn't the romantic scenario he imagined.

Damn. How the hell was he ever going to tell her? Telling her about Chanku was going to be difficult enough.

Luc leaned over and picked Tia's blouse off the floor and then grabbed her denim skirt. Her bra was next, a black, lacy thing, then a tiny pair of black thong panties. Every item of clothing was imbued with her scent and her panties felt suspiciously damp. He hadn't imagined her arousal. He held the evidence in his hands.

It wasn't easy, but he resisted the desire to hold her panties to his nose. He couldn't risk it. Not now.

Not after what had happened earlier. He'd never come so close to losing control. Thank goodness Tia had stopped him. On the edge sexually, he'd been bare seconds from shifting. His behavior more wolf than human, his love-making ferocious, not tender.

He wondered if the bite on Tia's neck had left a mark. His mark.

Another thought intruded as he stood there in the middle of Tia's living room with her clothing clutched to his chest. Were the others from the pack invited to dinner tonight? Ulrich wouldn't do that to Tia and Luc, would he?

If so, Luc hoped the mark showed.

Lost in contemplation, Luc missed the sound of water shutting off, but the silence caught his attention. A door creaked. Luc glanced up sharply. Tia stood in the bathroom doorway, her wet hair wrapped in a fluffy yellow towel, her body wrapped in nothing more than a leftover wisp of steam.

She was all long legs and lean body. Her dark skin glowed bronze, her breasts swelled lushly from her chest, full and firm, the areolas dark as ripe plums and even more inviting. Her stomach was flat and her pubic hair nonexistent. She was, for all intents and purposes, a goddess.

Luc's lungs stopped working and his hands ceased to function. He dropped the clothes he was holding. They landed in a small, wrinkled heap on top of his loafers.

Tia's hands flew up to cover her mouth and halt a strangled scream. She made no attempt to cover either her breasts or her crotch. Luc spun around, turning his back to her.

"I'm sorry." He barely choked out the apology.

"Shit. You scared me half to death. I thought you locked the door on your way out. How'd you get in?"

"It was open. I'm really sorry." Luc thought he'd locked it, too. He'd have to check on that. After he got another look at Tia's body. No. He didn't need to see her. Not now. His heart couldn't take it. The damned thing felt like it might pound right out of his chest.

He heard a rustling behind him.

"You can turn around now."

Slowly Luc turned.

Tia had removed the towel from her head and wrapped it tightly around her body. Her dark blond hair hung in long, wet, curly tangles, partially covering the tops of her breasts.

Unfortunately, the towel covered the rest.

Luc cleared his throat. His voice still sounded unusually husky. "We need to check that door. I know I locked it when I left."

"Yeah." Tia sucked her lips between her teeth and stared straight at Luc. She made no attempt to go into her room.

He realized he was walking toward her, kicking aside and then stepping over the pile of clothes, reaching out to touch her. Tia gazed steadily at him, her amber eyes bright, her skin flushed an even darker hue.

Luc tangled one finger in her damp hair and tugged. She moved like a puppet on a string, lifted her lips to his for a long, slow kiss. The part of his brain that should be telling him to stop, at least ordering him to take it slow, remained curiously silent.

Tia moaned into his mouth. Her slim hands came up around his neck and her body flowed against his like hot wax. She was all invitation and warm, willing woman, her lips moving over his, her full breasts flattened against his light sweater.

He felt the damp towel through the knit, wondered if

her nipples had peaked. Luc groaned. *Damn.* He wanted her like he'd never wanted anything or anyone in his life. Not now, though. Not tonight. Not when he'd have to face Tia's father over the dinner table.

Not when so many secrets still existed between them.

Luc's secrets.

He kissed her again. Tia met him, lips parted and inviting, tongue sweeping across his. He suckled at her tongue and then thrust his own into her mouth. She sighed and opened for him, hinting at what she could do with lips and teeth and tongue.

Luc's cock ached, pulsing against the restraining zipper in his jeans. His balls drew up tight between his legs.

Tia whimpered against his throat. "Luc. I can't...I... My body is burning, Luc. I'm burning up."

Oh, God. She wasn't the only one.

Luc trailed kisses from her lips to the deep dimple in her cheek. He feathered tiny kisses along Tia's throat, licking the dark purple mark where he'd nipped her earlier. Something in the back of his mind cheered, some part that recognized his mark on her, a sign any other male Chanku would read as *No Trespassing.*

She knew he'd marked her, yet she hadn't said a word. Hadn't accused him of something so crass as leaving a love bite for all the world to see.

Now she begged him. Luc's heart pounded in his chest, his cock surged harder against his tight denim jeans and he swallowed a low, feral growl.

He wouldn't do what she expected, but he could do what she wanted. What she so obviously needed. Luc slipped his fingers along the column of her throat. Her blood pulsed, a rapid tempo fluttering against his fingertips. He kissed the throbbing pulse. Tia tilted her chin higher, giving him access.

Unwittingly baring her throat to him in an age-old gesture of submission.

The wolf in Luc rejoiced. He licked the mark he'd left, circling it slowly with his tongue, and then moved lower, kissing his way across her sharply defined collarbone, following the curve of her shoulders. His fingers slipped beneath the damp towel and traced the tender flesh where her right breast swelled from her rib cage. Tia moaned, arched her back, and thrust her chest forward.

Slowly tugging the towel away from her perfect breasts, Luc kissed his way down the length of Tia's body until he knelt in front of her, his hands planted firmly on her sleek hips, his mouth pressed to the smooth flesh just below her navel.

He butted at her belly button with his nose until she giggled, and then Luc raised his head. She watched him through heavy-lidded eyes. Her parted lips were moist as though she'd just run her tongue across them, her nostrils slightly flared.

Her tongue peeked out between her lips for just a moment. Soft and pink. Moist. As moist, as soft, as pink as the feast waiting for him between her thighs. Luc kissed her smooth mons, then leaned close and found her sweet honey with his tongue.

Tia feared her knees might buckle. Blindly she reached for Luc, grabbed his shoulders and buried her fingers in the soft cotton knit of his sweater. He nudged her thighs with his chin, spreading her legs wide, licking the crease between thigh and groin. He moved higher. His mouth left a burning trail along her rib cage as his tongue and lips discovered each ridge and hollow.

He found her navel and swirled inside with the tip of his tongue. Tia whimpered, the sound vibrating somewhere deep in her throat. She closed her eyes against the pleasure, even though she wanted to watch him, to capture the image of his dark hair sliding over her belly, his strong arms supporting her thighs, his beautiful mouth making her body sing.

She couldn't. Her eyes fluttered shut with the exquisite sensations Luc created, the damp trail from his kisses cooled by his breath, the clasp of his strong hands squeezing her buttocks, supporting her. He'd so easily found the perfect rhythm between mouth and hands, teeth and tongue.

Tiny nips and lush licks across her belly. Kisses over her freshly shaved mons, the brush of his smooth chin against her greedy, desperate clit. She thrust her hips forward and he followed her lead, dipping his head to tongue between her moist labia.

Tia cried out, a choked scream that ended in a moaning sigh as Luc turned his attention to her clit and the hidden depths between her legs. She felt the rush of hot cream against her inner thighs, the tension building deep inside her womb. The moist sounds of his lips and tongue, wet, impossibly lush sounds made her tremble even more as Luc feasted on her.

His fingers tightened on her buttocks. Luc held her close to his mouth, practically lifting her off the floor as he worked wonders with his mouth. His tongue snaked in and out of her cunt, long strokes that ended with the very tip invading the tiny hood around her clit.

Each time she tensed, well aware too much pressure could bring pain as well as pleasure. Each time Luc took her to the edge, then soothed her with his lips, sucking lightly on the tiny bundle of nerves and laving it with his tongue.

Once, twice, again . . . the same sweeping pressure, the anticipation of pain, the gentle, perfect caress before repeating the process.

His hands followed their own agenda. Luc's fingers searched and then pressed between her cheeks, slipping from vagina to ass, probing deeper, harder, pressing steadily against her tightly muscled anus, rubbing her fluids back and forth, softening her, readying her body for one more intimate invasion.

Crying now, her fingers twisted in his softly knit sweater, she mewled like a lost pup. Overwhelmed by sensation, Tia reached for something beyond, something barely imagined and not understood until now.

She reached for Luc. Felt his mind just as his tongue jabbed sharply into her slick pussy, felt his love as his forefinger breached her bottom. Like a bolt of lightning, sensation upon sensation rocked her world as knowledge filled her soul. Tia's cries cut off. She screamed, a long, low, drawn-out howl of pure, unadulterated pleasure, and then fell forward as Luc sat back on his heels to catch her. They tumbled gently to the floor.

Time paused. Tia's heart fluttered. Her mind blossomed with unanswered questions, unexpected sensations.

The first thing she heard, past the sound of her own labored breathing, was Luc's bark of triumphant laughter. Sprawled on his back on the living room floor, he held Tia against his chest. Her legs were spread wide, her breasts pressed against his chest and thick tangles of her damp hair covered part of his face.

Luc's left hand caressed her back. The fingers of his right hand swept slowly up and down the crease between her legs. Bathed in her slick fluids, he trailed back and forth from clit to ass, bringing her back, holding her on the edge of yet another climax.

Her body hummed, still aroused and needy, but her thoughts spun wildly out of control. She forced herself beyond the unbelievably erotic decadence of lying naked across Luc's fully clothed body, wriggled enough to free her arms from beneath her own weight and pressed down on the floor on either side of Luc's shoulders. Raising up, reluctantly lifting her breasts away from his hard chest, she glared at him.

"Just what the hell do you think you're doing?"

His fingers never broke rhythm. "Why? Don't you like it?" She felt his chest rumble with another deep chuckle as his fingers slipped deep inside her pliant, needy vagina.

For some odd reason his comment irritated the hell out of her.

"That's not the point. What happened?"

He laughed out loud this time. "I gave you one hell of an orgasm—at least that's what it looks like from this vantage point."

"You gave me something more, Luc."

He frowned. The sweep of his fingers between her legs stilled. "What are you talking about?"

"I saw something, right before I came. Something I can't explain. I saw me, through your eyes." She rolled away from Luc's suddenly loose grasp and sat beside him, legs folded Indian fashion. Luc raised up on his elbows and studied her. His hair was mussed, his lips swollen and glistening from his feast, but his eyes glittered, intent and watchful.

His amber eyes. Beautiful, golden eyes, just like the wolf of her dreams.

Tia shoved her mussed hair back over her shoulders and glared at him. None of this made sense. It had to make sense, or she'd think she was going nuts. "Explain this. . . . I was licking between my own legs. I felt my labia against my own tongue, tasted my own juices. At the same time, I was aware of the granddaddy of all hard-ons. I was in your head, Luc. Don't deny it. How the hell did that happen? And why, when I was in your head, did I feel like I was . . ." She looked away and locked her teeth together to keep her chin from trembling. "I was something else. Something not altogether human. Can you explain that, Luc? Tell me I'm not imagining what happened. Either that or I'll know I'm going crazy. Tell me."

Chapter 5

Shit. He hadn't expected that, not so soon, not in human form and especially not without the supplement. Hadn't even considered it. Luc glanced at his watch and then back at Tia. She looked indignant, angry, a little confused, and so gloriously sexy Luc was afraid he'd shoot his load right there in his pants.

If he didn't find release soon, it might happen anyway. His cock twitched with Tia's comment, but his erection didn't subside. Unfortunately, they were running late for dinner. The graphic image of Ulrich impatiently pacing while he waited for his daughter was all it took to bring Luc's raging libido somewhat under control.

"Well?" Tia glared at him, though the effect wasn't nearly as ferocious as it could have been, not with her sitting there with her knees spread wide, her crossed ankles barely covering her glistening pussy and her glorious breasts staring straight at him, the nipples still stiff and distended from her orgasm.

Luc licked the taste of Tia from his lips. He swallowed and looked away and then shifted into a sitting position across from her. He rubbed his hand across his mouth and jaw, aware that his face was still damp and shining from her fluids.

She watched him, waiting. Luc wasn't quite ready to meet her intense gaze, so he studied his hands instead and tried to ignore the erection that obviously had no intention of completely subsiding, visions of Ulrich or not.

Luc cleared his throat, buying time, but there really was no way out of this discussion, at least no honorable way, so he clasped his hands together in his lap and decided to start at the beginning.

"A little background, okay? Bear with me. When I was a kid, I had amazing dreams. They were so real, I'd wake up, expecting my arms and legs would be covered with coarse, black fur." He looked up, caught Tia's gaze. "I used to dream I was a wolf. The dreams were so real, so much a part of my childhood, they set me apart from the other kids. Actually changed my perception of myself."

Tia's soft gasp made him smile and he wondered what her dreams were like. "As I got older, every time I thought of the dreams, I'd get so damned horny I couldn't think straight. I remember masturbating from the time I was a kid, and I was sexually active with any willing partners I could find from the time I hit puberty. I didn't care if they were male or female or multiples of either, so long as they eased that needy itch I had. The odd thing, though: No matter how good the sex was, it was never enough. There was always something missing."

He laughed, a short bark of sound that sounded strangled in his own ears. As vivid as the memories were, they were mostly unpleasant and far from easy to speak of out loud. "I was a total fuck-up, constantly searching for pleasure but never finding true satisfaction, and I didn't care who I hurt along the way."

A soft hand touched his knee. Luc felt Tia's heat even through the heavy denim jeans. "I'm sorry, but I don't understand. Luc, where are you going with this? I want to know what happened tonight . . . to me."

He smiled and shook his head, but he didn't look up. Instead he concentrated on the spot where her palm had briefly lingered. "There's a reason for the whole pathetic tale. Be patient. I'm getting there." He glanced up and grinned at her, but there were so many questions in Tia's eyes, he had to look away.

"I joined the marines right out of high school. Boot camp was wonderful. For the first time in my life, I had somewhere to direct all that sexual energy." This time when Luc raised his head and grinned at Tia, she smiled back. He had the feeling she was beginning to understand exactly how he'd felt.

"I was a damned good marine. My unit went to Granada in 1983. The invasion was short and bloody, but for the first time I felt as though I belonged somewhere. I wasn't just part of a military unit. I was part of a pack. It even had its hierarchy—alpha, beta, omega."

Now Tia watched him intently. Her lips were parted, her eyes narrowed. He was inordinately pleased to see that she ran her hands up and down her forearms in what might have been a nervous habit.

Or something much, much more.

"Another thing that sort of set me apart." He watched her hands rubbing, scratching up and down her arms. "Beginning when I was a kid, around the time I hit puberty, actually, sometimes I'd feel like my bones wanted to crawl out of my skin. It was worse when I dreamed. I'd wake up in the morning with bloody streaks on my arms where I'd clawed at my skin, sort of like what you're doing now."

Tia's gaze flashed to her arms. She hadn't drawn blood, but there were raw, dark red streaks along the tops of her arms. She covered them with her hands. When she looked back at Luc, her lips trembled.

"I didn't like the politics in the military, so when my

tour of duty was up I joined the San Francisco Police Department. That's where I met your father. He's the one who finally made everything clear for me."

Luc stood up and reached out for Tia. Confusion darkened her eyes, but she took his hand. "Look, I hate to keep your dad waiting, and we're running late. We can continue this conversation on the way over."

"But Luc, I . . ." She blinked, caught off guard by his abrupt change in conversation. Frowning, Tia grabbed his hand with both of hers as if she could force him to say more.

He leaned over and kissed her on the tip of the nose. So much rested on what he said to her, how he said it. Luc took a deep breath, let it out, then brushed his hand over her tangled hair. "Go get dressed. Just be thinking about something else—something really important. Those bedtime stories your mom used to tell you, the stories about the Chanku? Sweetie, I hate to rock your world, but they're not make-believe. They're real. Now get ready. We're running late."

They're not make-believe? Now what the hell did Luc mean by that? Tia ripped the brush through her snarled hair with one hand and aimed the hair drier with the other. Her body trembled, but she wasn't sure if it was the aftereffect of her orgasm or her absolute fury with Luc for leaving her hanging with more questions than answers.

I was sexually active with any willing partners I could find from the time I hit puberty. I didn't care if they were male or female partners or multiples of either. He'd thrown out that line as if it was no big deal he'd screwed another guy—or guys, or had group sex.

Well, damnit. She sure as hell wasn't going to criticize him. Tia'd been just as active, only she'd always felt guilty and wondered what was wrong with her after an evening of sex with multiple partners. Her longtime affair with Shannon Murphy had left her wondering if she was lesbian or straight.

Damn. Tia hoped Shannon was okay, hoped she was managing without Tia. They'd been a team for so long, even when things weren't going all that well. An old memory of Shannon floated through her mind and Tia paused to smile at her reflection. When they'd headed off to Briarwood, they'd called themselves the M&M girls. . . . *Melts in your mouth . . . or in your hand.*

Of course, no one had any idea the reference was to anything other than Mason and Murphy.

Even so, Shannon's mouth between her legs had never had the same explosive effect as Luc's. Tia pictured Shannon, her long, auburn hair draped over Tia's belly, her lips and chin wet with Tia's fluids. Thinking of Shannon's mouth on her almost always turned Tia from cold to hot in a heartbeat.

Right now it paled beside the image of Luc in bed with another man. She saw him lying back while a nameless, faceless man sucked his cock, and then wondered if Luc ever took the bottom position in anal sex.

No, she thought. Not *Lucien Stone.* He'd be on top. An alpha male all the way.

Or alpha wolf.

It was all too easy to see Luc as a wolf. Her wolf, the one who haunted her dreams. As the familiar image materialized in her mind, Tia's body reacted with a gush of hot cream between her legs. She dropped the hair drier and grabbed the tile counter for balance. The drier swung just above the linoleum floor, hanging by the cord, hot air blowing against her calves.

Damn him!

Ripping the plug out of the wall, Tia wound the cord around the drier before stuffing it in an empty drawer. Her hair snapped and crackled with static electricity, so she twisted it into a messy knot at the back of her head, stuck in a decorated chopstick to hold it in place, and then dug through her makeup kit for a lipstick. Holding the dark plum tip to her lips, Tia stared at the reflection of her shaking fingers in the mirror. Hell. There was no way she'd get that color where it belonged.

She stared at the thick lipstick case and knew exactly where she'd like to shove it about now.

They're not make-believe.

Her mother's soft voice echoed in Tia's mind. Camille Mason had drawn the stories of her mythical Chanku so clearly, Tia had believed.

If what Luc said were true, she had every reason to believe. But it couldn't be. Shape-shifting was impossible. Physically impossible. Genetically impossible. Psychologically impossible.

It was the only explanation.

Damn his eyes!

Eyes that looked remarkably like the wolf in Tia's dreams . . . Tia's father's . . . like her mother's . . . like her own.

Moving as if her arms and legs were only partially connected, Tia pulled her formfitting, raspberry-red halter-top dress over her head and slipped on a pair of matching high-heeled sandals.

She raised her chin and stared for a long moment at her reflection in the mirror. Luc's love bite stood out plain as day. She'd thought of covering it with makeup, but then decided she'd rather see Luc explain it to her father.

Running her hands down her sides, Tia smoothed out the sleek, stretchy satin. She wasn't wearing a bra and she'd skipped wearing panties as well. This dress showed everything, right down to her puckered nipples.

Wearing it, she felt sexy, strong, and very much in control.

You ain't seen nuttin' yet, Lucien Stone.

Drop a bomb like that on her and then clam up, would he? Well, maybe it was time Luc figured out just which one of them was really alpha.

With a knowing smile on her face, Tia opened the bathroom door and marched out to confront Luc.

Luc tried to think of something witty to say and almost swallowed his tongue instead. Tia stood in the bathroom doorway wearing a tight red dress that clung to her full breasts and perfectly rounded ass as if it had been painted on her. His bite mark showed dark purple, almost black on the tender skin beneath her left ear.

She hadn't attempted to cover it with makeup. Did that mean she accepted his claim, recognized his status? Smiling, hoping for the best, Luc stepped forward to take her arm.

Tia raised her hand. He stopped in midstride.

"Not one more step, Lucien Stone. I'm not going anywhere with you until you explain all the little non sequiturs you just dropped in my lap."

He shook his head. "Your dad really hates it if people are late. We can talk in the car."

"Too fucking bad. We talk here or I don't go. My father can wait. This can't."

So much for accepting my claim. . . .

"We can talk on the way." He reached for her once again. She backed away, glaring at him through narrowed eyes.

Obviously, she wasn't willing to wait any longer.

"Ah, hell, Tia. I don't even know where to start."

"Try the most obvious point. What do you mean the stories aren't make-believe?"

Luc raked his fingers through his hair. "Your father should be the one to tell you this, not me."

"You're here. He's not. Besides, he's had twenty-six fucking years to tell me and hasn't. You brought it up. Now talk."

She was utterly magnificent. As Luc watched, her hair slowly unwound and fell out of its twist, cascading over her shoulders in thick, blond ringlets. The chopstick clattered to the floor. Tia shook her head and swept her hand through the mass of hair, pushing it back over her shoulder. The action brought her breasts up high, gave a regal tilt to the long column of her throat. She looked like an avenging angel.

A dark angel, all fire and passion, her amber eyes flashing, jaw clenched.

He couldn't *not* tell her, but he didn't have to like it.

But he did, damnit. He liked it very much. Luc wanted to be the one, the only one she turned to. For knowledge, for friendship. For sex.

Luc jammed his hands in his pockets, took a deep breath, and planted his feet. "Okay. You want the truth? Here's the abbreviated version. Chanku are real. They're a separate species from human, but the differences are hidden until they add certain nutritional supplements to their diet. Once you ingest the proper nutrients, a combination of grasses from Tibet where the Chanku originated, the body goes through physiological changes that render it other than human, changes that allow the body to shift form from human to wolf. There are a lot of genetically perfect Chanku walking among us who have no idea who or what they are because they've never eaten the supplement that implements the shift. They know they're a little different, but they don't know why. Maybe they dream of wolves or maybe they just feel like they have to fuck everything in sight, only they never feel as though they've screwed the right one. They feel different, apart from the rest of society, yet they're always searching for something, searching for their pack. Recognize anything so far?"

Tia stepped back, as though his clipped tirade frightened her. Her stance went from aggressive to vulnerable in a heartbeat.

Luc took a deep breath and softened his tone. "Tia, I am Chanku. I have the ability to shift from human to wolf at will. So does your father. So did your mother."

Tia's eyes went wide. She clapped a hand over her mouth and then dragged her fingers slowly down the curve of her throat to rest over her heart. "My mother? She was Chanku and I didn't know it? The stories really were true?"

Luc nodded. "The gene is passed through the mother. We know it's a sex-linked gene, carried on the X chromosome. It doesn't matter whether or not the father is Chanku, though I imagine it makes the bloodline even stronger if, as in your case, he is. There's a lot we don't know, a lot your father is trying to find out. We have a couple of scientists studying it, but it's not like we can turn this project over to a large group and still retain anonymity. What we do know is, if the mother is Chanku, whether she ever activates the genetics or not, her children will carry the genes as well. However, unless they get the right combination of Tibetan grasses, the Chanku physiology doesn't manifest itself. We used to add the grasses to our meals but your father has managed to synthesize the supplement down to a pill form we take once a day."

"You're kidding, right? A little one-a-day vitamin turns you into a wolf? I find that hard to believe." Tia threw her hands in the air. Luc hoped it was a safe alternative to taking a swing at him. "I find this entire story unbelievable. It's a fairy tale, right? Besides, you left me out of the equation, Luc. What about me?" Tia planted her hands on her hips and thrust her chin forward.

She might look tough, but Luc realized Tia trembled from head to toe, no matter how hard she seemed to fight it. Her bravado was all for show. Her bravery in the face of so much touched him more than anything else about her. Luc's voice softened. He remembered that night so clearly when Ulrich first shifted in front of him, how terrified he'd been. How relieved.

Tia had no idea how her life was about to change. "You, too, Tia. You are Chanku. Not yet awakened, not yet able to shift, but still not entirely human. The fact you were able to link with me proves that. I imagine it's because both your parents were Chanku instead of just one. There's so much more you need to know. C'mon. Ulrich will fill you in on the details."

Tia bent over at the waist and picked her chopstick off the floor, grabbed her mussed hair, and twisted it back into a knot at the base of her neck. As she fastened it in place, she glared at Luc. "Well? Aren't you going to show me first?"

"Show you what?" He knew, of course. Knew she had to see to believe, had to watch the shift before it finally made sense. Just as he'd watched Ulrich that first time, scared silly and wanting so hard to believe it was true.

He couldn't do it, not right now, not when his cock was hard and his need for her escalating with each move she made, each defiant word she uttered. Control as a man was so much easier. The beast didn't always understand the need for restraint.

For that matter, his human side wasn't doing all that well.

Tia blinked. Obviously, she didn't believe he could be so obtuse, but there was no way Luc could tell her the whole truth, that if he shifted now, it wouldn't be sex. It would be bestial rape, pure and simple.

"The wolf, damn you. You expect me to believe you, to merely accept your word that you can shift from human to wolf, but you're not willing to prove it?"

He stared at Tia, using his eyes to intimidate her. From the set of her jaw, it wasn't working. His cock grew harder and he clenched his hands into fists to keep from reaching for her. She was everything he wanted in a mate. Powerful, strong-willed, a true alpha bitch in every sense of the word. When he shifted, Luc wanted time to show Tia everything. Time to make love to her the way he needed.

"Later. We don't have time right now. I promise you'll see the wolf tonight." He stepped forward and gently took her arm. She didn't fight him this time, but she glared at Luc as if he were the foulest being on the face of the earth.

He caught her message, loud and clear. She felt as if he'd betrayed her, as if he'd ripped apart her known universe and dropped her into something dark and frightening and then left her without answers.

In many ways, he had. He'd also shown her the first steps to something glorious, but now was not the time. Both of them needed patience.

Grabbing Tia's handbag off a small table near the front door, Luc handed it to her. Tia took it without comment. Her body radiated anger and fear in equal parts. Luc paused just outside the door as he carefully checked the locks and then turned to face her.

"Believe what you want," he said, his sense of injustice fading, "but I would advise you not to blame the messenger. Please don't blame your father either. He did what he thought was right. It wasn't easy for him either when your mother died. He did his best."

Luc took both Tia's hands in his, leaned close, and kissed her cold, unresponsive lips. "Sweetie, what you're about to discover is nothing short of miraculous. C'mon. Your father's waiting."

Traffic through the city was heavy. Tia sat quietly beside Luc, but her mind raced through everything that had happened tonight. They'd not even discussed the sex, the amazing, mind-blowing orgasm she'd experienced. Nothing she and Shannon had done had ever come close. No other partner had left her feeling the way Luc had tonight.

She'd never imagined what it would feel like from the man's point of view. Her body still hummed with arousal, her pussy clenched in a slow, constant rhythm, and her heart had yet to settle down, either because of or in spite of everything Luc had told her.

Tia knew he thought she was mad at him. That wasn't it at all, but he didn't need to know that right now. He deserved a little bit of confusion after what he'd dumped on her. She stared out the window, resting her chin on her closed knuckles, and thought of her father, of all the years she'd lived away from him.

His choice as well as hers.

Ulrich hadn't wanted her close. She'd always thought it was her developing sexuality that made him nervous. That wasn't it at all. Obviously, he didn't want her to know about her heritage, the fact that she might have the amazing abilities Luc described so matter-of-factly.

Why had he kept it a secret?

Tia had always loved her father. Looked on him with total hero worship, yet at the same time, felt as if he never quite knew what to do with her.

Now, to learn what they had in common, to learn there was an entire world he'd kept hidden from her, hurt as deeply as losing her mother had so many years ago. Why hadn't he told her? Had he left it up to Luc out of cowardice, or was her discovery tonight a terrible mistake?

Who was Ulrich Mason? Obviously, he wasn't the man she'd thought he was. Pack Dynamics wasn't merely a detective agency either. She still needed to question Luc about that, unless her father finally chose to be honest with her.

Feeling as if her heart had been ripped from her chest, Tia watched the blocks pass slowly and wondered exactly what she would say when she faced Ulrich Mason tonight.

A car cut in front of them and Luc hit the brakes. Tia turned and noticed that, while he was still paying attention to his driving, Luc had that same, faraway look she'd seen earlier at the airport, when she was almost sure he and her father had somehow been communicating.

"What are you telling my father?"

"Huh?" Luc swung his head in her direction. "What do you mean?"

"I know you can communicate telepathically. I noticed it earlier but didn't realize what was going on until I experienced the link with you. You're doing the same thing now. What did you tell him?"

Luc was at least honest enough to look ashamed, and he didn't deny her accusation. "We call it mindtalking. I told him to be ready to answer a lot of questions. I also wanted to know who would be at the house. I was hoping just the three of us. It's not. He's invited the rest of the pack to meet you."

"Some of them are your lovers, aren't they?" Tia wasn't sure where that question came from, but suddenly his answer seemed terribly important. She folded her arms over her chest, afraid Luc would notice her hands shaking if she didn't.

Luc's jaw tensed, but he kept his eyes on the road ahead. "All of them are my lovers. Except Ulrich. He finds his sex outside the pack. It's his way of remaining loyal to your mother's memory and maintaining authority within the pack. He doesn't fuck other Chanku." Luc swung his head in Tia's direction. "There. Is that what you wanted to know? Are you happy now?"

Tia threw her hands in the air. "Hey. Don't get mad at me. The only way I'm going to learn a damned thing is if I ask questions. You're sure not volunteering much."

"Ask away, sweetheart."

The surprising venom in Luc's words left Tia feeling hollow inside. They rode the rest of the way to Ulrich's house in silence.

Chapter 6

Luc found a parking space about half a block from Ulrich's house in the Marina District, got out, and opened the door for Tia. She pointedly ignored his outstretched hand and climbed out without his aid. He raised an eyebrow in a mocking salute. She gritted her teeth and looked away. When she walked beside Luc, Tia was careful not to touch him.

Her anger simmered just below the surface, held in check by sheer willpower. How the hell did he expect her to react? The first time she sees Luc in ten years and he proceeds to tell her he can shift from human to wolf, that *she'll* be able to do the same damned thing after taking some stupid pill every day. Even worse, he'd gone down on her with the most talented tongue she'd ever experienced, had given her the orgasm of her life, and it obviously meant nothing to him.

Why did it mean so much to her?

Tia flushed hot and cold, arousal outweighing anger in a heartbeat. Her nipples beaded against the silky fabric of her dress and her pussy clenched in reaction. Luc glanced sharply in her direction. With his damned wolf senses he probably smelled the cream between her thighs. She knew he could see her tits.

She thrust her aching breasts forward and picked up her pace. Luc rolled his eyes and grabbed her arm, hurrying her along the sidewalk. The sharp *tap tap tap* of her high heels seemed to echo in her head. She wanted to tug her arm loose, but they were already at her father's house. The same house she'd grown up in. Where her mother had lived and they'd all been the perfect family, together.

A perfect family, divided by secrets.

Ulrich waited on the front porch.

He met Tia and Luc at the top of the stairs. Light spilled out around him and Tia thought he looked like a Norse god with his thick, white hair and commanding stance. She tamped down her anger and smiled, but instead of the welcoming hug Tia expected, her father motioned them to a dark alcove on the left side of the porch.

"Thank you, Luc." He reached out and shook Luc's hand, but his gaze was fixed on Tia. "First of all, before we go in, sweetie, I have to apologize. This is all my fault, so, please, don't blame Luc. It was cowardly of me to ask Luc to tell you about Chanku, but . . ."

"Why?" Tia swallowed back an unwelcome lump in her throat. "All these years, so many occasions. Why didn't you say anything?"

Her father grabbed both her hands and squeezed them tightly. "A lot of reasons. Mostly I was lost without your mother. I had no idea how to relate to a little girl, much less a young woman. A father hates to acknowledge his daughter's sexuality. I knew, once you became fully Chanku, there would be no stopping you if you were anything like Camille."

His eyes lit up at the mention of her mother's name. Tia bit back tears when Ulrich smiled a very private little smile, and continued. "At least when you and Shannon went off to school, you had each other for sex. I figured that relationship would keep you out of trouble until I managed enough courage to tell you about your true nature."

"You knew about me and Shannon?" Shocked and embarrassed, Tia tried to free her hands from her father's grasp, but he held them firmly.

"Of course. I may be fairly obtuse about a lot of things, but I'm not stupid. You and Shannon are both sensual creatures and your mutual attraction was obvious. I'm not sure, but I believe Shannon's mother was Chanku, which would explain why you were so good together. Tess Murphy and your mother were close, though she died before I had a chance to meet her."

Ulrich relaxed his grip and Tia's hands slipped free. Rattled by his admission, she stepped back, putting distance between herself and both men. A girl, no matter how old she was, did not discuss her sex life with her father. That was way high on the *too much information* scale.

Tia took a deep, steadying breath, clenching and unclenching both fists. She realized she was looking to Luc for the answers her father should have given her. "Okay. Where do we go from here?"

"That's up to your father." Luc obviously turned to Ulrich for guidance. Tia was struck with how much Luc appeared to admire her father. How much her father obviously loved and trusted Luc. The shaft of jealousy that speared through her came as an unwelcome surprise.

"We start her on the supplement tonight. It should take about two weeks, though since she's full-blooded Chanku, it'll probably happen a lot sooner."

Luc nodded in agreement. "She'll need to have someone with her, in case the supplement works faster than we expect. I'd hate to see her attempt a change on her own."

Ulrich glanced at Tia and then turned back to Luc. "Is there room in her place where you can stay? If not, I know your apartment is large enough."

Anger swirling like a live thing inside, Tia glared first at Luc and then at her father. "I'm standing right here, gentlemen. Please don't talk about me as if I'm not."

Her father stopped in the midst of opening his mouth and sighed. "You're right. I'm sorry. I've known this day would come. Instead of preparing for it, I've pretended it wouldn't happen. Denial is truly the coward's way."

"Dad, don't you think I should have been given a choice?"

Tia felt Luc's arm slide around her waist. He gave her a slight squeeze. She glanced at him and realized he sided with her on this issue. His approval felt like a warm wrap against a cool night. Any anger she'd held against him dissipated on the cool evening breeze.

"That was Luc's feeling as well, for what it's worth. I should have said something before now. There really wasn't a choice. You are your mother's daughter. You're my daughter. You *are* Chanku. I was wrong and I'm sorry. This day was coming, no matter how much I tried to delay it." Ulrich sighed deeply, then smiled. "Tianna, I think it's time for you to meet the rest of the pack."

Overwhelmed with the questions she wanted to ask, Tia meekly followed her father. Her dress brushed across her thighs, reminding her that she'd skipped underwear to tantalize Luc, not to attract complete strangers.

She never would have dressed so provocatively if she'd known what waited for her inside her father's house. Four absolutely gorgeous men stood as she entered. Each one tall, athletic, dark haired, all with piercing amber eyes.

In some ways, each might have been Luc's brother, though every man had something to set him apart from the others. The one thing they all appeared to have in common was their blatant sensuality and obvious sexual interest—interest directed entirely at Tia.

She turned to Luc when she felt his body stiffen beside her. His jaw had set in a grim line and possessiveness radiated from every pore. She almost laughed aloud. The balance of power appeared to have shifted, and Luc obviously didn't like it one bit. Tia straightened her shoulders and sucked in her tummy, aware of the rapt attention she received from four sets of amber eyes.

Such sustained interest of four powerful males was intoxicating, undeniably arousing. Tia's nipples pebbled beneath her dress, beading up against the tight bodice. Once more she felt moisture gathering between her legs. Was it knowing Luc was jealous of the other men, or her body reacting to something else, something dark and exciting?

Would they scent her arousal, know exactly how her body responded to their presence? She couldn't shake another subtle thought insinuating itself into her mind, something dark and arousing. Luc and these men had known one another intimately. What would it be like to join them, to be one female among five desirable men?

To be the object of their combined desire? The target for all that male attention?

The thought barely registered, but somehow Luc must have sensed her interest. Tia felt his displeasure in the tightness of his arm around her waist, the rigid stance of his body beside hers.

She turned and smiled sweetly at him, savoring his discomfort. It was the least he deserved.

Luc returned her smile with a knowing frown. He knew exactly what she was up to. Tia licked her lips and looked toward her father.

Ulrich stood beside the four men like a proud father introducing his children. He showed no sign that he was aware each man must be contemplating how to get between his daughter's legs, but Tia was certain Ulrich knew exactly what was going on in the minds of every one of them.

Once again Tia was struck by the close relationship between her father and the men he worked with. The family bond seemed stronger among them than the one he felt for his own flesh and blood.

It had to be the bond of nature, the fact that these six men were all Chanku.

Would Tia know this bond when she finally became Chanku?

Her father stepped forward. "Gentlemen, I want you to meet my daughter, Tianna. She will be, but is not yet, one of us. Luc will lead Tia through the change. Is that understood?"

Tia felt Luc relax beside her, though his arm never left her waist. It rested firmly, possessively, around her hips.

Her father smiled at her and then turned proudly to his men. "Sweetie, this big guy is AJ, the one next to him is Jake, here's Mik, and we call this moose Tinker. He's the baby."

All the men nodded in welcome, but Tinker, a gorgeous mountain of a man standing over six and a half feet tall, the only one in the room with skin darker than Tia's, stepped forward and took her hand. Tia's fingers disappeared completely within his. As they shook hands, Tia felt Luc's arm tighten around her waist once more, but he didn't say anything.

Tinker's voice was soft and low, not at all what Tia would have expected, considering his size. He grinned over his shoulder at her father. "Not anymore, Boss. Looks like Tia's the new baby in the bunch, and about damned time. It's a pleasure to meet you, Tia. Luc, you need any help getting Tia through her first shift, you let me know, okay?"

Tinker winked. Luc growled. The sound was low and menacing and hard to hear, but not one of the men missed it. Tinker stepped quickly back, his demeanor immediately deferential, almost submissive, even though he had at least two inches and eighty pounds on Luc.

Tia's breath caught as all the bits and pieces began to fall into place. The dynamics of the group followed that of a wolf pack in the wild. Her father was the leader, Luc an alpha among the younger men, yet he still deferred to Ulrich.

Which led to another question. What the hell was Pack Dynamics? Tia turned to her father and caught his attention. "Dad, everyone here works for you, right? It's not just the shared genetics. . . . Explain Pack Dynamics. What is it?"

"A detective agency." Ulrich's answer came a bit too quickly.

"Let's try a little of that honesty you were talking about, okay? As far as the general public is concerned, I'll accept your answer. As your daughter and a potential member of your pack, what is it, really?"

"We occasionally do some work for the government." Luc's answer led to more questions. Tia turned to ask for a better explanation, when her father motioned them all into the dining room for dinner.

Tia leaned over and whispered in Luc's ear. "Saved by the bell?"

He merely grinned, bumped her hip with his, and guided her into the next room.

Conversation at the table was more relaxed, but it never returned to Pack Dynamics. Tia learned how each of the men had met her father. Mik, or Miguel, was the only Hispanic of the pack. He and AJ had come directly out of prison to work for Pack Dynamics, which made Tia think of Ulrich rescuing dogs from the pound. Their lives had not been easy, from the stories they told.

Both men obviously worshipped Ulrich, but he'd given them the first real home they'd known. Tinker, like Luc, had been in the military and served in Afghanistan, while Jake, a quiet, contemplative man, was a paramedic in his younger years. Each man had admitted to feeling separate from society before Ulrich recognized the Chanku nature hidden beneath troubled spirits.

Finally, as Mik and AJ cleared away the dishes, Tia turned to Luc. "You've never said how you and Dad met. How did he know you were Chanku?"

Luc's head snapped around at her question. He opened his mouth, paused, and then took a deep breath. "I was a cop on the San Francisco force. We met during an investigation."

"Oh." Tia watched Luc as he handed his dish to AJ and wondered what he was hiding. Why did she feel as though Luc offered more secrets than answers?

Ulrich got up and walked around the table to stand beside Tia. He held a small jar filled with plain brown capsules the size of vitamin pills. "I want you to take one of these every day, without fail. Stay close to Luc. After a few days, you'll be aware of perceptual changes, a stronger sense of smell, sharper hearing, even a difference in your physical strength. I want you to tell Luc anything you feel, anything that is at all different. Here, take one now." He placed the bottle in Tia's outstretched hand. She stared down at the innocuous-looking pills and then back at her father.

So many questions. Before they overwhelmed her, Tia flipped open the bottle, took a capsule, and popped it into her mouth. She chased it with a swallow of wine, wondering once more what she was getting into.

A phone rang. Ulrich shared a quick glance with Luc and then went into his office to answer it. A moment later, he returned.

"Gentlemen, we have an emergency."

AJ and Mik stepped out of the kitchen. Mik had a towel wrapped around his waist and a dish in his hand. For some reason, Tia found herself concentrating on the normalcy of the scene, the absolute domesticity.

"There's been a kidnapping, a member of the President's cabinet. Secretary of Homeland Security, Milton Bosworth, I believe. The pack is to meet with our contact at 0700 hours. Luc, I'm sorry, but you, AJ, Mik, and Jake—you're on this one. The jet's being readied now. Tinker, I want you to remain behind and keep an eye on my daughter."

"I'm a grown-up, Dad. I can take care of myself."

"No. There'll be no argument, especially since you've already started on the supplement. That goes for you as well, Luc."

Tia glanced at Luc, saw the anger in his eyes and the way he concentrated on Tinker. There obviously was a major conversation going on between them that Tia wasn't privy to.

She turned back to her father. He snapped his attention away from Luc and Tinker. "There's too much you don't know, Tia, and it's my fault, but there's no time to fill you in now. You can trust Tinker. When this job is done I'll answer any of your questions."

From the emotions swirling about her, Tia knew Ulrich's last statement was as much for Luc's benefit as her own.

"What about these?" She held up the bottle of capsules.

"Luc will be gone only a week. You should be fine, so continue taking them. Tinker can answer your questions. He went through his first shift just a little more than a year ago, so it's all going to be very fresh in his mind. I'll be available for emergencies, though as control, my time will be tied up until the mission is completed."

Ulrich stepped around the table as Tia stood up. He hugged her tightly against him and then turned away, toward his office. "Tinker, will you please take my daughter home? Contact me later, after she's settled."

Jake, AJ, and Mik followed Ulrich into the office. Tinker left the room and Tia suddenly was alone with Luc. Her heart pounded in her chest when he looked at her. There was a silent intensity about him as frightening as it was arousing.

"Tinker will keep you safe. He knows his boundaries and you can trust him. I'll be back as soon as I can.

Hopefully this won't take more than a few days. We have a lot to discuss."

Tia opened her mouth to say something, anything, but Luc covered her lips with his own. He dragged her body up against his and she felt him, hard and heavy against her belly, his cock a reminder of the orgasm he'd given and the satisfaction he'd not yet found.

Her head ached and then Luc was there, in her mind, a part of her thoughts.

One word. She heard just one word, not with her ears but with her mind, whispered in his voice, harsh with need, it raced along her spine, leaving shivers in its wake.

Mine.

Ulrich called Luc from the other room. Luc swept his tongue across Tia's mouth, as if taking one last taste for the road.

She looked into his amber eyes, her decision made without hesitation, and tried to project her thought in a single, powerful word.

Yours.

Luc blinked, then smiled. He nodded. Kissed her lightly on the tip of her nose. Then he turned, tossed his car keys to Tinker, who had reentered the room, and walked away with a confident, almost cocky step to join his packmates in Ulrich's office.

Tinker quietly took Tia's arm and led her from the house.

She hadn't realized the depth of her exhaustion until Tinker settled Tia into the front seat of Luc's Mercedes and helped her fasten the seat belt. She yawned, kicked her shoes off, and settled back into the soft leather seat. The little jar of pills was safely stashed in her handbag, but she was too tired to think of the implications of their use.

Tinker handled the heavy traffic and Luc's high-powered car with skill and confidence. Tia relaxed and let her eyes drift shut.

She didn't realize she'd fallen asleep until Tinker tapped her lightly on the shoulder. "I think this is your place, isn't it?"

Groggy, Tia scooted up in the seat and looked out the window. Her little apartment already felt like home. She nodded and gathered up her purse and shoes. Tinker opened her door, gave her a hand out, and then guided her up the steps to her front door.

Tia dug her keys out of her purse, but the moment she stuck the key in the lock, the door swung open on its hinges.

Tia glanced at the large man beside her. "I know it was locked when we left. Luc checked it."

"Stay here." Where he'd holstered the gun, Tia had no idea, but now it was firmly grasped in his huge right hand when Tinker slipped through the open doorway. He was gone a couple of minutes before he returned and slipped the pistol into a holster under his shirt, low on his back. "The place is all clear, but I'm staying here with you tonight. Come on in. I want you to call your landlord and let him know we're installing new locks on the doors and windows in the morning."

Tia nodded and followed Tinker into her home.

Chapter 7

Tinker checked the doors and windows once again and then met Tia in the kitchen. "Luc's gonna kill me for this, but there's something I need to do."

Tia looked up from the bottle of wine she was opening. Thank goodness the landlord had stocked the refrigerator before she arrived. "What?"

"Tia, I don't want to frighten you, but I need to shift. I can sense things as a wolf that I totally miss when I'm human. Do you mind?"

Mind? He had to be kidding! Tia shook her head, laughing. "Go ahead. I've been hearing about this all evening long and have yet to see it happen."

"Thanks." Tinker kicked off his shoes, shrugged out of his shirt, and unzipped his pants. Tia blinked. She hadn't really thought about where the clothes went when someone shifted.

Obviously they went right in the middle of her kitchen floor. Lucien Stone might be the one who held her interest, but there was no denying that the young man undressing in front of her had the body of a god.

A very large god.

She realized she was staring at Tinker's white boxer shorts and the way they contrasted with his dark chocolate skin, when he suddenly looped his thumbs beneath the elastic waist and shoved them down over his lean hips.

Tia gasped. She hadn't intended to make a sound, but the body Tinker uncovered was the most impressive she'd ever seen. She glanced up, literally tearing her eyes away from his partially tumescent cock rising from a nest of thick, dark hair.

Her gaze settled on his smile, which suddenly seemed to waver in front of her. His mouth and nose stretched forward at the same time his upper body seemed to turn in on itself and drop lower.

The shift happened in a heartbeat. Tia might have been frightened, but she realized as she witnessed the impossible that she'd seen this in her dreams, had lived with this knowledge buried somewhere deep in her genetic code.

Tinker sat on muscular haunches in front of her, a huge black wolf with golden highlights shining in his thick coat. He licked his muzzle with a long, pink tongue, and Tia thought of the dream that had haunted her for so many nights.

It wasn't Tinker she'd dreamed of. . . . No, her wolf was sleeker, not so muscular, not quite as tall.

Her wolf was definitely Lucien Stone.

Tinker stood up and shook like a big dog climbing out of a lake, then he came close enough to sniff Tia's hand.

"You're absolutely beautiful." She knew her voice sounded as if she'd run a mile, but it was all she could do to get sound past a throat constricted with awe.

Tinker opened his mouth wide, took another long sniff of her legs, and then whirled around and began to search the house once again. He raced from room to room, standing on his hind legs to check the casings around windows and the shelves and cabinets where an intruder might have touched.

Mesmerized, Tia watched while Tinker searched. After a few minutes it actually felt almost normal to have a large black wolf racing around her home. Shaking her head and grinning at what she was accepting so easily, Tia called her landlord, the school principal, to let him know she'd arrived and to ask if he'd been inside her apartment at all.

He said he'd stopped by the day before to stock the refrigerator and cupboards as a welcome gift from the school, but that was all. Tia made plans to meet with him the following day, then slowly hung up the phone.

So who the hell had been snooping through her apartment?

Lost in thought, Tia picked up Tinker's clothing and held the items against her chest. She ran the process of Tinker's shift through her mind once again, and smiled at the thought of his nude body morphing into the huge wolf now scouring her small apartment for clues. Damn. He was as beautiful a wolf as he was a man. Totally gorgeous.

And she was totally *not* aroused. Tia blinked, surprised at her own lack of interest. She'd admired his muscles, the long, strong length of him, even the extraordinary size of his cock and the heavy balls hanging beneath, but she'd looked on him out of curiosity, not desire.

If that had been Luc standing naked in front of her . . . Shivers ran along Tia's spine, imagining how she'd react, how he'd look. Not as big as Tinker, not as tall or muscular, but lean and strong, his shoulders broad, the muscles on his abdomen and chest neatly defined.

When he shifted, Luc would be black as night, his thick coat glistening, his teeth sharp, his beautiful amber eyes focused on Tia.

She held that image in her mind, even when, after a few more minutes, Tinker returned to the kitchen. Tia watched him shift back to human form. She tried to pick the exact moment when wolf became man, but it happened too quickly and so smoothly. Within seconds, Luc's packmate stood tall and naked in front of Tia.

She handed him his boxer shorts. He took them from her with a big grin and quickly stepped into them.

Tia smiled back at him. "That was absolutely amazing." She handed Tinker the rest of his clothes and then jumped up to sit on the kitchen counter while he finished dressing. "I grew up on stories of the Chanku, but until tonight I always thought my mother made them up. I had no idea. The fact that you—we—are real absolutely blows my mind. Did you find out anything?"

Tinker nodded as he finished dressing. "You definitely had a visitor. One person, male, and very nervous. His scent is so strong, I'm surprised we can't smell it even in our human form. He left the window in your bedroom unlatched, probably so he could break in later when you'd be sleeping. We need to go fasten it. Can't do latches with paws."

He held up his huge hands and laughed. Shaking her head, Tia hopped down off the counter and followed Tinker into the bedroom. She was inordinately thankful that this huge man would be sleeping on her couch until Luc returned.

Hiding deep in the shadows, out of sight of the landing pad, Luc checked his watch. Tia would be sleeping right now. Damn, he'd love to be beside her in that big four-poster bed of hers. Instead, he was swatting mosquitoes deep in the swamps of southern Florida, waiting on a helicopter to land on the only piece of solid ground for miles.

He'd never expected the operation to take three days. It would be at least another twenty-four hours before he and Jake finished the job, went through debriefing, and headed back to California.

Back to Tia.

A steady *thump thump thump* echoed on the still night air. Mik flashed a high-powered lantern, using a signal the pilot would be watching for.

The helicopter came in dark and landed without lights, guided only by the beam of Mik's flashlight. AJ shook hands with Secretary Milton Bosworth, the cabinet member he and Mik had just smuggled out of a booby-trapped cavern located deep beneath the swamp, and then turned the exhausted man over to members of the special operations team in the helicopter. Their job was to deliver him safely to operatives in Virginia, who would then return him to Washington, hopefully without the American public ever realizing that a member of the President's cabinet had been held for more than seventy-two hours, supposedly by al Qaeda terrorists working on American soil.

As successful as the mission had been, it left an uneasy feeling in Luc's mind. Something didn't click, but he wasn't sure what it was.

They'd gone in using their typical cover—two men as human handlers, two as Chanku. AJ and Mik lost the draw and pulled duty as humans. Luc and Jake shifted and remained in wolf form throughout the entire mission, changing to human form only after the rescue was complete.

They'd found their target, alone and unguarded, after two days of searching the jungle. As usual, intelligence had been incomplete. The ransom note, for want of a better description, had consisted of a recording by a man with a thick Middle Eastern accent. Experts had pegged him as a native of Jordan, but details were sketchy. They'd had enough to go on, though, to lead them to this Florida swamp filled with sinkholes and old caves. The limestone cavern, one of many in the area, was well hidden, the victim secured by leg chains in a fairly comfortable room, as cavern prisons went.

He'd been grateful for rescue, but more curious about the two wolves who'd found him than excited to be free. He'd offered no information on his captors, other than to say they were al Qaeda terrorists.

There'd been no sign of the bad guys. The victim had been well fed. Odors of cooking lingered in the cavern, easily discernible with sensitive Chanku noses.

The captive had definitely eaten well. The scent of bacon and eggs had made Luc's mouth water. They'd been on slim rations throughout the search, depending as much on their hunting skill as the food their two humans carried.

Luc watched the small jet take off and then contacted Ulrich. He and Jake planned to go back into the cavern. It wasn't in their orders, but Luc wanted the chance to look for evidence before the second group of special-operations forces currently on their way blew up the entire area.

He shook his head, trying to discern the niggling little questions hovering just out of reach. If he wasn't so tired, or so worried about Tia, Luc knew it would all become clear. Maybe one more run through the cavern would help.

Luc's radio came to life. "Mason here. What's your status?"

"The pigeon's headed home to roost. Jake and I are going hunting." Luc flashed a quick grin at his partner. Jake nodded and pulled his cap down over his eyes.

"Negative. Too dangerous."

Luc stared at the com unit. Since when had Ulrich Mason deemed a job too dangerous? "Looks clear. We marked all possible traps. Al Qaeda appears not to be an issue. The wolves want to check out the setup before the dogs arrive."

"You're needed here. Now."

Luc's heart went cold. "Tia?"

"Wait for a secure channel. Come home immediately."

Tia added an extra nail to the bookshelf, wiped her dusty hands on her long skirt, and stood back to admire her work. For some reason the shelf had come loose during the night. Thank goodness it had happened now, not after classes started, or she or the children could have been hurt.

When she'd entered the classroom to finish putting everything in order for the first day of school in a little more than a week, she'd been met by a scattered pile of biology books covering her desk and chair.

"Tinker, where are you when I need you?"

Tia refused to even think of Luc. She couldn't, not if she wanted to get any work done.

She really could have used Tinker about now, but he was spending the morning helping her father. She missed him. He was big and helpful and strong as an ox, not to mention easy on the eyes.

He treated Tia like a little sister, but she'd caught him staring avidly more than once. She'd even noticed he had an erection on a few occasions when they'd worked closely together on one project or another, something she'd decided to take as a compliment.

His obvious arousal and male interest didn't make her at all nervous. Though the bite mark Luc left on her neck had faded almost completely, Tinker obviously respected his leader's claim.

But did Tia? She still wasn't certain how she felt about Luc, about his possessive nature, his intensity. He acted as if, after one day together, she belonged to him, as if Tianna Mason were already his chosen mate.

Of course, even if she was, it was a little too soon to let him know that for sure.

So why in the hell had Tia said she was his before he left? Damn, it was all so confusing.

She'd been taking her pills, one every day like a damned vitamin. There were already changes, but not changes she'd felt comfortable telling Tinker about.

Ulrich's supplements were definitely doing something to her body, specifically her libido.

Tia grinned broadly as she pounded the nail into the

wall. No way was she going to try explaining her newest increased perception to her father . . . or to Luc. She'd never felt so horny in her life. Within two days of starting the supplements, she'd even found herself lusting after Tinker whenever he came near, though she'd managed—with great difficulty—to keep that lust under control.

At night she dreamed of Luc, of his mouth between her legs, of his cock stuffing her full. Her nights were filled with frustration until she took care of herself with her fingers or vibrator or both, hoping like hell Tinker couldn't hear either the humming from the vibrator or the moans she'd been unable to completely stifle.

Then Tinker would wander into the kitchen in the morning, half asleep and looking for a cup of coffee, and she'd feel the same rush of heat in her needy pussy that she had from dreams of Luc.

He'd told her Chanku were sensual beings. He hadn't mentioned twenty-four-hour-a-day lust!

A soft scratching at the classroom door caught Tia's attention. She felt a strange sensation, as if the hair on the back of her neck stood on end, and once again the skin over her arms seemed to crawl. She brushed her hands down her skirt and stared at the door. After all the odd little incidents since her arrival, Tia definitely felt more comfortable with Tinker close by.

Whether it was the supplements she faithfully took each morning or the fact that she was becoming a total ninny after her father's warnings and the break-in at her apartment, Tia had to admit she felt jumpy and skittish and not at all comfortable being here alone.

There'd been the phone calls with no one on the other end, the odd sense of being watched on a few occasions, the feeling she wasn't alone. Part of it might have been due to her heightened senses.

She glanced at her watch and realized it was almost noon. Tinker should be back within the next hour.

There was another quick thump against the door and then all went quiet. Tia walked across the room and carefully opened the classroom door. Two calico kittens belonging to the school principal's daughter played in the dust just outside. Sighing with relief, Tia squatted on the threshold and held her hand out to the nearest one.

It rolled to its belly, stood up, and scampered close. She laughed when the kitten's ears perked forward and it sniffed her fingers.

Suddenly, the kitten hissed and backed away. The fur on its back stood straight on end. With another hiss and a brave little swat at Tia's fingers, the kitten ran back across the yard to the principal's apartment. The second one followed close behind, its fuzzy tail standing straight.

"It recognizes the wolf in you."

"Holy shit!" Tia fell backward and landed on her butt. Still dressed in worn fatigues, Luc stood off to one side. He looked exhausted, and so dear Tia practically wept.

"When did you get home?" She took a deep breath to settle her pounding heart and smiled up at him, silently cataloging the fact that her short tank top was stained, her ankle-length, tie-dyed skirt was covered in dust, and she'd not put on any underwear after her shower this morning.

"Just now. I came straight here. I was headed for your apartment, but I saw you open the door here when I went by." Luc held out his hand. Tia grabbed on, fully aware of rough calluses and strength. Luc hauled her to her feet, directly into his arms.

His mouth against her lips felt right, as if they'd been lovers forever. Tia's body immediately found the hills and valleys of Luc's, so that they touched from toes to lips.

Her doubts of only a moment before fled beneath the pressure of his mouth against hers.

Luc's powerful legs contained Tia's and his cock rode against her mons with bruising strength. He walked her back into the classroom, still kissing and nibbling at her mouth, and then closed the door behind them. His hands slipped under her cropped tank top and left a trail of fire across her back along her ribs. He found her right breast, cupped her flesh in his rough palm, then pinched her nipple, hard.

Tia moaned and thrust her hips hard against Luc.

"No bra?"

She felt his smile against her mouth.

"No undies, either."

Luc's groan was all the answer Tia needed. Her arms looped tightly around his neck and she pressed hard against him, rubbing her pelvis slowly back and forth over the solid length of Luc's cock straining beneath his heavy canvas pants.

Luc grabbed Tia's waist and lifted her as if she weighed nothing at all, setting her on a raised work counter stretched across the back of the classroom. He spread her legs wide, shoved her long cotton skirt up into a multicolored twist past her thighs, and leaned close between her knees. Tia arched her back and closed her eyes. Her entire sex pulsed in anticipation, from womb to labia to needy clit. The cool air lightly brushed her damp folds as her awareness of Luc, her memory of his greedy mouth and hot tongue, propelled her to the edge of orgasm.

With his hands firmly planted on the countertop on either side of Tia's widely spread thighs, Luc licked his lips, anticipating the taste of Tia on his tongue.

He'd dreamed of this forever, it seemed, the flavors and textures of Tia's pussy. Her sweet ambrosia had hooked him from the very first taste. Was it only five days ago?

He looped his arms under her knees and drew her forward over the slick counter top, spreading her legs even wider.

She was open and ready, her pink folds glistening with dew, the tiny bud of her clit peeking out of its protective hood. Luc merely looked at her, inhaling her scent, recognizing the changes already taking place. What before had intrigued and excited him now drew him like an addictive drug.

Tia was more Chanku than even she appeared to realize. Her body's chemistry had changed; the scents, even the flavors, should be different.

Luc slowly leaned close. His tongue swept the length of her pussy, from perineum to just below her clitoris.

He'd save that for later.

She was wet and ready, her labia plump and glistening. The taste of her cream an addictive elixir. Luc's breathing faltered as he drew her scent deep into his lungs and found Tia once more with his tongue.

He'd been right. Subtly different, her taste was an aphrodisiac to the wolf in Luc. He clamped down on the almost overwhelming urge to shift, to take her as the wolf.

Not here. Not now. Not until Tia was ready.

Tia moaned as he lapped slowly between her legs, his tongue going deeper with each lick, his nose bumping unobtrusively at her clit. He felt her legs trembling and concentrated more on sucking her labia between his lips, then lightly tonguing her clitoris. She jerked her hips when he found that bundle of nerves with his lips and gently sucked, then laved her with the flat of his tongue.

Her moans turned to whimpers, soft pleas for more. He heard her fingernails scrabbling at the slick countertop and then felt them tangle in his hair. He fought a driving compulsion to straighten up and shove his throbbing cock between her legs.

No. Not now, not here. He repeated the words, a silent mantra, promising himself more, all of her, later.

For now, Luc fully intended to show Tia just what her body was capable of, how highly tuned her senses were becoming.

He grabbed her firm buttocks and lifted her closer to

his mouth, jabbing his tongue deep inside, licking his way out of her streaming cunt and then sucking and licking at her clit.

His fingers found the crack between her cheeks and rimmed her sensitive anus, putting pressure there as he used his mouth on her pussy.

He felt her body tense, heard the frantic need behind her whimpering cries. Her fluids filled his mouth and he lapped and sucked, driving her over the edge and beyond.

She cried out, a long, low cry of pleasure as she arched her back and clamped her knees against the sides of Luc's head. Her fingers pulled tightly in his hair, holding him close between her legs. He felt Tia's uncontrolled spasms, tasted the fresh flow of honey on his lips, thrust his tongue harder, deeper. . . .

"Hey, Tia! I heard Luc's ba—oh. Fuck."

Luc whipped around. Tinker stood in the doorway, a couple bags of takeout in his hand, a shocked grin on his face.

"Uh, I guess you already knew, eh?"

Instead of leaving, he shut the door behind him and leaned against it.

Tia raised her head, blinking owlishly, the breath huffing in and out of her mouth. She stared at Tinker for a long moment, as though trying to make sense of her situation. "Don't you think you should leave? At least until we're through?"

"Um . . . no. From what I understand, that's not the Chanku way."

Luc turned back to Tia and gave her one more possessive lick between her legs, then pulled down her skirt.

"What's he mean, Luc?" As if their situation had finally sunk in, Tia blushed furiously and scooted back against the wall, tucking her long skirt around her ankles until only her toes peeked out under the hem.

Luc wiped her juices off his face with a clean handkerchief. As embarrassed as Tia looked, he should have felt a little more remorseful, but she'd find out about this sooner or later. At some point he'd known all along he'd have to explain why Tinker's presence left him even more aroused.

It might as well be now.

Turning slowly, Luc smiled at Tia. Her answering frown practically screamed her confusion. He stroked her foot through the gauzy fabric of her skirt and rubbed the ends of her toes with his thumb. "What Tinker means is that the alpha female of a Chanku pack generally shares her favors with the entire pack, no matter what sex. She will breed only with her chosen mate, but she'll have sex with all the other adult members, either individually or in a group."

Luc expected at least a bit of shock. Instead, what he saw on Tia's face made his gut clench. She wasn't at all put off by the idea. In fact, if his nose was on target, she'd just climaxed thinking about the possibilities.

She stared at him for a long moment. He wished her thoughts weren't so thoroughly blocked. "How do you feel about that, Luc?"

"Until you and I are a mated pair, something that damned well better happen sooner than later, I'm not sharing you. After we mate, it's your call and I will embrace whatever you decide . . . or maybe I should say, whomever."

Tia blinked, wide-eyed. She glanced toward Tinker with what appeared to be an entirely new appreciation. Luc should have been jealous—he'd been jealous the first night she'd met the pack—but now he felt only pride, as well as an intense desire for his woman, stronger even than what he'd felt before.

Tia obviously had what she needed to function as Chanku, including the sensual nature of the beast. He wondered how close she was to shifting, how far the supplements had taken her.

Luc stood up and lifted Tia off the counter. "Well, what do you think?"

She turned and winked at Tinker and then looked up at Luc. Her lips curved in a provocative smile. "I think I'm really going to like being the alpha bitch in this pack."

Luc's decision already had been made on the way here, but Tia's response convinced him he was doing the right thing. "Good. Then pack your bags and get ready for a vacation. We're going somewhere private where I won't have to worry about a doofus like Tinker walking in at inappropriate moments."

Tinker laughed. "Hell, Luc. I thought my timing was extremely appropriate." His intense gaze was at odds to his light banter.

What's wrong?

Tia's in danger. I'm glad you mentioned a vacation. You need to get her away from here. Now.

Luc punched the big guy lightly on the shoulder. There was no time to question Tinker, but he'd learned to trust his packmate implicitly. "I'm taking her to the cabin. Let Ulrich know we'll be gone at least five days. I want you and the guys to come up on Wednesday." He glanced down at Tia and smiled at the confusion in her expression. This would work to everyone's advantage. "You and I need time alone. You may not realize it, but you're almost ready to make the shift."

Tia blinked and backed away. "Dad said it would take two weeks. It's not even been a whole week since I started the supplement." She rubbed her hands over her arms, the nervous gesture looking frantic, almost obsessive.

"Your skin feels like it's ready to burst, doesn't it? You're noticing some odd bouts of vertigo, sensory things that don't quite make sense . . . smells are more intense. You're aware of sounds you've never paid attention to before and you feel as if you could fuck anything on two legs . . . or four."

Tia stopped rubbing her arms and stared at Luc. She

should have laughed, but he'd hit too damned close to the truth. "How did you know?"

He'd thought so. Tia's look of surprise confirmed Luc's suspicions. "You're the first full-blooded Chanku we've seen. It's happening fast. I recognize the signs in you." He tipped up her chin with a fingertip and kissed her lightly on the mouth. "Tonight you'll run with me in the forest. Trust me."

Tia gazed at him with trust shaded by fear. He couldn't blame her. Luc had fears of his own. They would link, at some point. They had to, so he could show her how to shift.

Would he be able to hide his sins? Could he suppress the memories of that long-ago night in Golden Gate Park? Conceal the fatal gunshot that killed Camille Mason, the fact that he, Lucien Stone, had pulled the trigger?

He had to. This woman was destined to be his mate. Luc felt it in his heart, knew it in his mind. Knew just as well that Tia could never forgive the man who killed her mother.

Chapter 8

"What do you think?" Luc stood beside the open car door and stretched, raising his long arms over his head, arching his back and twisting around his head so that his long hair swept the collar on either side of his shirt.

Tia climbed stiffly out of the car and rubbed her arms. The evening air was cool, but her chill came from the inside. Fear, curiosity. Arousal.

Tia swallowed hard. She forced herself to look away from the sleek play of soft flannel shirt over rippling muscle, the sunlight shimmering off his sleek, dark hair. It took every bit of willpower she possessed.

Luc could very well be right. She might actually be ready. Tia knew something was changing. Her body, her perceptions, her sensual nature. Sitting so close to Luc on the long drive had left her antsy and aroused. She'd laughed when he'd told her the Chanku were a sensual species.

No kidding.

Tia shuddered and tried to draw her raging libido under control, but it wasn't easy. Not when her pussy kept clenching and releasing, not when her nipples hurt from staying tight and puckered against her shirt for the entire ride up the mountain.

She turned in a full circle, doing her utmost to appreciate the wild beauty of the setting. It wasn't easy when all she could think of were the sleeping arrangements and how her body needed, wanted.

The cabin nestled in a thick stand of mixed fir and pine at the edge of a meadow. Huge, barren mountain peaks towered over the small clearing, their tops frosted with remnants of last season's snow, now turning pink with the dying rays of the evening sun.

The air at this elevation was fresh and clean, with just a hint of fall coolness. Aspen growing along the creeks had begun the yearly shift from green to gold. There was no sound other than the soft sigh of wind in the trees, the chatter of blue jays in the nearby woods. After the constant noise and bustle of San Francisco, this spot felt like heaven.

Quietly ripe with potential, the perfect setting to discover a new self, to explore a new lover. Tia smiled at Luc. "It's beautiful. Impressive. I've never been this high in the mountains before."

Never been this high, period.

She tilted her glance sideways at Luc and wondered how this night would end. Sex had always been so easy and uncomplicated for her. Not with this man. No, Luc expected more from Tia than any lover before.

Not even Shannon had asked for her soul.

Luc watched her over the roof of the car. Tia felt it again, the odd pressure in her head as though Luc tried to communicate telepathically. He'd said it would happen, that suddenly she would discover how to open her thoughts, accept her need to communicate on a level beyond verbal speech.

He'd called it "mindtalking."

Tia knew she was close. She'd managed that one word before Luc left, but try as she might, she'd not been able to communicate with Tinker during the long days he'd shadowed her.

Today, though, there'd been a sense of something or someone searching, pressing against her skull for much of the trip, but she'd not understood how to open her thoughts to him.

Would she have allowed him in, had she known how? It was all so confusing. Luc hadn't asked. Hadn't acknowledged his silent intrusion. Neither had Tia.

She'd hardly noticed the scenery on the trip up the mountainous roads. Her eyes might have looked, but her mind remained otherwise occupied. Luc had been so close, yet a million miles away. Tapping at a door she'd been unable to open.

It had taken them all afternoon to get here, to this wild slice of California mountain wilderness in the northeastern part of the state.

Tia had bubbled over with questions.

Luc hadn't answered any of them.

Of course, she hadn't asked. She couldn't. There were too many and nothing made sense. In the back of her mind, Tia accepted that there were some questions only her ability to shift would answer.

Luc had said she would run with the wolf tonight. Would she make love with him as well?

She shivered. She wasn't quite willing to think about that yet. "Who owns this place?" Tia reached into the backseat for the small sports bag filled with her belongings. Turning with the bag clutched to her chest, she glanced at Luc. Her stomach clenched, seeing him here in this wild setting, dressed so casually. He belonged here, not the city.

By tonight, he would belong to Tia as well. Or would he?

"Pack Dynamics is the registered owner, but since we're all owners of the company, it's ours. Yours as well, once you are fully Chanku. I imagine your father has already added you to the deeds for the properties we own."

Tia's heart beat faster. She felt poised on the edge of a

dark abyss, as if contemplating a leap into the void. Her life truly depended on her ability to survive the fall. Tia's arms itched and a shiver raced across her spine. She took a deep breath, nodded her understanding, and followed Luc into the cabin.

"Sorry I'm late, boss." Tinker slipped quietly into Ulrich's office and nodded at the other four men in the room before leaning against the back wall. "What's up?"

Ulrich stood behind his desk and studied his hands while the pack settled. He almost smiled at the tension in the room. If it had been anyone other than his daughter at the root of it, he might have.

"Have they gone?" He focused on Tinker, the least likely wolf of the entire pack, yet easily the most loyal. If not for Luc, Ulrich would have chosen Tinker as Tia's mate. A good man. A strong man. An even better wolf.

"Yeah. They should be at the cabin by now. The rest of us will join them in a couple days."

AJ, Mik, and Jake turned as one to stare at Tinker and then just as quickly looked back at Ulrich. Even AJ looked flustered, as if uncertain what would come next. Only Tinker seemed sure of himself.

Obviously, Tinker still needed to share Luc's plans with the pack. He certainly hadn't shared them with Ulrich.

Ulrich hadn't expected this so soon. Not all of them. Not with his baby. He bit back a snarl. Four sets of eyes turned to him in question. Ulrich ignored them. Let the damned beasts figure it out for themselves. He brushed his hands along his thighs, physically wiping his hands of the entire situation. Moving on to more important things.

"Okay. Enough on that. We need to discuss the mission. I've read your report and agree with Luc's summary. Something doesn't feel right. Our target was not forthcoming on details, evidence in the caves was a bit too easy to find, and Luc said all of you had a bad feeling about the entire operation . . . and that's merely regarding the obvious. Any comments, additions to your report?"

Tinker held up his hand. "I've got a comment, but it's not on this mission. It's about Tia."

"Is this really necessary right now?"

Tinker glared at him, practically a challenge. Ulrich almost took a step back in surprise, but caught himself in time. Tinker never challenged anyone, especially Ulrich. He nodded.

"I'm convinced someone is stalking Tia."

"What?" Ulrich glared at Tinker. "You said it was a false alarm, that the break-in was an isolated incident and Tia's sense of being watched just a case of nerves."

Tinker shrugged his shoulders. "I wasn't sure of my suspicions until this morning. She had a bookshelf give way in the classroom. A heavy one, right over her desk. If it had come down while she was sitting there, Tia could have been badly hurt. As you know, it's not the first incident, but easily the most dangerous."

Ulrich picked up a pencil and rolled it between his thumb and forefinger. "Could it have been an accident?"

Tinker shook his head. "Nope. Bolts generally don't saw halfway through themselves. Another thing: I recognized scent. Same guy as the one who tried to break into her apartment the first night."

The pencil snapped. "Anything else?"

AJ spoke up. "About the mission, not Tia. A feeling. A very strong feeling that something is not as it should be."

Jake and Mik muttered in agreement. "The entire mission felt like a setup, boss, but we couldn't figure out why." Jake shrugged his shoulders. "It just didn't feel right. Bosworth didn't feel right."

Ulrich nodded. "I've known Bosworth for years. Never liked or disliked the man either way, so I can't comment on him. I've had a similar sense of disorder. It's good Luc and Tia are gone. The cabin's as close to a safe house as we've got. Stay alert. If you think of anything, contact me."

Ulrich took a long look at the four young men crowding his office. Each of them was as a son to him, a member of his family, and he loved each one more than he ever thought he could love another man.

Yet the love he felt for these men paled beside the emotions tied up in Tia. She would always be his heart, his baby, his only link to Camille. He opened his mouth, coughed, cleared his throat, and realized he was too choked up to speak aloud.

Still, the words needed to be said. He was, after all, her father. Ulrich had known this day would come, but never expected it to happen so soon . . . for Tia to grow up so quickly.

To look so very much like her mother.

When you go to the cabin . . . when you are with Luc and Tia, remember this: She is my daughter. She is very precious to me.

Ulrich pinned every man, one after the other, with a look that should have left them shaking in their boots, not practically quivering in anticipation.

Sighing, he added, *Don't ever forget, Tia is my only daughter. If you hurt her, the world will not be big enough to hide you.*

The cabin was surprisingly large inside. Tia accepted the fact that her sudden interest in the floor plan was to keep from thinking of the night ahead, but she explored the bottom level with the large kitchen and common room dominated by a huge fireplace at one end, and then climbed the stairs to a spacious loft sleeping area while Luc unpacked the car and checked outside to make sure all was well.

Tia reached the top of the stairs and stopped in her tracks.

She'd expected lots of beds. Not four king-size mattresses shoved together across the floor to make *one* large bed.

A bed for five big men? Tia's stomach clenched, imagining Luc, Tinker, AJ, Jake, and Mik sprawled naked across the bedding. Five perfect bodies, limbs entwined, mouths and hands and cocks all working in perfect unison. Five perfect men, loving one another.

Loving Tia?

She grabbed the stair railing when her legs threatened to give way.

"Tia? You upstairs?"

"Uh . . . yeah. I'm here. I'm coming down." She really didn't want Luc to catch her here. Not the way her mind was working right now, the way her entire midsection felt as if it were clenching into one huge, impending orgasm.

She turned around and ran into Luc. He grabbed her waist to steady her. "You okay?"

Tia nodded.

"Good. It'll be dark soon. We should eat something light before I take you through your shift." He pulled back and looked more carefully. His eyes narrowed and Tia was certain his nostrils flared. "Are you sure you're okay?"

When she didn't answer, his gaze swept her body from crotch to chin and then he glanced over Tia's shoulder and laughed. "Ah . . . now I see what's going on. Our sleeping loft has left you speechless?"

Blushing, Tia shoved against his chest and stepped around Luc when he dropped his hands from her waist. "Only four beds? Where do you sleep?"

"Up here with the guys." He paused, just long enough to allow Tia's imagination full rein. "We generally only need two of the mattresses."

Tia snorted. Tried her best to play it cool. "That many?" She gave Luc a look similar to the one he'd just given her, but the image in her mind of all those sexy, sweaty bodies made it difficult to swallow. She wondered once more if Luc took the bottom or the top.

Definitely the top. With that visual planted firmly in her mind, Tia led the way down the stairs.

Luc barbecued steaks, though he really only warmed them over the fire. Tia had noticed an increased craving for meat just a day after starting the supplements, quite a change after her mostly vegetarian diet of the past. Tonight she cut into the blood-rare beef and savored every bite.

Luc ate quietly, sipping at his wine and barely touching the salad she'd made. He looked up, chewing slowly, and swallowed. "Why do you block me?"

"What?" Tia swallowed a sip of wine and set down the glass. "I don't understand."

"In order to show you how to shift, I'll need to do at least a simple link, enough to show you the physical steps to take you through the change. You've got a block like a brick wall around your thoughts."

"I don't mean to." Tia thought of the one time they had linked, during sex when she'd been high in the midst of orgasm. There'd been the sense of a shutter opening to allow light inside, only the light had been Lucien's thoughts.

She went there now, raising the shutters consciously this time. Opening her mind. *Like this?*

Exactly! Do you understand me? Do you think you can see what I want you to see?

It really was quite simple. If she'd only known! Tia stared at Luc, concentrated on the open shutter. *Yes. I'm certain I can. I hope I can. But I'm afraid.*

What if it didn't work? What if she ended up caught halfway between wolf and human? What if . . . "I don't know if I can do this. What if I'm not ready? It's barely been a week since I started the pills."

"If it's too soon, nothing will happen. We'll wait and try it again in a couple of days."

"Easy for you to say." She bit off a laugh that sounded more like a sob.

"I'm going to shift. Tinker said you've watched him shift a couple times, so you know what to expect. I want you to link with me and feel what I feel from the inside out."

Tia carefully wiped her mouth and pushed away her plate. It had happened so fast with Tinker, the change from human to wolf and back again. How would she ever do something so complex, changing bones and organs, even her brain!

"Luc? Does it hurt? I mean . . . your bones are changing, your entire body." Damn, she felt like such a baby, but until a week ago, she'd never once imagined anything at all like this.

Except in her dreams.

Luc shook his head. "I know it seems like it should hurt, but it doesn't. There's a sense of disorientation that lasts an instant. Your dad thinks it's at that moment when the human brain becomes wolf, or vice versa, that the other structures make the change as well. During the shift from one brain to another, there's no sensor for pain, so the body doesn't feel the change in bone and muscle and everything else." He flashed a sexy grin at Tia. "At least, that's the theory. Have you had enough to eat? Are you ready?"

Tia stood up and tossed her napkin on the table. "Ready as I'll ever be. Lead on."

Luc took her out on the deck. The sun had gone down and stars sprinkled across a midnight sky. The forest loomed black and threatening, and a bare slice of moon spread a pale glimmer of light over the meadow.

How would she see to run at night? What if she got lost in the woods, not even human, unsure how to return to her human form?

What if . . . ?

Tia spun around at the sound of a zipper. Luc already had his shirt and shoes off. He'd pushed his pants down his legs and was stepping out of them. Why hadn't she thought of this? Tinker had undressed first, too.

She'd never seen Luc completely naked before. He was beautiful, his body lean and sculpted, the muscles of thigh and chest, abdomen and arms sharply defined in the glow of light spilling from the large front window of the cabin.

His cock jutted forward from its tangle of dark hair, not fully erect, its tumescence merely hinting at ultimate length and width. Tinker might be a physically larger man than Luc, but he had nothing on this alpha male.

Trembling, her pussy clenching in unexpected arousal, Tia turned her back on Luc and forced the image of their naked bodies coupling from her mind. She had to concentrate on shifting, needed her full attention on Luc's instructions, not sex.

Impossible. She'd thought of little else with him since that first meeting in the airport just a week ago.

Blanking her mind to the inevitable, Tia quickly slipped out of her jeans and sweater, folded them carefully, and then removed her panties and bra and placed everything carefully on one of the deck chairs. The night air felt uncomfortably cold. Her teeth chattered, as much from the chill air as from nerves. Her nipples beaded and she wrapped her arms around herself. Luc stepped close and drew her into a hug.

He rubbed her cold arms with his extraordinarily hot hands. Tia wanted to concentrate on his words, his hands, anything but the length of his cock pressing against her belly.

Impossible. She pressed close to him, felt his erection grow firmer, longer, thicker. Then she heard Luc's soft chuckle.

"Suddenly I'm warm enough. You'll warm up when you've got fur. I'm going to shift. I want you in my head, feeling what I do, watching with your eyes, with your mind. Don't shift this time. Just watch."

He stepped away. *Are you with me?*

Tia nodded. *Yes.*

Shivering, she tightened her arms around her waist and watched as Luc smiled at her, then leaned over. By the time his hands touched the deck, they were wolf's paws with thick, dark nails. His powerful body stretched, his tail waved across his back like a flag. Luc looked up at her, amber eyes glowing, the face of the wolf in her dreams.

He'd told her to wait. She couldn't. Tia looked into Luc's beautiful eyes and her anxiety fled. She'd followed the shift in his mind and suddenly it all made perfect sense.

There was no pain or fear. Instead, Tia felt her world come together, as if she'd done this a thousand times before. She leaned forward as if to touch her toes. Her bones and muscles flowed smoothly from one being to another. There was a brief sense of disorientation, just as Luc described. Then she found herself looking up at the larger wolf and seeing delight in his eyes.

Tia held up one paw and then the other. Her coat was much lighter than Luc's, with more of a reddish tint. She no longer felt the chill in the air. Instead, the night was filled with scents and sounds unnoticed by her human senses.

Moonlight bathed the meadow in a brilliant glow as bright as the noonday sun. The trees no longer loomed dark and menacing. Though her colors weren't as sharp as with her human eyes, Tia felt as if she'd entered a multi-layered tapestry where sound and scent became an extension of sight.

Eyes wide with wonder, she turned to Luc. He sat quietly, watching her. *Are you ready to run?*

Oh, yes! Tia stood and shook herself, then followed Luc's leap from the deck to the soft meadow grass below. She'd always prided herself on keeping fit, but the four legs now powering her across the meadow and into the forest were beyond anything she'd ever imagined.

Luc yipped, a joyful sound of play, and streaked down a narrow trail with Tia in hot pursuit. She caught up to him near a small stream, nipped at his flank, and leapt over the water. A big-eared jackrabbit, startled by two wolves in the forest, took off running. Luc followed with Tia close on his heels. They leapt over fallen logs, scrabbled across rocks and under thorny blackberry vines where they lost their prey amid the brambles.

They raced on, running for the pure joy of speed, the sense of freedom and the unique beauty of their wild nature. Tia felt powerful, alert, and wild, yet still aware of that human part of her, alive with the wonder of Chanku.

Aware, too, of the sensuality of this marvelous form, the purity of motion, the perfection of her wolven body. The world of the deep forest teemed with scents and sounds never before experienced, an entire universe of sensation beyond her human perception.

As wolf, Tia felt it all. Reveled in the wonder of a new world layered closely upon the familiar. She breathed in the scents of moss and decay, of new growth and living things, but most of all, she celebrated the rush of feeling for Lucien, for his alpha status, his powerful wolven body clearing the trail ahead.

When she'd agreed to his claim, when he'd called her his own, Tia had no idea the commitment she'd made. Now the words made sense. As wolf, as Chanku, Tia understood the power of that single vow.

It wasn't for the night or for however long it worked. It was forever. Period. A bond so powerful even death could not sever the link.

Was she ready? Tia didn't know. Didn't want to think about it now, not with the wind in her face, the sights and scents of the night all around her, as foreign to this wondrous form as if she'd landed here from another planet.

Later. She'd think about it later. For now, Tia ran.

Finally, panting, tongues lolling and eyes glittering, Tia flopped down next to Luc in a marshy patch of grass. She stretched out full length in the damp carpet, rolling over to her back. Luc crept close, his muzzle mere inches from hers. His long tongue swept across her face and he nipped softly at her ear.

Before she could react to his nearness, his delicious scent, Luc sat back on his haunches. *It's almost dawn. We've run all night long. It's time to rest.*

I know. Now that we've stopped, I realize I'm really tired. How far is it? I have no idea where we are.

Follow me. Not far.

Tia trotted along behind Luc. It really wasn't all that far, as distance went. Not far at all. But she knew that this night, this experience, had taken her farther than she'd ever dreamed possible.

Luc had told her nothing would be the same once she shifted for the first time. That she would never again see the world through human eyes without weighing the view against her Chanku perception. Following his trail through the forest in the early light of dawn, Tia finally understood.

She understood something else, as well. Something Tia wasn't certain she was ready to accept, though the promise tugged at her heart, filled her thoughts.

She would follow Luc anywhere.

For as long as he wanted—wherever he went.

The shift from wolf to human felt rather anti-climactic. The moments following, anything but. Standing in the cool morning air, shivering without her heavy fur coat, Tia smiled uncertainly at Luc. Her body felt tight, her skin ultra-sensitive. Luc had said she would be more aroused just after her run than she'd ever been in her life.

He hadn't exaggerated. Alert to scents and sounds as never before, almost painfully receptive to her own body's needs and desires, Tia ached with a deep, overwhelming sexual hunger. She ran her tongue across her upper lip, tasted the salty flavor of sweat from their long run.

Tia tilted her head to the sky and inhaled, expanding her lungs. She recognized Luc's musky, male scent, like an aphrodisiac to her already highly stimulated libido. Wrapping her arms around her body for warmth, Tia caught herself gently massaging her elongated nipples, just for the sharp rush of desire that arrowed straight down between her legs. Like a fuse, lit and ready to explode, her body hummed with need and desire, her mind raced with the words she wanted to say, the questions she wanted to ask.

She couldn't. Not now, not with Luc merely a breath away, his naked body so close she felt the warmth radiating from his skin, smelled the dark forest and primal scents of the night just past.

Not with her own body ready to ignite, primed for sex, impatient and restless. She glanced at Luc, wondering why he hesitated, why he hadn't taken her here under the stars, beneath the moon. He looked different, somehow. More powerful . . . feral. His eyes glittered and there was a dark shadow of beard he'd not had the night before. A sheen of sweat glistened through the thick mat of hair on his chest. His shoulders seemed broader, his muscles larger, as if pumped from their run through the night. His overlong, dark hair was mussed and tousled, the inevitable question mark hanging forward across his forehead.

Tia swallowed, the sound audible in the still of the early morning. Swallowed and fought an overwhelming need to drop to her knees in front of Luc, to take his swollen cock, now standing so proudly erect, between her lips.

Arousal, hot and insistent, pooled in her belly, crawled across her limbs. She looked into Luc's eyes and read matching desire, a need every bit as powerful as her own. Giving in to carnal hunger, she licked her lips and smiled innocently, then slowly, surely, knelt before him and raised her head.

Luc's eyes widened when her mouth found the taut crown of his cock. She licked the dark head with the tip of her tongue, circling the tiny slit to taste the pale drops glistening at the tip. Luc's hands shot down and fisted in her hair when she sucked half of his length into her mouth. She tightened her lips around him and sucked hard and then raised her hand and cupped his heavy testicles in her palm. Luc moaned, a long, low sound of need and desire.

Sure now, more confident, Tia stretched her lips around Luc's engorged cock and sucked him deep and hard, inhaling the rich, musky scent of man and forest. His hips thrust forward. Tia closed her eyes and matched his rhythm, hollowing her cheeks with each pull and then slowly withdrawing. She clasped his taut buttock in one hand, softly caressed his balls with the other.

Luc's muscled thighs trembled and she smiled around his swollen cock, squeezing lightly as his testicles drew closer to his body. Confidence growing, Tia took him closer to the edge and then slowly, carefully dragged her mouth his full length before releasing him.

His cock bounced against his flat belly, erect and weeping, glistening from crown to base where she'd suckled him. Luc moaned when Tia nuzzled against the sensitive crease of his groin.

"I'm cold." She licked the inside of his thigh with a long, slow sweep of her tongue. He tasted so good, she did it again and then nuzzled the side of his hard cock, licked the soft, wrinkly sac holding his testicles. Luc groaned and thrust his hips forward, silently begging for more.

Tia planted a wet kiss on the rounded head of his cock. "Let's take this inside."

Before she'd even finished her sentence, Luc had Tia wrapped close against his chest and was rushing through the door into the warmth of the cabin.

Chapter 9

For twenty years he'd been Chanku. Run freely as the wolf, experienced the sensuality, the untamed, feral perception and heart-stopping thrill of a body so in tune with nature, so much a part of the whole, so powerful and agile that mere humanity was but a dull respite between life on four legs.

Tonight Luc had discovered an entirely new level of existence. Running, hunting, *being* wolf—with his bitch beside him.

They might not be mated, at least not yet, but he'd never felt so in tune with another creature, human or wolf, in his entire life, never felt desire so strong nor passion as hot. Now Luc carried her inside into his den. Tia snuggled against him, his willing captive, her scent arousing, her desire obviously as strong as his.

Luc buried the hated memories, the visual of Camille Mason standing at the edge of the thick foliage in Golden Gate Park, her eyes blazing as she stared intently at her killer. At him.

Buried the feel of the warm gun in his hand, the pressure of his finger against the smooth trigger, the sharp retort and even sharper recoil as he aimed, fired . . . killed.

Tia's fingers brushed across the stubble on Luc's jaw

and thoughts of that long-ago night fled. Luc bent to kiss her palm, then carried her on up the dark stairs. He flipped the wall switch in the loft, bathing the room in soft overhead lighting. Flecks of pitch on the log walls glistened like golden jewels and the corners disappeared in deep shadows.

Perfect. Everything about this moment was absolutely perfect. He'd thought her beautiful as a child; as a grown woman coming into her Chanku nature, Tia was absolutely magnificent.

In moments, she would be his.

Kiss me, Luc. Tia's arms tightened around his shoulders and she raised her lips to his. He tasted her, the fresh flavors of the forest, the flavors of the woman who had run beside him as a wolf.

In all the years since Ulrich had taken him through his first shift, Luc had imagined a woman as perfectly attuned to him as Tia. A woman such as his mentor had loved, Tia's mother.

Some nights, after more brandy than was prudent, Ulrich had talked passionately about his Camille.

About her sensuality, her limitless passion and free spirit. Their marriage had been an open one. With the Chanku ability to control reproduction, there'd been no risk of unwanted pregnancy. Their immunity to most human diseases removed that risk as well, which left both Camille and Ulrich open to fully explore their sensual natures.

Without guilt. Without risk. Each had taken numerous lovers, yet they'd loved one another unconditionally. Camille's need for risk-taking, though, went beyond sex. Running as a wolf in daylight, in Golden Gate Park, had gotten her killed.

Ulrich's anger still simmered beneath his words of love, though it was obvious that Camille had truly been his fantasy come to life . . . his one true mate.

Now Luc's fantasy nestled in his arms. A woman perfectly designed to be his mate. Even her flavors matched his dreams. He thrust his tongue into her mouth and tasted the dark woods and the chill night air. Her teeth scraped against his lips as she suckled him, drawing him deep into her mouth.

Groaning, Luc lowered Tia to the mattress nearest the door. Pale ivory sheets shimmered in the muted light, a perfect backdrop to her dark skin. Still kissing her, Luc pressed Tia's body against the sheets, rubbing his chest over her full breasts, abrading her tender skin with the hair covering his pectoral muscles and abdomen.

She arched against him, turned away her head to bare her throat. He nipped her, just below her left ear, marking her once more. She moaned. Luc sucked hard at the tiny bite, bringing blood to the surface. Creating a brand that would linger well for the next few days.

Mine!

Yours. Always yours, Luc. Please! Help me . . . I've never felt like this. I'm burning inside. I need you.

Luc pushed Tia's tangled hair back from her face. Her lips parted, her eyes were wide, almost frantic with desire. Hips undulating, her mons pressing against his engorged cock, she looped one long leg over his buttocks, pulling him even closer against her.

Luc grabbed her wrists in one hand and tugged her arms over her head, holding her still with the weight of his lower body. Slowly, methodically he plundered her mouth, nipping, licking, invading.

She kissed him frantically, arching her back to bring her breasts in contact with the thick hair on his chest. Her taut nipples brushed across his and Luc shuddered. He arched away, then slid back from Tia's mouth to capture one elusive nipple between his lips.

Sucking hard, pressing the sensitive point between his tongue and the roof of his mouth, he dragged a passionate scream from Tia. He laved that nipple gently with his tongue, then turned his head and grabbed the other, pulling it deep, sucking and licking until she bucked against him. Her sobs and needy cries made him even harder. With her hands still trapped in his strong grasp, Tia drew up her knees and raised her pussy, connecting with the sensitive underside of his cock.

Slick and smooth, she tilted her pelvis and rubbed against him, dragging her fluid-drenched labia back and forth along the length of his cock. Heat on the upstroke, then cold when the night air touched his hot flesh as she slipped away. Over and over, rubbing hard against him, faster, her cries more frantic, her body jerking against his, each motion punctuated by incoherent sobs of need and pleasure that brought Luc nearly to the edge.

His own breath coming in short, sharp gasps, he reached down and grabbed his cock, fumbling in his haste to get inside her swollen cunt. Finally, as she slipped low against the root of his penis, her buttocks resting on his balls, Luc tilted his hips just enough to find entrance.

He almost came with his first thrust. She was hot and wet and so damned tight, her needy flesh giving way almost reluctantly before his long, slow glide deep inside. Muscles held him like a hot, wet velvet glove, but the slick layer of lubricating moisture eased his way. It took forever, yet lasted barely a heartbeat before Luc felt the head of his cock touch the mouth to her womb. His balls rested solidly against her perfect ass, caught in the tight cleft between her buttocks and thighs.

Still holding her arms above her head with one hand, Luc shifted his hips to better position himself within Tia's welcoming passage. Seating himself firmly, he planted the crown of his cock directly over her cervix and tilted his hips a fraction more.

Tia arched her back and screamed. Her pussy tightened, holding his cock in a living vise, squeezing and undulating around him. Caught by surprise, it was all he could do to keep from joining her climax.

Instead, Luc slowly withdrew and then just as slowly filled her again. Her muscles clenched and spasmed around him, sucking hard against his cock. Tia whimpered and wrapped both legs tightly about his hips. Luc released her hands and knelt back between her legs, lifting her buttocks in his broad palms, arching her back as he raised her to meet him. He thrust hard and fast, sliding in and out amid the sounds of Tia's fervent cries and the wet slap of flesh against flesh.

He opened his mind, careful to keep those necessary barriers in place, and searched for Tia. She was there, a screaming crescendo of sensation and lust, arousal beyond imagining, passion spiraling out of control. As he linked with her, a second climax shattered Tia's body and sent shock waves through her mind.

Every nuance of Tia's passion crossed the link, became part of Luc's experience, senses added atop his own, blended layer upon layer to become more of the whole, more powerful, more intense.

He felt every thrust deep inside her pussy, experienced the pleasure/pain of his huge cock forcing its way past tissues not accustomed to a man of his dimensions. Felt the broad head bump against her cervix, only this time he sensed it through Tia's body, not his own.

He would have pulled away, afraid of hurting her, but he knew, because of the link, how she reveled in the pain, needed the sense of being filled beyond what her body should have accepted. Wanted the perception of submission, needed his domination, from the weight of his body holding her down to the tight grasp of his hands bruising her buttocks.

Tia needed his lips, his teeth, his thrusting tongue plundering her mouth, savaging her breasts. Her body cried out for his hard cock pounding against the entrance of her womb. Her heels dug into the small of his back, her sharp nails raked his shoulders.

More. She wanted more, wanted her cunt stuffed full of him, filled and stretched to the limit, wanted his mouth on her breasts, his teeth biting at her nipples. She wanted Luc. Only Luc. Forever, Luc.

He felt it then, the tight curl low in his gut, the painful throbbing in his balls. Going with it, accepting and giving up the struggle for control, Luc threw his head back and howled his own climax, an orgasm so powerful, so perfect, his entire sense of being existed only in those parts where their bodies connected.

Pumping his hips hard between her legs, Luc drove deep and long and still he came, filling Tia with his seed, marking her within as he'd marked her without.

Mine! he might have shouted, knew he filled her mind, her heart with his claim. Black spots danced in front of his eyes, flashes of light as if consciousness waned. Tia sprawled beneath him, trembling in the aftermath of her orgasm. Her tight sheath clenching, squeezing, increasing his.

Tia's eyes were closed, her lips parted. She was more lovely than anything or anyone Luc had ever seen in his life. Precious to him, unique among women. He couldn't recall ever feeling as complete, as sated, in his life. Luc slowly lowered himself to lay beside her, but Tia caught him with one slim hand to the side of his face.

No. Don't go. I want to feel your weight. Want to keep you inside me for just a little longer.

Carefully, Luc lowered himself back over her body, nestling his hips firmly into the perfect cradle of her thighs. His head rested on the pillow beside hers, his lips pressed against her throat. The mark he'd left burned a deep reddish purple. He licked it with the tip of his tongue, tasting salt, tasting Tia.

Luc still felt the clenching, rhythmic spasms of Tia's

vaginal muscles, milking him of every last drop. His cock was no longer so hard, but still he filled her.

Their chests expanded as one, their hearts beat a syncopated rhythm, stuttering in and out of time together. Luc nuzzled the soft skin beneath Tia's ear, kissed her jaw, and then leaned close and kissed her gently on the lips.

He felt as if his world had finally, after a lifetime, come together. He wondered if Tia felt it as he did, if she realized what had just happened between them?

He tried to speak, but there was no sound. Tried to focus and realized his eyes swam with tears. Raised his head back just enough to see Tia's face, and saw the glistening silver tracks pouring from her eyes.

He smiled and brushed away a tear. Instead of looking at him, she turned her head away, but he saw her smile. Knew she understood.

I love you. He wanted to say it aloud, to shout it from the rooftops, echo the words off the granite walls of the stark Sierra Nevada mountains guarding this small cabin, but his throat felt uncharacteristically tight. His chest burned and he knew his heart must be feeling as blindsided as the rest of him. Luc opened his mouth to try once more to speak, but Tia's finger pressed against his lips.

It's so soon. How can you be sure?

Luc frowned. Hadn't she felt what he'd felt? Didn't she realize how special this was?

I'm sure, Tia. He pushed down with his arms, raised himself away from her warm and welcoming body. His cock slipped slowly from its warm, wet resting place. Her vaginal muscles tightened, grabbed him as though trying to keep him from leaving.

Luc felt a surge of blood rushing to that unruly yet terribly needy part of him. Looked down and watched himself swell once more. He tilted his hips forward and filled Tia again.

He felt her soft sigh as well as heard it. Slowly, softly, he thrust in and then pulled just as slowly out of her hot, wet pussy. Gone was the frantic pace, the overwhelming need to dominate, to fill her beyond what her body could take.

This time he made love to her. Reverently, showing Tia with each tilt of his hips, each gentle kiss to her breasts and throat, just how much he truly cared, how deeply he loved her.

She looped her arms around his neck and smiled, but when Luc tried to link, her mind was blocked. It hit him then, what she was doing. She thought she was through, that her last huge orgasm was all she would feel tonight. This was for Luc and she expected nothing more than what it would take for him to come inside her once more.

What man could ignore a subtle dare like that? Grinning, feeling a step closer to actually understanding this fascinating woman the little girl had become, Luc leaned over and carefully drew one taut nipple into his mouth.

He felt Tia's heart flutter beneath his lips as he suckled and nipped at the sensitive flesh. He licked first one nipple and then the other, biting gently, then squeezing each one tightly between his lips.

Tia's breath hitched in her throat and a flush spread across her dark skin. Smiling, Luc continued giving attention to her breasts, but his right hand journeyed south, cupping the smooth globe of her buttock, finding the crease between her cheeks.

Thrusting slowly with easy, shallow forays into her tight, slick pussy, Luc sensed the moment Tia realized he was going to make her come again. She tilted her hips to take him deeper. Spread her legs to bring him closer.

He traced the crease between her cheeks, pausing longer and longer on each pass over her tight sphincter, pressing just a little bit harder, timing the thrusts of his finger to the more powerful thrusts of his cock.

Tia whimpered and her body twisted. Luc tried to link, but the block remained. He drove his cock in deeper, harder, pressed against her ass with his finger and then dipped his fingers into her pussy from behind, finding her lubricating fluids, dragging them back over her perineum, and pressing once more against the tight ring of muscle.

Luc pulled up her knees and rocked back on his heels, dragging Tia with him. She wrapped her legs around his waist as once more Luc grabbed her buttocks and held her while he pounded inside. This time his middle finger breached her ass and he stretched her tight opening, forcing his finger past the first and then the second knuckle.

Tia whimpered and strained against him. Luc felt his cock through the wall of tissues and thrust harder, faster, matching each move between his finger and his cock.

He added a second finger as Tia strained against him, pinning her to his body. Like a piston now, driving into her, holding her prisoner front and rear, he tilted his hips to put pressure directly on her swollen clit with each inward thrust.

Her body stiffened, tightened around his cock and his fingers. Her tiny whimpers went from choppy and breathless to one long, harsh cry. Pumping hard, Luc emptied himself in her clenching body, slipped his fingers free, and fell with her to the twisted sheets.

This time there was no gentle collapse. He fell, full weight over her heaving breasts, until Tia giggled and shoved weakly at his chest.

"Okay. I give." She barely gasped the words, but Luc understood.

Laughing, he rolled to one side. "Wanna go for round three?"

She turned her head on the pillow and looked at him out of narrowed eyes. "Is this some kind of contest?"

"Don't tell me you didn't enjoy yourself." Luc raised himself on one elbow in order to see her better. He picked up a twisted length of hair and tickled Tia's nose.

She batted away his hand.

"Why are you blocking me?"

Tia blinked, but she didn't look away. "I don't know. I'm not doing it on purpose. I think it's too much, too soon. Too intimate. When we made love and linked, I felt you. I *was* you. I felt the pressure in your cock pressed deep inside me, I knew how your balls ached when you held back an orgasm that was screaming to get out. I . . ." She sighed. "I'm not ready for this much intimacy this suddenly, Luc. I've only learned today what it feels like to run through the woods on four legs. You've known for twenty years. I remember you as an adult when I was a kid. Suddenly we're on even ground, but it feels terribly shaky to me. Give me time to adjust, okay?"

She brushed the side of his face with long, gentle fingers. Luc turned and kissed each one. She'd figure it out before too long. There wasn't a shred of doubt in his mind. She would love him as he loved her. Tia would be his mate for all time.

She had to. He leaned over and kissed her mouth, tasted the flavors that already made his heart whole, and knew there was no other woman in all the world who could complete him as Tia could.

Luc slept soundly beside her. Tia stared wide-eyed into the darkness. Her body still hummed with the strength of her orgasm . . . make that *orgasms*. *Damn*. She'd never come so hard or so often in her life. It would be easy to credit it to Luc's amazing technique, but there was more to tonight than mere ability as a lover.

A sense of wonder filled her. Not only had she shifted, become a wolf, and run through the night beside this man, she'd let him into her soul. Tia brought her fingers to her lips and rubbed them slowly across the sensitive surface. Luc kissed her like he meant it. Made love to her as if she were the only woman in his world.

He said he loved her. Luc couldn't love her. Not after such a short time.

You've loved him since you were a kid.

There *was* that. She'd followed him like a stray puppy when she was small, fantasized over him when she was a prepubescent teen. Loved him, heart and soul, when she elected to go away to school with Shannon rather than stay home and have him break her heart.

Why was it so hard to accept the fact that her fantasy was coming true?

It had been easier to accept the fact that Chanku were more than mythical creatures than it was to believe in Luc's love. Of course, watching Tinker shift from man to wolf that first time had been pretty convincing, as far as myths went.

Tia smiled with the memory. Her pussy clenched as the image of Tinker's beautiful, dark, and dangerous nude body filled her mind.

Therein lies the quandary.

How could she tell Luc she loved him when thoughts of Tinker turned her on? How could she commit to one man when she'd been fantasizing about sex with all five? Luc had had twenty years to accustom himself to Chanku sensuality, to the concept of sexual freedom while loving one mate.

No matter what her heart believed, it was going to take time for Tia's head to accept. Until she fully understood this new reality, Tia knew she couldn't truly give all her love to Lucien Stone.

Not yet.

Rolling over, Tia pressed her body close along Luc's back. Already he felt familiar and wonderfully dear to her. In her heart, for now, he was her mate.

Once they mated as wolves, Luc would be hers for all time. The explanation had seemed so simple when he first described it.

Chanku mated for life, yet did not consider themselves fully bonded until they'd come together as wolves. She pictured Luc taking her as a wolf, fucking her hard and fast in the deep, dark woods, his cock locking them together during climax, claws raking her sides as he held her. . . . The visual image made her pussy clench, made her chest feel tight.

Not yet. It wasn't the act that frightened her. It wasn't even the commitment. No, Tia knew that if she searched her heart, she would find it was doubt that Luc really, truly loved her.

He couldn't fall in love in days. Not a love with the ability to last a lifetime. What if they bonded and he grew tired of her? Would he be trapped forever with a woman he loathed? Someday soon, she might be ready. Someday when she believed his words of love. For now, Tia figured she'd take what she could get. Sighing, she snuggled close against Luc's warm back and drifted slowly into sleep.

Chapter 10

Luc woke Tia in the early afternoon hours, sliding his cock deep inside her pussy from behind, bringing her out of sleep with a slow, steady, wonderful invasion of her body. Wrapped in his embrace, both breasts cupped in his warm palms, Tia groaned and snuggled her bottom close against Luc's belly.

He slowly thrust his hips forward and then just as slowly withdrew. She felt as though he went even deeper from this angle, filled her more completely.

Tia leaned her cheek against Luc's arm and nuzzled. She pressed her hips back, rubbing her buttocks against his belly. A shaft of sunlight caught her eyes and she blinked. Tia realized the sun was already past its zenith. They'd slept away most of the day. She kissed Luc's wrist, running her tongue along the tendons and raised veins. "I could get used to waking up like this."

"Please do." He kissed the back of her neck, licked over the tender spot where he'd left a noticeable bite the night before, and tilted his hips, thrusting his cock deeper, harder. "I intend to wake up like this every day for the rest of our lives."

"That's a long time." She was no closer this afternoon to a declaration of love than she'd been the night before.

Luc slowly withdrew until the tip of his cock rested at the mouth of her pussy. With glacial slowness he filled her once more. "It'll never be long enough. I don't think I can ever get enough of this . . . of you."

"Mmmm . . . feels so good." She couldn't answer him, wouldn't. Not yet. Not until she was sure. He pinched her nipples and tugged. His palms were hot where they cupped the full sides of her breasts, her nipples burned when he pulled and squeezed. Tia wriggled and pressed her butt close to Luc's belly, but it wasn't enough.

Luc must have sensed her need, or maybe it was his frustration over her lack of reply. Suddenly he was lifting Tia to her knees without breaking rhythm. Raising her buttocks, kneeling behind her with his cock deep inside her weeping pussy while Tia rested her cheek on her crossed arms.

Each stroke took him deeper. His hands clutched at her hips with bruising strength and he slammed into her, filling her with each downward thrust, leaving her empty and wanting each time he withdrew.

His thoughts slammed into her every bit as hard. She felt his frustration and anger with every bruising penetration. *We can have more, Tia. Imagine me covering you, my wolven body holding you, my swollen cock locking us together, tying us together for a lifetime. You won't be satisfied until you submit. I know this, Tia. I know you.*

She felt her own anger boil to the surface. *No, Luc. You don't know me.* Tia raised up on her forearms and turned to glare at him. Luc's chest glistened where sunlight from an open window caught the beads of sweat in his dark hair. A menacing scowl twisted his face, but his eyes practically shimmered with arousal, with a fierce need to dominate. To take her in any way he could.

Damn, she couldn't remember ever being this turned on in her life! No man had ever made her feel this way. None had dared.

Luc drove into her harder, faster. Tia braced her shoulders and spread her legs wider. His cock rammed hard against her cervix, but pleasure far outweighed the pain of such deep and thorough penetration.

Tia met his intensity with her own. Yes, she would take him—on her terms and her terms only. She practically snarled at Luc as her body shuddered beneath each searing thrust.

Anger gave her strength, desire powered her need. She blasted him with her thoughts. *You know the sixteen-year-old, the child. You haven't got a clue who the woman is, what she can do, how she thinks. When you finally know her, then we'll talk of two wolves fucking. Not before.*

Luc shifted. Between one heartbeat and the next he changed from man to wolf. Tia rolled away from him before he completed the shift, pulled free of his cock, turned and faced him from her corner of the mattress, like a fighter facing an opponent on the opposite side of boxing ring.

Hair hanging in tangles, chest heaving, she knew she must look like a dark, naked witch. No matter.

She would not shift. No way in hell would she let him take her like this. Not now. Not yet. Her pussy throbbed, her breasts ached, and shocked laughter bubbled in her throat. *Damn you! That's cheating!*

Luc stood on all fours at the end of the mattress, wolven head hanging low, eyes narrowed, his pink cock glistening beneath his belly. Almost sheepishly he sat back on his haunches, panting. *You can't fault me for trying. . . .*

Oh, but I can. Tia leaned back against the wall, her legs sprawled out in front of her on the tumbled sheets. She sent him a long, slow, seductive smile and then palmed her breast with one hand. Luc's head came up, but he didn't shift back. His cock swelled once more, bumping against his furred belly. He watched her every move.

Tia plucked at her nipple with one hand while she slipped the fingers of her other hand slowly between her legs. Closing her eyes, Tia leaned back and stroked herself. The wet, sucking sounds of her fingers dipping into her engorged pussy and then rubbing around her swollen clit seemed overly loud to Tia's ears. She rubbed her left palm over her right nipple, broadcasting loudly in her mind how she imagined Luc's hand there, imagined his rough calluses on her tender flesh.

The wolf whimpered and then lay down on the mattress with his nose on his paws. Tia grinned, lowered her eyelids until she barely saw through the narrow slits, and concentrated on her pleasure. It was really enjoyable, knowing how horny Luc was, how much he wanted her. She dipped her fingers in and out of her streaming cunt, circled her clit, and then repeated the process. Slowly, very methodically, and with great drama, Tia brought herself to climax. Gasping, sighing, and collapsing weakly against the wall, she finally opened her eyes and smirked at Luc.

He watched, panting, from his end of the mattress. After a moment, he sat up. His cock bobbed against his belly with each breath he took. The knot at its base had forced its way past his sheath and Tia knew it took every ounce of Luc's willpower not to take her. Stoically, he held his position at the far side of the mattress from her.

Biting back a smile, legs trembling from the force of her orgasm, Tia held out her wet fingers for Luc. Ears back, he leaned close and licked each one clean of her cream. When he was through, Tia stroked him between the ears and then stood up. "Good boy. Now behave or you can go outside. I'm going to have some breakfast. Care to join me?"

By the time Luc got out of the shower and dried off, he was beginning to see the humor in the situation, in spite of the fact that he had a hard-on that could drive nails. Damn, but she pissed him off! He had to admit, though, Tia had gotten the last word.

She was absolutely right. He didn't know her. Not as she was now. He'd loved the child as the daughter he might someday have, remembered the teenager with fondness, and had anticipated her promise as a beautiful adult. He'd heard stories from Ulrish of the woman she'd become, but he didn't really know Tia. He wanted her. He desired her as he'd never desired anyone in his life, but he had no idea what the adult Tia, the woman, was like.

She was a teacher. Luc had no idea what she taught. She'd studied in Boston, lived somewhere in that city for the past few years at least, but what had she done when she was there? What were her hobbies, her interests? She'd been with Shannon, her friend and lover, but why had they separated? What had really brought Tia home?

Luc slipped on a pair of worn denims and an old flannel shirt he found in the closet. The shirt hung loosely on his body, which meant it must have been one of Tinker's, but he rolled up the sleeves, tucked the tail into his jeans, and headed down the stairs.

Tia stood in front of the stove. She'd wrapped one of the guys' old bathrobes around herself and tied her hair back in a frizzy ponytail. When she looked up at him and smiled, Luc paused midstep.

She looked all of sixteen. Innocent, sweet, nothing like the alpha bitch who'd cut him off at the balls just a short time ago. Bemused and grinning like an idiot, Luc wandered into the kitchen, leaned over, and kissed her on the cheek she turned to him.

"I'm sorry."

Tia's head snapped around. "What? Did I just hear an apology?" She slapped her palm to her heart.

"Yeah. Don't get used to it." Luc leaned over and sniffed at the sausage cooking beside perfectly fried potatoes. His woman could cook? Another thing he didn't know about her.

"Well? What are you apologizing for?"

"Uh, well . . . pulling a switch in midbattle? You were right. That's cheating."

"All's fair in love and war." Tia smiled, turned back to the stove, and carefully rolled over the sausages to finish browning.

"Okay. I guess." Even more off-balance, Luc poured himself a cup of coffee. Tia was right. He didn't have a clue what she was really all about.

He had two more days before the guys arrived to discover exactly what made Tia tick.

This time when they shifted, the sun hadn't yet slipped behind the mountains. Instead of racing through the forest, Luc led Tia on a slow lope along a fairly well-marked trail. Less than a mile from the cabin, steam rose through the thick undergrowth in a low cloud, almost obscuring a small, crystal-clear pool.

Hot springs. The guys and I like to come here to soak after a long run.

Tia shifted at the water's edge as if it were something she'd done all her life. She rose to her feet and then glanced over her shoulder at Luc. He'd shifted as well. Naked, he could have been a forest god—all long, lean muscle and thick, dark hair. His cock was only partially erect and still impressive. No wonder she ached after sex with this man! Tia held her hand out to Luc and he took it, pulling her into a tight embrace for a deep, lingering kiss.

His taste was different immediately after his shift. Earthier, more in tune with the forest, the night, flavors on the edge of something wild yet natural.

When they finally broke apart, Luc held her close and stared at her for a long moment, as though memorizing her face. Tia blinked and licked her lips, tasting him on her mouth. That simple movement seemed to break whatever spell held him.

"C'mon." Luc led Tia into the pool. The water was warm and very still, except where springwater bubbled to the surface near one end. A faint sulfuric smell hung in the air, though the odor wasn't strong enough to ruin the beauty of the place. Luc eased down into the water, pulling Tia with him.

He showed her a submerged lip of rock where they could sit shoulders deep and let the warm water wash over their bodies.

Tia tilted back her head against the smooth stone and closed her eyes. Luc's arm crept around her shoulders and she leaned against him. *Unbelievable. This feels like heaven.*

So do you.

You never give up, do you? Tia grinned, opened one eye, and squinted at Luc.

Never. He hugged her against him. *You said I don't know you. You're right. Will you tell me?*

Tell you what?

Who you are. What you like. What you want. Most of all, what you need.

You really want to know? This time Tia pulled away and really stared at him. "You're serious, right?"

"Yeah. Very serious." He grinned and tapped her once on the end of the nose. "First question. What do you teach?"

"Little kids with learning disabilities. Children who don't fit in, who need extra help keeping up."

"Why? I would think that's really difficult."

"It is, but it's worth it." She looked away, remembering. "I was one of those kids. I had my mother to help me when I was small, but when she was gone, there was no one. . . . I always felt different, sort of the odd girl out. Not only was I biracial, I didn't have a mother and I was always just different." She turned to Luc and smiled. "I imagine some of the difference I felt was being Chanku, but obviously I didn't know that until this week. Anyway, I was miserable until I got a wonderful teacher in the fourth grade who took extra time with me. She made me feel as though I mattered, as though I counted for something. I want to do that for kids who have trouble adjusting to what life throws at them. I don't remember my mother well enough to know what she was like, so I want to be like my teacher. She was my role model. I want to be like her."

Luc's silence caught Tia's attention. She turned to him and mentally ventured across the gap to see what he was thinking.

Luc's thoughts were thoroughly blocked. Tia frowned, confused. He'd never blocked her before. Not once.

"Luc? Are you listening to me?"

He blinked as if he'd been a million miles away. "I'm sorry. I guess I never thought of you having any sort of learning problems. You were always such a bright little thing, so inquisitive."

"My mother's death was hard on me. Harder even than my father realized. I shut down in a lot of ways, but when I look back now I realize it was the only way I could cope. Just this week I remember we used to speak without words. It was our secret, but I'd forgotten. Luc, I've forgotten so much about her. That's part of the reason I came back to San Francisco."

"What do you mean?"

"I intend to find out how my mother really died. I don't think anyone has ever told me the truth. There was some kind of cover-up, I'm absolutely convinced of that. Dad won't discuss her at all, but I know I'll never understand myself until I know more about my mother, about her death and her life. It's even more important, now that I know she was Chanku. It explains so much, yet leaves me with even more questions."

Tia turned to face Luc and cupped his beard-roughened jaw in her palm. "Do you understand what I'm saying? Until I find out more about my mother's life and her death, I can't commit to life with you. I do love you, Luc. I know that, but I have to know the truth about my mother, or I'll never really feel as though I truly know myself. Please be patient with me. Try to understand."

Oh, he understood all right. He understood all too well. Tia raced ahead of him, her tail a dark flag waving in the night. She didn't have a clue about her mother and she wanted answers.

Thank God she didn't know about Luc's role in Camille's death. As fragile as she seemed right now, news like that could only harm her.

It would also destroy whatever hope Luc might carry within his heart for a future between the two of them.

Somehow he had to tell her the truth, but now was not the time. He had to do it right . . . pick the right time, the proper circumstances. So far Luc had managed to block all thoughts of Camille, of her funeral, of the final look in her glittering feral eyes just before the bullet took her life, but he couldn't do it forever. One day he would slip and Tia would learn the truth.

Mating was out of the question. He could never hide such a powerful memory during the total bonding he'd been told occurred during a Chanku mating. He couldn't imagine a more horrible thing, to bond Tia to him while sharing a memory of how he killed her mother.

She would hate him forever.

Yet be bound to him for just as long.

Tia would never forgive Luc for taking away her mother. Even if the adult Tia could understand what a horrible mistake Luc had made, the lost child in her past would hate with a mindless passion. He knew this, accepted the truth with a horrible pain in his heart.

Racing swiftly through the dark woods, Luc buried his memories, buried his guilt, and followed his woman through the night.

Tia ran as if racing the night could leave behind the horrible memories. She rarely allowed herself to think of her mother. It was too painful, but Luc had said he wanted to know, so she'd told him.

Damn him! So typically male. Acting concerned about her feelings, making her think he really cared until she actually spilled her guts and told him the truth. Now, when she needed him, needed his love and his reassurance, he blocked her, the walls so high and thick there was no getting through.

Was he so afraid of her emotions? So self-centered and selfish he couldn't deal with the fact that she had something important she needed to do before committing to him?

Once again Tia felt totally alone. She'd grown used to his constantly reassuring presence. Now she'd been set adrift from the one anchor she'd known since learning of her Chanku heritage.

So typical of a man, to abandon her when she'd finally decided to trust. Her father had been much the same, retreating into his shell of despair after her mother died. Throwing himself into Pack Dynamics and his new friends while Tia floundered. Abandoning the child who cried out for the one parent who had always been there, had always known the right thing to say, the right thing to do.

She'd never doubted that her father loved her. It just hadn't been enough, not when Camille had loved so completely. No one else's love had been enough to fill her mother's place in Tia's life. Not her father's, not Shannon's . . . not Luc's.

Definitely not Luc's.

Snarling into the wind, Tia raced through the darkness. Let Luc try to keep up. Adrenaline coursed through her system, and Tia put on an extra burst of speed. Trees blurred beside her. Small nocturnal animals scattered in her path.

Luc followed. Farther and farther behind, but still he followed. Though his thoughts were blocked, she sensed his presence. He was unhappy. In fact, he felt downright miserable.

Good. Let him suffer a bit for what he'd done, getting her to open up and then turning his back on her obvious need. He deserved to hurt, after what he'd done. Tia wished she could give him all her pain.

She'd love to give *anyone* her pain. It was so damned hard to carry it alone.

Miles later, lungs heaving, heart aching, Tia turned back toward the cabin. She sensed Luc nearby, but he stayed away from her. *Good.* At least he knew when to leave her alone.

There would be no mating in the woods tonight.

She flipped her bushy tail and sauntered up the front steps to the cabin. He could take her as a woman or not at all.

Luc watched Tia shift, making the change from wolf to woman in a graceful shimmer of light and motion. When she stood tall and searched the woods for him, he held his position behind the thick shrubs, out of her sight.

He wanted her. Wanted to feel the velvet clasp of her pussy around his cock, wanted the sweet taste of her lips, but he had no idea how she felt. If she would accept him as her lover even in human form.

There was no way in hell she would take him as a wolf. That dream had certainly been put on hold tonight. He opened his mind, searched carefully for her thoughts.

Found her, waiting, watching for him. Her body was ripe, her anger overwhelmed by arousal. He'd neglected to consider how hot she'd be after her run, how much she'd need sexual release after the shift.

Head high, thoughts still blocked, Luc trotted toward the house. The moment Tia saw him, he shifted, continuing his journey as a man on two legs. Slowly, Luc took each step up to the raised deck, his gaze never wavering until he met Tia at the top.

She stared back at him. The devastating sadness in her eyes came as a surprise. Luc held out his hand. She took hold of it. Tightened her fingers in his grasp. Tugged lightly until he followed her into the dark cabin.

Tia's mind was tightly closeted behind strong barriers. She guarded her thoughts just as he did, but she didn't try to contain her desire. He scented her arousal on the still night air. Accepted the fact that she needed him on the most basic level.

Needed him, but didn't really want him. Sighing, Luc followed her into the cabin and up the stairs to the loft. They had sex in the darkness, each locked behind their own barriers.

Luc's orgasm left him feeling tired and frustrated. Tia's left her in tears, sobbing quietly in the darkness. When he tried to hold her, to give comfort, she pulled away. Silently she rolled to one side and turned her back on him.

Sighing, wondering how he would find a way out of the hole he'd dug for himself, Luc lay awake in the dark beside Tia for a long time, reliving that fateful afternoon in Golden Gate Park.

Chapter 11

Tia leapt from the deck in human form, shifted to wolf in midair, and landed heavily on her side. Grunting, she picked herself up out of the dirt, shifted back to human form, and brushed the twigs and dirt out of her hair.

"Shit. Why in the hell can't I get that right?"

"You're trying too hard." Luc leaned on the railing, wearing worn blue jeans and no shirt. His chest glistened with perspiration, as if he were the one making the crappy falls, not her. "Just go with your instincts. Wolves are more like cats than you realize. If you try to direct your landing, you're going to keep falling. Don't fight it. Let the wolf take control."

"Easy for you to say." Tia snorted, wiped her bloodied hands along her bruised thighs, and stalked back up the steps. "You're standing there giving orders. I'm the one landing on my ass."

"Quit thinking like a girl. Think like a wolf." Luc folded his arms over his chest and glared at her. Tia glared back. If he would just open his mind, *show* her how to shift and land on all four feet, it would be so much easier. Instead he kept his damned barriers up and his thoughts hidden. Blocked, just as he'd been for the past two days.

He'd not even lowered the barriers during sex. She

missed the connection, missed Luc. Damn, but he pissed her off!

She would show him. This time Tia launched herself over the railing, fully expecting to break at least an arm if nothing worse, shifted on the fly, and suddenly found herself hitting the ground on all four feet.

She yipped, twirled around on her back legs, and was Tia again, grinning from ear to ear.

Luc raced down the steps and grabbed her in his arms. "You did it! Fantastic! That was absolutely perfect!" He held her close and kissed her.

She kissed him back. Bruised and hurting, she still wanted him. This kiss only reminded her of what she'd lost over the past couple of days.

All the exquisite sex in the world couldn't make up for the intimacy of making love with Lucien Stone when he shared his thoughts, his emotions, his every sensation.

Tia had had no idea how much she would miss that intimacy, that wonderful sense of belonging, until he'd taken it away.

She wanted Luc back, damnit! Wanted him to accept the fact that she had things to do before the final bonding he demanded. Then his lips moved over hers and she couldn't help but respond.

There was something terribly erotic about standing there in front of the cabin, the afternoon sun beating down on her naked body, caught in the embrace of a man who was still at least partially dressed.

Luc's jeans rubbed roughly against her belly; his chest hair abraded her sensitive nipples. Tia felt herself swelling, ripening to his touch. She wanted him. Not just his body, not merely his perfect mouth and his amazing cock. She wanted his heart, his mind. Now that he'd denied access to that most private part of him, she craved it.

Craved all of him. Groaning, she pressed against him, kissed his throat, his jaw, the corner of his mouth. Luc didn't kiss her back. Instead he raised his head and held very still. Then he slowly put Tia away from him.

"They're coming. The guys will be here in a couple minutes. Go put some clothes on."

Tia looked down at her body, ripe and ready for his. She saw the flush across her breasts, the way her nipples stood out hard and taut, an open invitation if ever there was one.

Her inner thighs glistened with her fluids, her clitoris visibly swollen below her flat belly. All in readiness for Luc, but when she raised her head to look at him, he was already turning away, picking her clothing off the deck, separating himself from her as completely as if he had physically severed flesh.

Sighing, Tia took the bundle of clothes Luc handed her and went inside the cabin to dress.

They sat on the deck after dinner and watched the sun go down over the mountains. It was the first time Tia had really had a chance to observe the other men of the pack without her father observing her.

Jake kept mostly to himself. A silent man, tall and strong, he carried an aura of sadness about him. Tia wondered about his story, wondered if he'd left someone behind in another life somewhere. He'd been with Luc the longest—part of Pack Dynamics for almost fifteen years. He was the first of the Chanku Luc had brought into the pack.

Mik and AJ obviously were a couple. How she'd missed that Tia wasn't sure, but the two men, both powerfully built and handsome as sin, had no qualms about their open affection for one another. They'd been prisoners serving time at Folsom when Ulrich discovered their Chanku genetics.

They'd been sentenced for assault, though Tia didn't know the particulars. Ulrich had discovered them somehow. She didn't know how that had happened, either, but he'd gotten their sentences reduced, brought them home to San Francisco, and taught them what it was like to live as wolves.

Now they were brothers of the pack and lovers. Tia wondered if they'd bonded as wolves, if their sexual relationship carried over from human to animal. The thought made her search out Luc.

He stood alone, off to one side, talking quietly to Tinker. Tia smiled and Tinker turned to catch her eye. Luc ignored her. She sighed and looked away. Somehow she needed to get Tinker aside and talk to him. At least he was her friend. After their week together, Tia thought of Tinker as the big brother she'd never had.

A very sexy big brother.

"Anyone up for a run?" Jake stood up and began peeling off his flannel shirt. The other men followed suit.

Tia didn't hesitate. She kicked off her shoes and began to take off her sweats without any thought of modesty, but as she slipped her sweatshirt over her head, Tia's eye caught Luc's.

He stared at her with such longing, she felt her heart break. What the hell was wrong with him? Why had he locked her out? From the look on his face, he wanted her. He missed her. Had all his protestations of love meant nothing?

She'd tried talking to him and he'd refused to explain. She'd tried forcing entrance into his thoughts and found his barriers insurmountable.

Tia turned away, removed her shirt, stepped out of her baggy pants, and folded her clothes neatly on her chair. Then, before the other men realized she'd even undressed, Tia leapt from the deck and shifted in midair, landing neatly on all fours before racing off into the forest.

The others followed. Tia heard the sounds of their soft landings behind her, felt the first stirrings of desire on a most primitive level.

This was her pack! Each of these men would defend her to the death, would protect her young, see to her comfort. She felt a growing bond to them, a sense of family more powerful than anything she could recall, even though most of them were practically strangers to her.

Strangers except for Luc, yet now he was the most distant of them all. She glanced back and saw him running at the rear of the pack, his ears back, head low. He appeared to hold himself separate from the others as though he were blocking his thoughts from his pack brothers as well.

The night closed in around them and they ran long and hard. AJ scared up an old buck. The animal lumbered off, its awkward gate from some type of injury slowing its escape. Reacting on instincts she'd never suspected, Tia's haunches bunched and she leapt, going for the animal's throat.

She dodged his swinging antlers and clamped her jaws down hard on the tough hide, bringing the buck to his knees. Tinker hit the animal from behind, cleanly snapping its neck.

Tia had never killed before. Even her mousetraps were designed for live release. Now the scent of hot blood unexpectedly aroused her. She tore at the warm flesh and practically shuddered with delight when hot blood filled her mouth.

The others slunk around the warm body, snapping and growling, but they didn't come near. Tia snarled, instinctively guarding the kill until she'd eaten her fill. The human part of her mind was amazed when the males backed off, whining and reverting to their purely animal roots.

The wolf in her rejoiced. Even Luc accepted her alpha status.

Tia fed just long enough to establish her position and then backed away and left the steaming carcass to the rest of the pack. They snarled and growled, fighting over the meat even though they'd eaten well at dinner.

Another level of Chanku existence opened to Tia. Another bit of knowledge to file away for future reference.

She had the ability to kill. Her teeth had found the animal's throat first. Instinctively, she'd known exactly what to do. How to use her weight, her strength. Her powerful jaws and compact body had brought the buck to his knees, where Tinker had finished it quickly, mercifully.

Luc had watched, standing back from the hunt but not participating. Tia felt his presence and was comforted by the fact that he watched her so carefully.

His silence, though, made her feel lonelier than ever.

After the kill, they ran slower, ending up at the hot spring where they cleaned their bloody coats in the warm water and then shifted to human form and back to wolf again.

Amazingly, their fur was dry after the second shift.

Neat trick, eh?

Startled by Luc's familiar voice in her mind, Tia spun around. He stood behind her, tongue lolling, the expression on his face as close to a smile as a wolf could have.

Before Tia could answer, Tinker's voice spoke clearly in her head. *Very neat. C'mon. Let's head back.*

Why? Tia glanced at Luc, noted the grim line to his jaw. She wasn't tired and they'd only run for a few hours. *Why do we have to go back?*

Luc nudged her shoulder, moved Tia away from the others. He put his muzzle close to hers. When he touched her like this, they could communicate privately without the others overhearing.

They want you. Haven't you noticed the tension? The fact that every damned guy has a hard-on? You're the star attraction tonight, sweetheart. A fresh kill makes the sex drive even stronger . . . and it was already boiling.

Tia should have been insulted by the tone of Luc's message. Should have felt some trepidation of sexually entertaining four men she hardly knew.

Instead she swept her tongue across Luc's muzzle, obviously surprising him. *You're the one who told me this is the Chanku way. You invited them up here with me as the main attraction. Don't try to make me feel guilty for acting according to my nature.*

Luc stared at her and then nodded his broad head, lowered his gaze in what could almost have been a submissive gesture, and looked away—directly at AJ and Mik.

Tia turned as well. What the hell were they doing? She sat back on her haunches to watch while the two males tumbled in the grass, nipping and playing like a couple of big puppies.

Mik yipped and then tackled AJ. AJ feinted, rolled under Mik, and came out on top. He mounted the other wolf, subduing him with powerful jaws locked on his neck, and his front legs looped over Mik's rib cage.

Suddenly it dawned on her. This was all about sex. Tia glanced at Luc, but his attention was riveted on the two wolves. Caught up in what she could only describe as lupine foreplay, Tia felt her own arousal growing, along with her curiosity. Within seconds AJ had stabbed Mik with his wolven cock, entering his ass so easily it was obvious they'd done this many times before. Pumping hard and fast, AJ dragged his claws over Mik's rough coat. Mik yipped and growled, but made no attempt to get away from his mate.

She'd wondered, ever since Luc had told her they'd all been intimate with one another, if any of the men had sex in wolf form. Now she knew. Mik and AJ were a bonded pair—mates as well as lovers.

Fascinated, both dreading and desiring sex as a wolf with Luc, Tia's excitement built as the two wolves coupled. Agitated, heart pounding, Tia's desire flamed out of control. She shifted back and forth, one front foot to the other. Tiny whimpers escaped from deep in her throat. She sensed her body readying itself for sex with Luc, felt the driving need to run with him, to mate.

This whole scene went beyond belief; her response to the bestial yet beautiful act between two men in wolf form tugged at a consciousness buried deep inside her Chanku nature.

Tia turned to Luc, forcing her attention away from the sight of AJ's strong haunches bunching and thrusting, of Mik's powerful front claws buried in the deep moss as he held his body steady for AJ's rhythmic assault.

Did Luc's body shiver with desire? Was he as turned on by his pack mates as Tia? She studied Luc, well aware he watched Mik and AJ, not Tia. Luc's cock extended, pink and glistening, raising up against his belly. His eyes glinted in the moonlight.

Tia glanced across the small area at Jake. He appeared just as involved, his entire being focused on AJ and Mik. From the size of his extended cock, Jake obviously was as aroused as Tia, as Luc. So was Tinker, sitting near Jake on the far side of the small meadow, poised as if to leap on the two men, his massive wolven shoulders flexing, the low sounds coming from his throat caught halfway between a snarl and a whimper.

Tia ran her tongue along the coarse fur on Luc's shoulder. His head jerked around and he glared at her, as though he resented being interrupted in the midst of the carnal display before them.

This is what you meant, isn't it? The powerful need to mate as wolves. I didn't understand it before, but I'm totally turned on by Mik and AJ. Luc, it feels right. I want to make love with you. I want Tinker and Jake, AJ and Mik in my bed as well, but only in human form. You will always be the first, the only one who mates me as Chanku. That's what you've been trying to tell me, isn't it? Luc, don't shut me out! This is all so new to me.

Luc stared into her eyes without answering and then turned his back to her, turned his attention to the two wolves fucking in the meadow. Three sharp yips punctuated what must have been a mutual climax. Tia glanced back in time to see Mik turn his head over his shoulder to nip at AJ; then both of them tumbled to one side to lie on the mossy ground. They'd obviously both climaxed. Now they lay on their sides, rib cages heaving with each deep breath, tongues lolling and eyes half closed. Tia imagined how they must feel, tied now with AJ's knotted cock clenched tightly inside Mik.

Luc's mental voice, void of any inflection, brought Tia back to him.

We both knew what tonight would bring. I wanted you bound to me first. You denied me, denied a need both of us feel. The others will know you're still available to mate. It makes things . . . complicated.

Damn him! Tia stood up on all fours and felt her hackles rising along her back.

No, Luc. You make things complicated. I'm yours. I told you that in the beginning. I do not go back on my word, nor can I change the way I feel, no matter how much you piss me off.

His mental laughter startled her. *Oh, I piss you off, do I? Good. You have the same effect on me. C'mon. Let's head back to the house.*

Tia glanced over her shoulder at the two wolves lying in the soft grass. AJ licked Mik's muzzle, his long tongue wrapping slowly around the other wolf's snout. They were still tightly locked together. Tia didn't know that much about wolf physiology, but if AJ's cock was knotted inside Mik's ass, they could be there for quite a while longer.

Tia heard a rustle in the grass beside her and realized Luc was already running down the pathway leading back to the cabin. She trotted along behind Luc, content to give him the lead, glancing back only once at the two wolves still lying together, panting.

What about Mik and AJ?

They know where to find us. Serves them right for getting tied so early in the evening. Luc turned his head and yipped. *Tinker? Jake! Let's go.*

Instead of feeling nervous as they drew closer to the cabin, Tia's arousal grew with each step. Her sense of her body, of her sexuality and need, expanded, enveloped, and tantalized her. It was a new experience, feeling sensual in this four-legged form. So aware of herself as both woman and wolf.

So aware of Luc. She had no desire to be mounted by either Jake or Tinker, though from their close proximity as they raced down the trail, neither of them would mind in the least.

She wanted Luc. Feeling contrary and somewhat foolish, Tia wished now she'd mated with him when they'd had the chance. Wished she'd taken him as a wolf, established their relationship so the others would know and accept.

Maybe then she wouldn't feel the sense of separation between Luc and herself. She wanted him inside her head where he belonged, not running ahead with his black tail waving like a flag, his thoughts closed to her, his heart not yet hers.

Still, there was that little matter of control, of dominance, of his assumption she would do whatever he wanted whenever he demanded. Not a good way to establish a relationship with someone destined to be your mate for life.

The cabin came into sight, windows glowing with the few lights they'd left on, front door open. Tia raced up the front steps and shifted as she ran through the door. Hot and sweaty, she actually wanted to be clean more than she wanted sex.

"I'm going to take a shower. Be out in a minute."

She left the three of them, still in wolven form, milling about the front room. Conflicted, confused, aroused, a little bit frightened, Tia closed the bathroom door behind her and then carefully flipped the lock.

The woman in the mirror seemed a stranger. Her hair looked different. As tangled as is was, the tightly frizzed curls that had been the bane of her existence looked smoother, not nearly so tight.

She wondered if shifting changed even the texture of her hair. It had certainly changed her perception of the world around her, of herself. Why should hair be any different?

Tia's lips seemed fuller, her eyes darker; her skin glowed with perspiration and her muscles were pumped up from the exertion of their long run. Her nipples stood erect, her clitoris swollen well beyond its protective hood. She looked exactly the way she felt, like desire personified, a woman who must have sex, who needed the feel of a man deep inside.

Right now any one of the men in the next room would satisfy. It had nothing to do with Luc, everything to do with acceding to her body's needs.

Sliding one hand across her breasts and down between her legs, Tia found her hot pussy and pressed inside with two fingers. She was already wet and ready, her body as aroused by the run through the woods as by thoughts of the hours yet to come. Smiling, she stepped into the shower.

The hot water beating against her skin like a thousand tiny fingers and tongues did nothing to ease her excitement. Washing her hair, something that usually left Tia relaxed and enervated, had somehow become stimulating and exhilarating. Rinsing the soap from her body with the handheld shower, she was tempted to ease the ache between her thighs with a well-directed spray.

Then she thought of the five strong men waiting for her, and put the showerhead back in its cradle.

When Tia stepped out of the bathroom about fifteen minutes later, the front room was empty. She'd thrown a bathrobe over herself, wrapped her hair in a towel. Her legs and pussy were shaved smooth, but she'd decided not to worry about her suddenly wavy hair and lack of makeup.

She figured no one would notice.

A light glowed from the loft. Taking a deep breath, she started up the stairs, wondering. Were AJ and Mik back yet? Would Tinker make love to her while the others watched? Would they all want to do something at once?

What was expected of her? She'd had sex with multiple partners in the past, but they'd all been familiar to her, lovers and friends, typical twentysomethings with healthy libidos and few inhibitions.

Suddenly Tia was filled with inhibitions. She paused on the staircase, took a deep breath, and realized she was every bit as nervous as she was aroused.

Nervous was okay, considering. Arousal was good. Her nipples rubbed against the soft terry-cloth robe; her pussy clenched. She felt the release of lubricating moisture between her legs, the first tremors of excitement, of expectation. Tightening the towel around her wet hair, Tia ran up the stairs.

Luc waited on the big mattress. Alone. Naked . . . and very, very aroused.

Chapter 12

"Disappointed it's just me?" Luc lay partially sprawled on the farthest mattress across the room, propped up against the wall, legs widespread, his fist wrapped around what had to be the biggest erection Tia had ever seen.

She tried to answer, licked her lips, and realized her mouth had gone completely dry. She shook her head in denial. How could any woman be disappointed with someone like Luc waiting for her?

Long and lean, his chest covered with dark hair, his eyes glinting in the muted light, he could have sprung from any desperate woman's wet dream. Tia stopped at the edge of the first mattress and stared with unabashed appreciation.

She hadn't realized she'd felt quite so desperate.

Luc continued stroking himself, as if the slow progress of his right hand sliding up and down his cock were merely an afterthought. "I asked the others to wait. I hope you don't mind."

Was that a hint of insecurity she sensed? It couldn't be. Not from Luc. "No." She barely choked out the word. "No, I don't mind at all."

Tia reached for the corded tie at her waist, slipped the knot free, and let the loose terry-cloth robe slide off her shoulders. It puddled at her feet. She caught herself running her hands up and down her forearms, in time with Luc's fist.

The crawling flesh, the sense of skin too tight that had always plagued her, was gone. Instead Tia felt the frisson of arousal, a desperate carnal need fed by the night's run through the forest, fueled by this vision of Luc—flaring to life, growing inside, spreading.

Slowly, as if she approached a wild thing, Tia knelt on the edge of the mattress and crawled across it on her hands and knees until she knelt between Luc's outspread legs.

"Here," she whispered, reaching for his swollen cock. "Let me."

Luc stared at her for a long moment. His fist stopped moving but stayed in place. Tia felt him touching her mind and opened her thoughts to his. He retreated the instant her blocks came down. Blinking, she licked her dry lips one more time.

"What do you want of me, Luc? I can't read your mind when you won't let me in. I can't give you everything you want, not yet, but you seem to want something more that I don't understand."

He smiled at her, but it was a sad smile filled with longing. "I think I want what I can never really have. For now, though, I'll take as much as you can give me."

Blinking back tears, Tia leaned forward and placed her hand over his big fist. The knuckles felt rough, his fingers long and callused. She dipped her head and took the crown of his weeping cock between her lips.

Luc sighed and moved his hand out from under Tia's, away from his cock to Tia's shoulder. She circled the base of his penis with her hand, felt the pulsing strength in him, the heat. At the same time, she was aware of the gentle glide of Luc's fingers over her shoulder, noticed the tremor in them and wondered if she were the cause.

Wrapping her lips around the entire head of Luc's cock, she slowly pulled him into her mouth. The tip felt smooth as silk, damp with his pre-cum, hot against her tongue. She gently raked the underside with her teeth, sucked him deeper, hollowing her cheeks with the effort.

Luc groaned. His hips lifted almost imperceptibly, begging for more. Both his hands stroked her shoulders now, roamed across her collarbones, delved beneath the twisted towel holding her damp mass of tangled hair. The towel slipped free, slowly unwinding and falling across her back. Her hair spilled down around her shoulders.

Tia leaned forward, dragging the damp strands across Luc's groin. She tongued the length of his cock, squeezed gently with her fingers and licked the tiny slit at the end. Her other hand explored, tracing the thick muscles at the top of his thigh, slipping between his legs and catching the taut pouch holding his testicles. Cupping them in her palm, she gently massaged the solid orbs within his sac, licked the hot length of his cock and nibbled the sensitive head.

Though she wouldn't have thought it possible, Tia was sure he grew larger, harder. Luc's breath whistled between his teeth as she increased her pace, applied more pressure.

Gasping for breath, Luc grabbed Tia by the shoulders, dragged her the length of his body, and captured her mouth with his.

Kissing him, sucking his tongue deep inside just as she'd done with his cock, Tia still managed to clasp his erection in her hand and guide him between her legs.

Luc lifted his hips and buried himself deep inside her pussy with a single, well-directed thrust. Tia felt her inner muscles clench and tighten around his huge length, holding Luc as tightly as he'd held himself within his own fist.

Tia placed her hands on Luc's chest and rocked back on his thighs, closing her eyes with pleasure as she forced his cock even deeper, stuffing herself as full as her body would allow. When she felt Luc's solid crown rest against the mouth of her womb, she shifted her hips, adjusted her thighs along his waist, seating him all the way. When Tia flexed her muscles around him, she felt his cock jerk in response.

Luc's hands smoothed the skin over her rib cage, found her breasts. His fingers pinched her sensitive nipples and tugged, dragging her close to his chest so that she lay draped across him.

Lifting his hips, penetrating her deep and hard with each thrust, Luc quickly found a rhythm that threatened Tia's control. One hand slipped between their bellies and he stroked her needy clit, applying just enough pressure to take Tia higher, sliding his finger back and forth in perfect time to the movement of his hips, the thrust of his cock.

Heat built, a twisting, needy fire threatening to consume her, spreading from her gut to her fingers and toes, coiling deep inside and coming back to coalesce in a white-hot explosion of pure, unadulterated lust.

One moment Tia had been cognizant of everything Luc did to excite her, the next found her spiraling out of control, arching her back up and away from his chest, opening her mouth to scream—hearing instead the blood-chilling cry of a she-wolf in heat.

Sobbing, breath coming in short, sharp gasps, Tia fell forward on Luc's chest just as he tensed, groaned, and filled her already flowing cunt with his seed. His muscles strained beneath hers, his chest labored, his arms clamped tightly around her waist.

Body loose and trembling, heart thudding, eyes closing, Tia drifted on a pillow of warm, breathing body and pure sensation. She felt Luc's cock as it continued to spasm inside her and concentrated on just that one point of existence.

Luc's heart slowed its thundering rush. Though he'd kept his barriers high and strong, Tia felt loved, worshipped.

Claimed.

She nuzzled the thick hair on his chest, sighed against

his warm body, and drifted even deeper, further away from questions without answers, from confusion and turmoil.

Drifted to a place where warm hands soothed her, stroked her body, massaged her breasts, her buttocks. Where everything was warm and breathing and so peaceful, and she lay in a field of calm, surrounded by heat and comfort.

Her body was lifted by unseen hands. Tia whimpered, loath to part with her lover. Her pussy clenched helplessly when Luc's softened penis slipped from her needy folds.

Before she could feel true loss, lips found her breasts, long fingers stretched between her legs, massaged her aching clit so gently that the greedy bit of flesh rose once more in search of attention.

Moaning, caught somewhere between dreams and a reality too perfect to consciously acknowledge, Tia sprawled on her back, legs spread wide, arms over her head. She inhaled and smelled only freshly showered bodies, the astringent scent of aftershave, the warm musk of clean male.

The mouths on her breasts continued their deep suckling, the fingers between her legs touched her softly, tenderly. More hands massaged her buttocks and gently worked the sore muscles of her thighs and calves.

Something warm and wet and very soft rubbed lightly between her legs. A washcloth . . . it had to be a washcloth cleaning the spill of Luc's semen, the stickiness of her own fluids from her inner thighs, away from her sensitive pussy.

The flat of a warm, damp tongue replaced the washcloth. Tia whimpered, arched her back, and opened her legs farther. Strong hands grasped her thighs, slipped around to her buttocks and spread her cheeks, parted her legs, opened her to full lips, a thick, powerful tongue, nipping teeth.

Still the mouths at each breast suckled. Hands continued to stroke her sides, her back, her breasts . . . her legs.

She should open her eyes, should come away from this

amazing dream, but a blunt fingertip prodded her ass and another mouth found her lips, and it was too marvelous, too arousing to end such a lush fantasy.

A mouth worked steadily between her legs, a thick finger probed her tight sphincter and slipped inside, matching the rhythm of the tongue in her pussy. The suction on her nipples grew more intense. Sharp nips and then steady pressure, fingers massaging and shaping each swollen globe.

Something smooth brushed her lips and left a trail of moisture. Tia smiled at the salty taste, opened her mouth, and drew a large cock between her lips. Not Luc's. The taste was different, the shape and size unfamiliar, but she sucked harder, drawing him into her mouth as the fantasy slowly gave way to reality.

Still, she didn't open her eyes. Who was this? Which of her packmates slowly, carefully fucked her mouth? Tia felt muscled thighs at either side of her face, the soft brush of testicles against her nose on each downward thrust.

The lips and tongue between her legs grew more insistent. Another tongue stroked her belly, licked her smooth mons. Who was it? Was it the same person whose finger breached her ass?

Someone else must be suckling her breasts . . . but who?

Where was Luc? She didn't feel him in the hands and mouths, lips and tongues worshipping her body. Tia opened her mind and sensed a lush haze of carnal thoughts all wound so tightly together the source was lost, the overall message practically omnipotent.

The cock in her mouth grew more insistent, and she clasped it at the base with both hands, controlling the depth and pressure of each thrust.

The finger in her bottom slipped free and a large cock found its way into her waiting pussy, filling her slowly, stretching her soft tissues until she thought she might burst. The lips and hands abandoned her breasts as the one fucking her mouth leaned forward and licked her belly again, slowly filled her mouth with cock, and ran his tongue once more across her smooth mons. Then he slipped himself free of her lips and moved aside.

Only one man filled Tia now, thrusting harder, stronger, his deep-throated groans of pleasure turning her on as much as the powerful rhythm taking her close to the edge. Tia opened her eyes and looked into Tinker's dark face. His eyes were closed, his mouth twisted in a tight grimace as he pumped hard and fast, lifting her hips in his huge hands, digging his fingers into her buttocks and filling her with the solid length of his cock. His balls slapped her butt on every downward thrust, the thick length of his penis dragged perfectly across her clitoris.

Gasping, grabbing at his strong arms and lifting her hips to meet him, Tia climaxed hard and fast. Tinker followed, bellowing like a mad bull, his hips jerking and twisting with each spasm of his release.

She'd not linked with him, felt no connection other than the meeting of their bodies. Now Tinker rolled away to one side, slipping free of her wet pussy with a soft sucking noise. Tia felt the thick cream of their release running slowly down the crease between her cheeks, but before the moisture could touch the rumpled sheets, Mik was there with a soft cloth, bathing her gently, smiling at her with a knowing grin.

Tia opened her mind to Mik's and found carnal images so explicit, so personal, she almost giggled. He saw the two of them in every position possible, but Tia discovered that what Mik wanted most was to come in her mouth. He wanted to feel her lips on him, her mouth suckling him as he climaxed.

His cock was swollen and wet. Tia knew at once Mik was the one she'd already taken in her mouth. That left AJ and Jake . . . and Luc. She turned her head, but Luc was gone.

Jake waited off to one side, reminding her of Luc and

the way he'd looked when she'd first come into the loft tonight. Naked, his beautiful body gleaming in the low light, Jake slowly stroked his swollen cock, rolling the foreskin over the bulbous head, and then, with slow deliberation, pulling it back to repeat the process.

When Tia caught his eye, he winked at her but never broke the slow, steady rhythm as he watched her and pleasured himself.

The sight, the intensity of his gaze, the soft sweep of Mik's damp washcloth between her legs had Tia panting and squirming within moments. AJ crawled close to her, nudged Mik aside, grabbed her hips, flipped Tia over on her belly, and then thrust his cock between her folds without any preparation at all.

She didn't need it. Wet and ready, Tia arched her back, taking him deep inside. Mik scooted around to her front and knelt before Tia. She grinned, raised herself up on her hands and knees, and, without a word, took his cock deep in her mouth. At this angle, Tia knew she could swallow him down her throat, though it wasn't her favorite way to take a man.

Mik seemed to sense exactly what she wanted. He pulled back until just the head remained between Tia's lips, allowing her to determine how deep, how hard. With AJ filling her pussy and Mik slowly, carefully fucking her mouth, Tia's body trembled on the edge of yet another climax.

Still, in the back of her mind, she wondered where Luc had gone, why he'd left the room. Did it bother him to watch her with the rest of his packmates, even though he'd orchestrated this entire evening?

With his thoughts blocked the past two days, she'd had no way of reading him. When would he open to her again, open the way he'd opened at the beginning? Worry about Luc threatened to take her out of the moment, but AJ reached around and found her clit, softly plucking and rubbing the sensitive organ between his fingers. Luc's image faded from her thoughts and she concentrated on the two men loving her. Mik tensed as Tia compressed her lips around his cock and then tried to pull out of her mouth before he came.

Tia held him between her lips, taking him even deeper, sucking hard and stroking him with her tongue until he stiffened and convulsed, his audible gasps of pleasure turning her on even more. Tia's mouth filled with the warm, salty taste of Mik's cum and she swallowed quickly, taking everything he gave. As Mik's spasms turned to tiny pulses, AJ's fingers compressed Tia's clit and he rammed his cock deep inside.

Tia arched her back, turned Mik's shrinking cock loose, and screamed, joining both men in yet another climax. Laughing, weak, and trembling, she fell to the mattress with AJ still clasped to her hips. Mik's cock hung limply between his legs, the shiny skin damp from her mouth.

Tia looked up and realized Jake still watched her. His cock was huge, caught in his broad fist, the head as large as a plum and just as dark. Slowly, Jake rolled to his knees and crawled across the tumbled sheets to Tia.

The look in his amber eyes was dark, intense, totally feral. His thoughts remained thoroughly blocked yet obviously focused on only Tia. He leaned over and kissed her, mindless of Mik's semen on her lips. Jake palmed her breast and gently lifted her away from Mik. Mesmerized by Jake's dark gaze, Tia allowed him to pull her to her knees and position her on the mattress with a tall stack of pillows under her belly.

Then Jake knelt behind her and carefully spread her thighs, checking to make sure her legs were firmly planted. He ran his forefinger from her tailbone to her navel and then slowly made the journey back to her ass. He pressed her tight sphincter a couple of times, as though testing her muscles.

Then he repeated the process.

The slow deliberation of his movements turned her on more than mere touch might have. Tia moaned and shifted her hips under Jake's slow exploration.

He stroked her again, dipping into her wet and weeping pussy, twirling his thick finger around in her cream, dragging her fluids up the crease in her butt to press at her sphincter. He pressed slowly, firmly. This time he breached the sensitive opening.

Tia grunted when he inserted one finger and then two and thrust slowly, in and out. With the third, she felt impaled on his hand, yet her body grew hotter, wetter.

The others watched. She felt their arousal, heard their loud, panting breaths. Knew even Luc was aware of Jake's deliberate motions, though he still hadn't come into the room.

Jake's fingers continued their slow and steady thrusts deep inside her bottom. His other hand swept over her thigh, across her groin to cup her smooth mons. One finger raked her suddenly needy clit and Tia whimpered.

She opened her thoughts to Jake's but read only need and dark desire. He saw them fucking hard and fast, saw his huge cock penetrating her anally, making her come more than once with his hands, his mouth.

The vision he shared made her hotter, took her higher. Tia shuddered. Jake's three fingers slipped in and out of her ass, bringing Tia closer to orgasm. The pressure on her clit was so gentle, she barely felt it. She wanted more, wanted Jake inside her. Once more she found his thoughts, but the visual had changed.

This time Jake saw her as a she-wolf, his bitch.

Saw himself mounting her, taking her vaginally, not anally, filling her with his wolven cock, swelling and tying them together, binding Tia to him for all time.

His fingers slipped quickly out of her ass. She felt the

pressure of Jake's human cock breaching her pussy, sensed his impending shift to wolf.

"No. You can't! I won't!" She spun away, twisting out of Jake's grasp just as he became the wolf. Snarling his frustration, Jake swung his big head back and forth, watching AJ, Mik, and Tinker. The three of them paused as if suspended in time, caught by their mate's unexpected shift.

Tia pressed back against the wall, almost at the same spot where Jake had waited. The sound of footsteps pounded on the stairs, followed by the hair-raising snarl of an enraged wolf and Jake's angry growl as Luc flew into the room, teeth bared, eyes glinting.

He went straight for Jake's throat. Tia screamed. Tinker grabbed her by the arm and dragged her out of the way.

"No! Let me go. . . . Luc will kill him. We can't let him!" Tia struggled in Tinker's strong grasp. She had no more effect than a fly swatting at an elephant.

"He damned well can kill him if he wants, and it's not our place to stop him. C'mon. This is no place for you."

Tinker barely had time to pull Tia down the stairs before Jake, as wolf, came flying down behind them. His neck was bleeding, but it was obvious the wound wasn't serious. Luc followed and then unexpectedly stopped at the back door to watch as Jake raced across the meadow.

When Luc turned around, he was once again human. He leaned against the door frame, his lean, naked body all hard muscle and taut sinew. Though his chest was heaving with each breath he took, his stance appeared unnaturally calm, considering what had just occurred. "Well, I certainly didn't expect that." He glanced at Tia. His expression remained tight, unreadable. His thoughts were totally blocked, just as they'd been for the past couple days. He shook his head. "But I should have. I blew it. I'm sorry. I should have realized Jake would try to force the issue. It's really not his fault. We all need . . . all want . . ." Luc rubbed his hand over his eyes. Speaking as much to himself as to Tia, he added, "We should have bonded first. Maybe not. I don't know. Hell, I'll go find him. Jake's going to feel really bad about this."

Jake's going to feel bad! Practically sputtering her outrage, Tia pulled out of Tinker's grasp.

Luc shifted and was out the door before she could get to him. AJ and Mik seemed to reach the same conclusion at the same time. Shifting as they ran, the two men followed Luc.

The cabin seemed unnaturally quiet with all of them gone. Tia rounded on the one man remaining. The words, the anger and hurt, spilled out of her. "What the hell is going on? What about me? Jake tried to force me to bond with him. That's rape. Luc's more upset about Jake's feelings than he is about me? I thought I meant something to Luc. He said he loved me. If that's the way he shows love, I want no part of him."

Tinker held his arms wide and Tia threw herself against his broad chest. No matter that he was naked, that she was as well. He was Tinker and he seemed to be the only one who really cared about her, the only one who listened.

He rested his chin on top of her head and hugged her close. Sobbing, Tia nestled against him, heart pounding, eyes burning, but somewhat calmed by the soft sweep of Tinker's big, warm palm along her spine.

Tia reached for Tinker's thoughts. There was no way she could tell him in words how much his friendship meant, no way beyond the mental communication that was quickly becoming as natural to Tia as speech.

Tinker's mind was open, but he seemed faraway. Tia realized he was lost in memory, reliving something that had happened elsewhere. Tinker's thoughts were clearly visible, inviting her to look, though on some level Tia knew, as she looked, that she broke every rule Luc had taught her, every Chanku law of privacy.

Tia saw Luc, saw him sitting with a beer in his hand in

what appeared to be a small bar. A large, dark hand grabbed a beer next to Luc's. *Tinker.* Of course! Tia saw whatever happened in Tinker's memories from his point of view.

The mellow strains of good jazz played in the background. Dim lights, soft voices wove in and out of Tinker's thoughts.

Luc wasn't drunk, but he seemed morose and upset. He stared at his beer, then finally turned and looked at Tinker. For once, Luc's mind was open, his thoughts unblocked . . . for Tinker, not for Tia. Now, though, they were clear, each one a shard of glass cutting into her heart.

How can I tell Tia I did it, Tink? How can I ever admit to her I'm the one who killed her mother?

Luc's words seared themselves on her brain. Tia froze, her body turned to ice, her muscles went rigid. Tinker's blocks snapped into place and the visual of Luc disappeared.

"Shit, sweetie. What the fuck were you doing in my head?" His voice raised and menacing, Tinker held Tia away from him. His big hands clasping her upper arms with bruising strength were all that kept her from falling to the floor. "You don't do that. Ever. Do you hear me? That's a hateful, horrible thing you just did, going into my head without permission."

At Tia's shocked gasp, Tinker shook his head. "No, I could never hate you, but a man's thoughts are private. You stay out of my head unless you're invited in. Understand?"

Tia expected him to shake her like a child. Furious, his face twisted in anger, he was nothing like the wonderful man who'd loved her so sweetly.

Right now he looked mad enough to take a swing at her. She didn't care. It didn't matter if he hated her for what she'd done. All Tia could think of was what she'd seen, the words she'd heard.

She raised her head and glared at Tinker. "Is it true? Did Luc really do it? Did he kill my mother?"

All the steam seemed to go out of the big man. Tinker glanced away and sighed. "I think you need to talk to Luc about it. It's not my place to tell his story. I should have been more careful with my memories. You're not supposed to go messin' in somebody's head without permission." He rubbed Tia's arms where he'd grabbed her but couldn't—or wouldn't—look her in the eye.

Tia stepped back, out of Tinker's reach. Outrage warred with pain, misery with righteous anger and shock. Her body trembled, her heart ached. "I'm sorry I intruded, Tinker, but if I hadn't, would anyone ever have told me the truth? Believe me, I'd ask Luc in person if I could." She clenched her fists, breathing hard. "I'd love to ask Luc what the fuck's going on, but he's out checking on poor Jake, someone he obviously cares about a lot more than he does me."

Her decision was made before she thought it through. "I'm out of here. You tell Luc I . . . I . . . oh, shit." She would not cry. Not now, not for a man who'd lied to her.

Not for the man who killed her mother.

Tia slapped her hand to her mouth, suddenly nauseous. Luc? How could he? Bending double, she cried out, a long, low wail of anguish and rage.

Tinker reached for her, but she broke from his grasp, raced up the stairs with Tinker right behind her, and grabbed the sports bag she'd used as a suitcase. Tia threw on a pair of jeans, grabbed a sweatshirt and sandals, and stuffed the rest of her things in the bag.

Tinker was pulling his jeans over his massive thighs when she stalked past him.

"Tell him I—"

"I'm telling him nothing, sweetie. I'm going with you. No way in hell are you driving these roads in the shape you're in. Now get your stuff. If you're determined to leave, I'm driving." He threw a sweatshirt over his head and slipped his feet into loafers without any socks.

Tia tried to take a deep breath, but her chest hurt. Her body ached from so much sex, her heart was a throbbing lead weight barely supported by her ribs. She wanted to run away by herself, she wanted to slap Luc's face and tell him just how much he'd hurt her, how much she hated him.

She wanted to curl up in a tight little ball and hide from herself, from what she had missed, from what she'd become.

First, though, Tia wanted to talk to her father. If Luc had done this horrible thing, if he actually had killed Tia's mother and then lied to her, Ulrich's lies were worse. He'd obviously known what happened all along, yet he'd let Tia live in ignorance of the truth.

He'd known about Luc yet treated him like a beloved son, probably loved Luc more than he loved his own daughter. Even worse, Ulrich had let her fall in love with her mother's murderer.

That was the greatest sin of all.

Chapter 13

Coward! He was nothing but a coward, chasing after Jake when he should be back at the cabin holding Tia. Loving her, letting her know how much she meant to him. Not nose-to-the-ground, frustration driving him through thick undergrowth and over boggy marshes. Luc forced the stricken look on Tia's face from his mind and tried to concentrate on his rampant anger with Jake.

AJ and Mik followed, off to his left and a bit behind, loyal backup no matter what was to come. Damn, he loved Jake. Had been brother, lover, friend to Jake for almost fifteen years. How could his own pack mate have betrayed him like this?

How could Luc have betrayed Tia? *Damn.*

Jake's actions might be inexcusable, but Luc's were unforgivable. Tia needed him. Luc could master Jake at any time, could easily remind him of his status within the pack. Besting Jake at battle was a no-brainer.

Winning Tia would take all his skill and more. It would take the truth.

Still Luc ran, following Jake's trail, avoiding the inevitable, focusing on something he understood, something he could fight out in the open without subterfuge, without lies.

Lies. Everything he had with Tia was based on lies. His love for her might be pure and honest, but the person he presented, the man he wanted her to love, didn't exist anywhere but in Tia's heart.

The real man, the Chanku who loved Tia, was a coward. A liar and a craven son of a bitch.

Until he could be completely honest with Tia, there would always be a wall between them. Once she knew the truth, there would be no need for walls. . . . She'd be so far out of his reach, it wouldn't matter anymore.

Head down, nose to the trail, Luc focused on what he could handle—he followed Jake's spoor.

Luc, we got trouble. Big trouble.

Tinker's mental call barely registered, as though Luc had gone farther from the cabin than he realized. He paused in his search for Jake. Tinker's mental touch should be much clearer.

Where are you? What's up?

I'm with Tia, headed for her father's house. She knows about her mother, about you. I'm sorry, man. She got into my head when I wasn't paying attention. She's one pissed Chanku bitch.

Luc's heart felt like lead in his chest. It was over. Everything he'd dreamed, everything he'd hoped for . . . over.

Shit. Okay. . . . AJ, Mik, and I'll head back. We'll leave Jake here to cool his heels for a while. Serves him right. And Tink . . . thanks. Don't feel so bad. It's not your fault.

No, it wasn't Tinker's fault at all. It was all Luc's. Why hadn't he told her when he'd had the chance?

Feeling as if his entire world were spinning helplessly out of control, Luc signaled to AJ and Mik. He turned and headed back to the cabin. They would leave Jake to fend for himself for a while. It was probably better this way. Luc really didn't feel like teaching anyone a lesson, not when he was the one most in need of learning.

* * *

Tia's heart still raced; her fingertips tingled as if she'd run long and hard. Instead, she sat next to Tinker in the front seat of his SUV as they drove the long road back to San Francisco. She was anxious, verging on tears, and fighting an impossible desire to shift and race through the forest, to run as far and fast from her misery as her Chanku body would allow.

The morning sun was already high in the sky by the time they reached the valley floor and headed west to San Francisco. Tinker hadn't spoken to her since they'd gotten into the car. His mental blocks were high and tight, but Tia hadn't done more than a cursory mind check to see if he was angry with her.

He wasn't really mad at all. Just terribly sad and feeling guilty. Why, when Tinker had nothing at all to feel guilty about? He'd done nothing wrong. It wasn't his place to tell Luc's story, no matter what he'd known.

Tia's mind whirled with unanswered questions, anger with her father, with Luc. Had all of them known? Jake? Mik and AJ? Had every man hidden the truth from Tia? How could they call her a packmate if every one of them lied to her?

Tia glanced at Tinker. He appeared loose and relaxed, one arm draped over the steering wheel, his body sprawled to one side in the dark leather seat. He stared straight ahead, skillfully maneuvering the big vehicle through the morning rush-hour traffic. Only the tic in his right jaw showed Tia how upset he was. She wondered what he'd told Luc.

Tia had to assume he'd communicated with Luc. Not that it mattered. She hated Luc, hated the lies he'd told her, the way he'd made her love him. She never wanted to see Luc again, not after what he'd done to her.

Oh, God. Biting back a moan, Tia tightened her arm across her midsection. Her stomach cramped in pain, her heart hurt.

Luc! She'd never be able to trust him, never be able to want his touch, his kisses. His love. Ulrich's image flashed into her thoughts. She'd always thought her father loved her. He couldn't, not if he'd been able to live a lie for the past twenty years. She wasn't sure which betrayal hurt more—Luc's or Ulrich's. No matter. Once Tia had it out with her father, she fully intended to give notice at school and head back to Boston.

Run home to Shannon with her tail between her legs and a story her friend would never believe. At least, Shannon wouldn't believe it until Tia shifted and showed her exactly what a Chanku could do! She would take plenty of the supplements with her, enough to share. Tia wondered if her father was right, that Shannon might be Chanku. Wouldn't that be something to share with her friend, her longtime lover? It certainly would explain a lot, especially the relationship the girls had shared for so many years.

Concentrating on Shannon, imagining her reaction, kept Tia's thoughts off Luc for at least another ten minutes . . . but they still had at least an hour and a half before she and Tinker reached San Francisco.

Suddenly Tinker straightened up in his seat, pulled the vehicle out of the fast lane, and found a wide spot on the side of the road next to a cornfield. Before Tia could ask what was wrong, he'd jumped out of the SUV, leaped over a small irrigation ditch, and disappeared into the field of standing corn.

Tia waited for a few moments, assuming Tinker had merely heeded a call to nature. When he didn't return, she grabbed the keys from the ignition and followed his trail away from the freeway, across the ditch, and into the corn.

Just a few steps through the dry, dusty stalks took Tia into a totally different world. Even the sounds of the nearby freeway were muted, lost in the crackling, crunchy whisper of dry stalks blowing in the morning breeze.

She turned slowly, amazed at how lost she felt, how alone.

"Tinker? Where are you?"

A low whine caught Tia's attention. She pushed straight ahead through the stalks and found the huge wolf she recognized as her friend. He glanced quickly at her and then cocked his head, as though listening for something.

Shift. Open your senses. Listen.

Okay. She could do that. Sticking the keys in her pocket, Tia slipped out of her clothes and placed them next to the pile of Tinker's things. Within seconds she'd shifted.

Her senses were stronger as Chanku, her hearing more acute. Her mind better able to read the mental speech of the pack.

Luc's voice was there, faint but still understandable. Tia cringed and threw up her mental blocks, unwilling to let him into her thoughts. Tinker snarled at Tia.

Frowning, Tia dropped the block, sat back, and listened.

She heard it then, a faint cry for help. Her father's voice! Struggling to understand, Tia filtered out the other voices, other sounds. Words caught like filaments of spiderweb on a soft breeze, hung just long enough to tease and then drifted away.

Chanku. Montana. Anton something. She couldn't understand. *Help. Hurry. . . .*

Frustrated, Tia whimpered, listened. Felt a sharp pain, as if she'd been dealt a blow to her head. She flinched, saw Tinker do the same. Listened harder, heard nothing.

Luc's voice broke the silence. She might hate him, but if he had any idea what had just happened . . .

Someone's got the boss. Ulrich's not sure who. Their faces were covered. I sense pain, now nothing. He's been knocked out, drugged, maybe. AJ, Mik, and I are about an hour behind you. We'll meet at Ulrich's and go from there.

Jake? Tinker's soft question hung in Tia's mind.

He'll figure out a way to get back. It'll give him time to think.

Time to think. Would there ever be enough time to think, to understand what was happening? Learning about Luc's connection to her mother's death without knowing any details, fearing for her father's safety. At the same time, she felt like smacking Luc for lying to her, remembering the soft touch of his lips on hers, her body's response to his lovemaking.

Remembering her response to sex with all the men. Tia hadn't allowed herself to think about last night, couldn't without fighting the tears that clogged her throat, made her eyes burn, her heart hurt.

Now, though, it was the least threatening thing to occupy her mind as Tinker sped down the freeway, taking them to Ulrich's home. She glanced to her left, noticed that Tinker's jaw was still clenched, his big football lineman's body not nearly so relaxed. Now, though, he looked like a man dealing with something he understood.

Tia almost smiled. A kidnapping was familiar; her problems with Luc probably scared Tinker half to death. She reached out and touched his muscular forearm, remembering how gentle he'd been with her last night. He'd made love to her so beautifully, so perfectly, yet they'd not said a word to one another about the experience. When her fingers closed over his arm, Tinker jerked his head to the right, as though her touch had shocked him out of deep thought.

"Sorry. Didn't meant to startle you. Thank you, Tink. For last night. You helped make what could have been an awkward experience something beautiful, something I'll treasure in spite of what Jake did. Thanks, too, for taking me home, for being my friend. I know this has to be so awkward for you, and I'm sorry to involve you."

He laughed. "Last night was all my pleasure, sweetie.

That's something I intend to do again and again . . . and then again, so get used to it. As far as the other, well, your father's been like family to me. Luc is my brother. So are AJ, Mik, and even Jake, though I'd like to wring his scrawny neck." He grinned at Tia. "I never even saw that move of his coming, but Jake's the quiet type. Don't always know what the man's thinking. He shouldn't have done that. I'm just thankful you're as quick as you are, or we could have had one hell of a problem. We all know you're Luc's."

Tia looked down and folded her hands tightly in her lap. "Not anymore, Tink. Not any man's. I'm going to go back to Boston as soon as we get Daddy back. I don't belong here. I've caused trouble between Luc and Jake, maybe even put my father in danger. Maybe what happened to him is my fault, too. I know someone's been watching me. Doing things in the classroom, in my apartment. Maybe it's connected."

"Don't blame yourself, sweetie." Tinker reached over and squeezed her shoulder. "There's a lot of folks out to get your dad. It comes with the territory. There've been other attempts, and we've never failed him. You're not going anywhere. You and Luc will work this out. Trust me and trust him. You don't know the details about your mom. When you do, you'll understand."

Would she? Tia couldn't imagine any scenario where her mother's death would make sense. Why hadn't her father told her the truth?

Why hadn't Luc?

Something Tinker said suddenly lodged in her mind. "Other attempts? What other attempts?"

Tinker at least had the good grace to look ashamed. "Um, you're aware Pack Dynamics isn't your typical detective agency, right?"

"Duh. I figured that out right away. Luc confirmed it. What's with the other attempts?"

"We do quite a bit of secret work for the government—more so, now that terrorist activity has escalated. There's been more than one attack stopped because of our intervention. Never makes the papers, doesn't show up on the nightly news. Chanku work so far undercover, even the President hasn't got a clue."

Tinker hit the brakes to avoid slowing traffic as they wound closer into the city. He grinned at Tia. "Your dad's made a lot of enemies over the years. It's part of the job. There's always someone wanting a little payback. There's the risk of someone finding out about Chanku. Lots of reasons for your dad to remain alert. This time he slipped up, but we'll get him back. We won't know who's behind this one until we have more facts, but when we find out, we'll get him."

"When we heard him, it wasn't really clear, but I heard some names I didn't recognize. Anton something? I think I heard him say Montana. Do you think that's where they're taking him?"

Tinker nodded. "Could be, though Anton Cheval is one of the good guys. He's the alpha leader of the Chanku pack in Montana, a man reputed to have powers that go way beyond the typical Chanku. I've never met him, just heard about him. I imagine your dad mentioned him because he wants us to contact Cheval for help. He's got three packmates. . . . In fact, I think one of them is your cousin, a woman named Keisha?"

"Keisha? Oh, my God! I remember her. . . . Our moms were sisters. She's older than me, but she used to come over to play when I was really little. She would make fun of my hair because it was so blond and frizzy, yet my skin was almost as dark as hers." Tia laughed, amazed to think Keisha was only a phone call away. "I'd forgotten all about her. She's Chanku, too?"

"Yep. Gorgeous, tough as nails. Takes her role as alpha bitch to heart, from what I've heard. She's a landscape architect, but she's decided to get out of the city and live way off in the woods in Montana. She was assaulted, badly hurt about a year ago. I think she's had it with the big city."

Tia shuddered. "I don't blame her. With all the weird stuff happening in my classroom and apartment, I can understand not wanting to stay in the city. You said there are four in the pack. Are the others men?"

"Not all. Two men and two women." Tinker grinned at Tia. "When Luc told us what your dad said about the Montana pack, we were all jealous as hell. You're the first Chanku female any of us has ever seen, much less been with. I can see why Jake did what he did, even though I can't forgive him for it. He was wrong, but after loving you, sweetie, I can't imagine settling for a plain old ordinary woman. And as much as I love my mates, they're chopped liver next to you."

Tia laughed. She punched Tinker lightly on the shoulder and settled back in the soft leather seat, grinning broadly for the first time today. This long trip down the mountain certainly wasn't anything like she'd expected when they left the cabin early that morning. She had no right to suddenly feel so lighthearted, even hopeful.

The skyscrapers of San Francisco loomed in the distance. Sunlight glinted off the bay and fog swirled and twisted over the hills surrounding the city. Maybe Tinker was right. Maybe she did need to give Luc a chance to tell his side of the story. Once they got her dad back, once they figured out who was behind the rash of incidents around Tia, maybe then she'd be willing to listen.

Ulrich's apartment was trashed. There was no other way to describe it. Tia's first reaction was to call the police. Tinker stopped her.

"Can't do that, sweetie. There would be too many questions we can't answer. Too great a risk. We have the man power, the skills, and the training. We handle this on our own."

Tinker gave her a quick squeeze and then headed straight for Ulrich's office, with Tia following. He stopped in front of the computer printer. A single sheet of paper lay in the tray.

"I figured they would leave something here." He picked it up and read the single line typed across the middle of the page. 'Do not call authorities. You will be contacted tomorrow.'"

"That's all?"

"Yep. We wait."

Tia nodded and then wandered aimlessly into her father's bedroom. She hadn't been in this room since she was a child, but it still felt the same, smelled the same. Her father's aftershave, the musty smell of books piled on every flat surface, stashed in boxes and on bookshelves.

The mattress lay halfway off the bed, as though he'd been taken while still asleep. Drawers hung open on the large dresser, and one had been pulled out entirely. It lay on the floor, the wood splintered and the contents scattered.

Tia leaned over and picked up a small framed picture. The glass was cracked, but she could still make out the smiling faces of her mother and herself. She looked about four years old in the snapshot. Camille's arms were wrapped tightly around her waist, the fingers interlaced over Tia's round, little tummy. She wished she could remember when the picture was taken, how it had felt to have her mom's arms around her.

She couldn't. The memories were too vague, the feelings too far away, overlaid by too much sorrow, too many years of loss. Tia continued staring at the picture long after it disappeared behind the watery blur of her tears.

Strong fingers carefully lifted the framed photo from her hands. Blinking away her tears, Tia turned, expecting

Tinker. Luc stood directly behind her, his expression solemn, his eyes wary.

With a choked sob, Tia threw her arms around his waist and pressed her face against his soft leather coat. He drew her into a warm and comforting hug. She felt the weight of his chin resting on top of her head, took a deep breath, and inhaled his familiar scent.

His voice sounded rough. It rumbled over her ragged nerve endings, teased her frayed senses. "I'm so sorry. Sorry about your dad, especially about what happened to your mom. I know just saying it isn't enough. It never will be, but please know I've carried this burden with me for more than twenty years. I'll always carry it."

Tia jerked out of his embrace and wrapped her arms around herself, suddenly chilled to the bone. Damn him. Then why his lame apology? Words but no explanations? Tia felt her anger, a lifetime of hurt bursting to the surface, a sense of rage unlike anything she'd ever known. Voice trembling, she glared at him. "I've lived with it for just as long. Tell your story to that little girl who lost her mother, who's wanted to know the truth for all these years!"

She brushed the back of her hand across her face, smearing aside hot tears and then covering her mouth with her fist. *Damn.* It hurt worse now than when her mother had died! "Why didn't you tell me? You've known from the beginning how much I wanted the truth. You've lied to me. My father's lied. Just as well he's not here, because he's every bit as guilty as you are. You should have told me. If you loved me the way you said you do, you would have been honest with me." She couldn't help the bitter edge to her words. Wasn't sure if she wanted to call them back or not.

"I couldn't." Luc jammed his hands in his pockets, looked anywhere but at Tia before finally turning his steady gaze back on her. His eyes glittered, his normally tan skin was ashen. "I was a coward. There's no excuse. I don't know if you can ever forgive me. I hope you will . . . hope you'll be able to, someday."

Tia heard the hope in his voice. The silent entreaty behind his words. She still didn't know what had happened, still didn't know the whole truth, but it was too much, her anger and hurt running too deep.

What she saw in Luc's eyes hurt even more. It was obvious that he suffered, that he hurt as badly as she did, but it wasn't enough. Would it ever be? Tia had to look away before she could find her voice, and when she spoke, her words sounded as cold as she felt.

"Help me find my father. Please."

Luc nodded. His entire body seemed to sag. "We'll find him. Tinker's looking for the phone number for the Montana pack. We all heard Ulrich mention them before we lost contact, so maybe they can help us."

AJ walked into the room with a single file card from Ulrich's Rolodex. "Tink found it. Here it is. Anton Cheval. He's the one."

"Thanks." Luc grabbed the card from AJ's outstretched hand and headed for Ulrich's office. Tia stood alone in her father's bedroom and watched him walk away. A dark wolf raced into the room, his nose to the ground.

Mik, looking for clues. AJ quickly stripped out of his clothes, shifted, and joined his partner. Tia stood by helplessly, unsure what she should be doing. She stayed out of the way as both Chanku made a thorough search of her father's bedroom before heading toward the main part of the house.

Tia followed. Tinker was going through papers on her father's desk, Luc talking quietly to someone on the phone. AJ and Mik moved on into the front room. Tia walked slowly about the office, picking up papers scattered on the floor, righting fallen lamps, straightening pictures hanging crookedly on the walls.

Moving from room to room, trying to put her father's

home right again. Trying to clean up the broken glass, find a place for the bits and pieces of her father's life. All the while, she wondered if she would ever be able to put her own life back together again. If what was broken could ever again be made whole.

Chapter 14

A private jet, courtesy of the Montana pack, waited for Luc, Tinker, and Tia on the tarmac at San Francisco International Airport. AJ and Mik would stay at Ulrich's to wait for the kidnappers' call. They would also be there to fill in Jake on what had happened, should he return. Luc had his cell phone and they all had Anton Cheval's numbers.

The flight into Montana was quiet, uneventful, and very tense. Tia sat by herself, claiming exhaustion, but spent the first half of the trip staring out the window at the thick clouds between the plane and the ground.

She needed sleep, couldn't remember the last time she'd slept. The past forty-eight hours had been filled with Luc's training, her run with the pack, a night of unbelievable sex, and her horrible discovery about her mother, followed by the long trip down the mountain with Tinker to her father's empty home.

Now Tia's anxious world revolved around worry for her father and an unresolved anger only he could appease. Was Ulrich all right? Had his kidnappers hurt him? Did he have his supplements with him? She'd never asked how long they could go without the essential combination of nutrients needed to become and remain Chanku.

Tia had no idea what would happen if she missed a pill, and she wasn't about to take a chance. They went everywhere with her. Would she revert to a plain, ordinary human again? Would her abilities disappear altogether, those amazingly enhanced senses that allowed her to see, smell, and hear her world in the manner of Chanku?

Why hadn't her father told her the truth? Looking back, Tia realized her life since her mother's death had been filled with lies of omission. The fact Ulrich knew she wasn't even human should have warranted at least a conversation or two.

Crap. This all felt so unreal. Ulrich knew how much Tia hungered for any information about her mother, yet he'd refused to discuss Camille's death, had actually befriended the man who killed his wife, and treated him like a son.

Then he'd gone and put that same man in Tia's life. He'd thrown Luc at her like bait. Like a fool, she'd fallen for him, taken him hook, line, and sinker. Tia rubbed her burning eyes and tried to ignore the hollow ache in the pit of her stomach, the lump of pain in her throat. Of the two men in the world Tia loved most, both had lied.

Her chin quivered. She caught her lip between her teeth and held the tears at bay. So many questions without answers. So much to try to understand. Too much, and all of it hurt.

Sighing, Tia rolled her head to one side, scrunched herself in the comfortable seat, and stared blindly out the window. The small jet sped onward, heading toward the rugged mountains of Montana and a private airstrip belonging to their Chanku hosts.

Luc wandered to the back of the jet to check on Tia. She slept soundly, her usual tangle of hair appearing smoother, more touchable than he recalled. He searched the overhead rack and found a warm blanket. Tucking it around her shoulders, hearing her soft, sleepy sigh as she snuggled her face against the woven folds, made Luc's heart ache.

Would he ever regain what he had lost? He smoothed Tia's hair out of her eyes, watched her sleep for a moment longer, and then slowly walked back to his seat beside Tinker.

"Didja find Jake?" Tinker's soft question caught Luc off guard. He hadn't even thought of their packmate, still alone at the cabin, for all he knew.

"No. This thing with Ulrich took precedence. I left him a note, said there'd been trouble, that the boss was kidnapped. I figure he'll either stay up there or make his way back to the city. It's up to him."

For that matter, Jake could stay gone permanently. Luc felt as if he'd lost a brother. The man he thought he'd loved had never existed.

Tinker sighed loudly, sounding as exasperated as Luc felt. "He's one of us, Luc. No matter what he's done, he's a part of each one of us. He'll apologize eventually, and we're going to forgive him. We have to. We're all he's got, and we need him as much as he needs us."

Luc swung his head around slowly and stared at Tinker for a long moment. Thank goodness for this guy, sometimes the only reasonable one among them. "How did you get so smart? You're still a wet-behind-the-ears kid."

"I have a lot of experience as the odd man out." Tinker's sad smile spoke volumes. "Jake doesn't. He's used to being your second, the one who guards your back the same way you watch his. I don't believe what he did to Tia was planned. I don't think it was part of his conscious mind at all. If you ask me, what happened scared the shit out of him. That's why he ran."

Tinker scooted around in his seat so that he faced Luc. "Think about it. AJ and Mik have each other. I've gotten to know Tia as a friend. Jake sees her as only a woman. An available female. You hadn't mated her and the wolf in him couldn't afford to pass up the opportunity. We all have our human roots, but at heart we're still wolves. We're nothin' more than animals. Put yourself in Jake's place."

Luc was still running Tinker's comments through his head when they touched down at a small private airstrip in Montana. A shiny black SUV waited at the end of the runway, the only vehicle in sight. Long shadows of late afternoon stretched across the smooth asphalt and lost themselves in the thick forest surrounding the runway.

Luc turned to go awaken Tia, but she was already standing and reaching for her bags. She glanced his direction and then quickly looked away. Luc shouldered his own bag and followed Tinker out the door at the front of the plane.

A small, dark-skinned man waited beside the vehicle, a large black Hummer. He tipped his baseball cap, introduced himself as Oliver, an employee of Cheval's, and then opened the back door of the imposing vehicle. His English accent seemed strangely out of place in the midst of the Montana mountains.

Tia sat in the back beside Tinker, studiously avoiding Luc. Luc took the seat up front with Oliver as they sped away from the airstrip. He lost all sense of direction as they meandered along a series of mountain roads.

None of them spoke audibly. Mentally, they discussed what AJ and Mik had sensed, the possible number of kidnappers, their ethnicities. Luc had discovered an ability to pick out various ethnic groups by scent when he was in his wolf form. He knew the differences were tied into diet and drink, but the distinct odors often gave him clues a normal human nose would miss.

The others possessed the same ability.

AJ and Mik had searched carefully and then shared the information with Tinker and Luc before they left. The unique smells and scents typical of many of their terrorist targets were missing. They'd sensed stale cigarette smoke, bacon grease and onions, and, very faintly, coffee, beneath the rancid odor of sweat and fear.

It had taken at least four men to abduct Ulrich. That much they knew for certain. They'd obviously had breakfast first and knew enough about Ulrich to realize he would be sleeping late into the morning. Did they know he was Chanku? That he ran through the park for most of the night?

Where his captors had taken him, and why, remained a mystery.

Luc turned over the information in his mind. They'd fully expected Middle Eastern terrorists, especially after their most recent raid in Florida. What didn't compute? What clue was he overlooking?

Tinker? Didn't you say AJ smelled bacon?

Tia's soft mental question yanked Luc out of his contemplation.

Yeah. They'd all eaten a big breakfast just before they hit. Sausage, too, I think.

Pork sausage?

I think so.

"Bingo." Luc snapped his fingers as the missing pieces fell into place. He turned around in his seat and smiled at Tia. For the first time today, she returned his smile with one of her own. "Good job, sweetheart."

Tinker looked from one to the other. "Would you mind filling in this poor schmuck on what's going on?"

"The hit in Florida, the one blamed on Jordanian terrorists? Damn, I wish Jake was here, because he was the second wolf. AJ and Mik were on two legs, but ya know what they were bitching about, what they smelled in that cave?"

"Bacon." Tinker grinned broadly. "Knowing those two and their bottomless pits at breakfast time, I bet they smelled bacon and eggs, and you had to listen to them bitch about it the whole time. Am I right?"

"You got it." Luc shook his head. "No self-respecting Middle Eastern terrorist is going to feed his captive bacon . . . or eat it himself." His smile was grim. "Something else I just remembered about Florida. There was no scent of fear. Whoever 'kidnapped' Secretary Bosworth wasn't at all nervous. Nerves, fear . . . put off a stench . . . a strong, acrid odor." Luc slammed down his fist on the back of the seat. "*Damn*. I wish I wasn't working on secondhand information. I should have been the one sniffing around Ulrich's place. I might have been able to find a connection."

"Between the raid in Florida and my father's kidnapping?" Tia leaned forward in her seat. "I don't understand."

Luc glanced at Oliver, but the small man stared straight ahead, presumably concentrating on his driving and completely ignoring the conversation around him. "We all had a feeling the kidnapping in Florida was a setup. We never saw any sign of Secretary Bosworth's captors, though we picked up the scents of others. Bosworth was more interested in Jake and me on four legs than he was in being freed. He kept talking about how we seemed almost human, how we didn't look like regular wolves. He's a member of the President's cabinet but not privy to Pack Dynamics."

"You think he's trying to find out more about the Chanku?" Tia's glance shifted from Tinker to Luc. "Do you think he might be behind my father's kidnapping?"

Luc shook his head. "I'm not ready to jump to conclusions yet, but if Cheval has the connections and the talents Ulrich seems to think he's got, we'll put him on it. I'll get in touch with our Washington contact and put out some feelers as well." He turned to the driver. "How much farther to Cheval's?"

The little man smiled. "We're here," he said, turning a long, sweeping corner.

The home seemed to grow up out of the stone that surrounded it, a huge, flowing structure built of rock and cedar logs, nestled in a dark forest of old-growth fir and pine. Stark mountains rose majestically behind the roofline, and a broad deck appeared to encircle the entire structure.

Standing on the deck in the last rays of the setting sun were four tall figures, two men and two women. The Montana pack Luc had heard of but never met. Luc glanced at Tia and then back at the four, immediately identifying Anton Cheval by his commanding presence. The man beside him would be the once famous magician, Stefan Aragat, the auburn-haired beauty his mate, Alexandria Olanet.

The woman standing beside Anton Cheval stole the breath from Luc's lungs. It wasn't her beauty or her regal bearing that shocked him to the core.

No. It was the fact she could have been Camille Mason's twin. She was an exact match to Tia's mother. The family resemblance was so strong, it made Luc's heart clench. He took a deep breath, tried to ignore the butterflies zinging through his gut. He had to put Camille's death out of his mind, for Tia's sake as well as his own.

If Keisha knew about Luc's role in her aunt's death, it could affect her desire to help, could affect the entire operation. Recovering Ulrich depended on their ability to work together, two autonomous Chanku packs, each unused to cooperating with strangers.

Luc hadn't let any of his packmates know of his fears, that alphas fought much easier than they cooperated. Keisha's resemblance to Tia's mother complicated things even more.

As the three of them piled out of the vehicle, Luc's gaze shifted to Tia and then back to Cheval. The look of speculation in the other man's eyes raised the nonexistent hackles along Luc's neck.

Another complication he hadn't thought of. Just because Cheval and Aragat were already mated didn't mean they wouldn't want to add another woman to their pack. With that thought uppermost in his mind, Luc headed up the steps to the deck.

Tia crawled out of the backseat and stretched. Her gaze slid from Luc—and the narrowed cast to his eyes—to the four strangers standing on the deck above them.

Sudden recognition swamped her, stopped the breath in her lungs, choked back the words she wanted to say. *Keisha?* The beautiful African-American woman standing proudly beside the tallest of the four reminded Tia so much of her mother, she felt faint. *Oh, my God! Keisha!* Dropping her bag, Tia raced up the steps into the woman's welcoming embrace.

Look at you! Keisha Rialto's familiar voice settled in Tia's mind like a warm, comforting blanket. The arms wrapping tightly around Tia's waist were the embrace of the mother she'd lost so long ago.

Without warning, Tia burst into tears.

Tia? Luc stood beside her, holding her bag in his hand. Tinker hovered right beside him, radiating anxiety and worry.

I'm okay. Don't worry. It's just . . . Tia covered her eyes with her hand, struggling for control.

Keisha gave her another tight squeeze. *It's been a long time, sweetie. A very long time. C'mon. You can meet the rest of the guys later.*

Embarrassed, overjoyed, and exhausted, Tia allowed Keisha to lead her into the house, away from the others. She cast one quick glance at Luc and Tinker, silently assuring them she would be okay, and then entered the house with her cousin.

* * *

Luc's heart rate slowed imperceptibly with Tia's reassuring thought. Tinker waited on the step just behind him, a solid presence of support. Luc and Anton Cheval faced off across the deck while Cheval's two remaining pack mates stood silently to one side. The air practically hummed with tension. Luc's chest felt tight; his heart thundered.

He'd never faced another true alpha before, the leader of a separate pack with all its inherent rules and taboos . . . rules Luc wasn't even sure he understood.

Though Ulrich remained their leader, Luc had long held the role of Pack Dynamics' functioning alpha. Looking at the powerful Chanku facing him, Luc wondered which one of them would rise victorious, should there be an actual battle between them.

He really, *really* didn't want to have to find out.

After a long, taut moment, Cheval nodded his head. The man standing beside him, so similar to Cheval's tall, lean build and dramatic coloring that they might have been brothers, took a step back. His arm remained wrapped possessively around the waist of the auburn-haired beauty at his side.

Cheval's amber eyes glittered as he held out his hand. "Lucien Stone? I am Anton Cheval." He took Luc's hand in a firm grip. "I've looked forward to meeting all of you, but certainly not under such trying circumstances."

Though every word was civil, Luc recognized the danger lurking just beneath Cheval's skin. When Cheval turned and acknowledged the man and woman standing beside him, there was pride as well as a warning in his voice. "My packmates, Stefan Aragat, his mate, Alexandria Olanet. I'll introduce you to Keisha, my mate, when she and her cousin return."

Luc silently acknowledged Cheval's emphasis on the word *mate*. With Tinker standing huge and menacing behind him, Luc appreciated the alpha's obvious concern.

He'd had a moment of major unease when Tia left with her cousin. How would he have felt if another male outside his pack had shown such interest?

Luc introduced Tinker, smiling inwardly at the stiff formality from his normally affable friend. Necessary, given their protective, possessive natures, but almost comical, considering the situation facing them. Luc's voice was serious when he added, "I appreciate your willingness to help."

Cheval nodded, then led them inside the house, where a spacious room with couches and chairs made a comfortable sitting area. "Oliver will take your bags to your rooms. I've given you a connecting suite at the back of the residence. You'll have privacy and access outside, should you wish to run. You'll also have complete access to one another's rooms."

Left unspoken was the fact that any other bedroom in the house would remain off-limits. Grinning to himself, Luc took a seat near the large window overlooking the drive they'd just traveled. There obviously was a lot he needed to learn about pack interaction. For now, though, he had to focus on the issue at hand. "I don't even know where to begin. We have so little to go on."

"Actually, we have more than you realize." Without asking their preference, Cheval poured brandy, offered a goblet to each of the men.

Luc gratefully accepted his. Stefan Aragat took the seat next to him. That's when Luc noticed Aragat's woman had not joined them, and wondered if they were just being cautious. Did Luc and his men represent a threat to this tight-knit pack?

Luc took a sip of the brandy. For some reason, memories of that night so long ago when Ulrich first told him about the Chanku came to mind.

Something in Cheval's arrogant posture, his supreme self-confidence, reminded Luc of his mentor. Given the faith he'd always had in Ulrich, it gave him a sense of hope that this might turn out well after all. "Mason's been missing for less than twelve hours," Luc said. "According to the note the kidnappers left, we're to be contacted tomorrow. Two of our pack mates have remained at Ulrich's home to take the call. We checked for clues. I have whatever scents and other information the two gathered. Unfortunately, I didn't gather clues on my own."

"No problem." Cheval took a sip of his brandy. "Actually, I've already scanned your thoughts and have the information from . . ." He paused a moment. "Ah, Mik and AJ?"

Already scanned? Luc glanced from Cheval to Aragat and back again to Cheval. "I don't understand? Why didn't I sense an intrusion? I should have felt you in my mind."

Cheval shook his head. "Actually, no. You would have if I'd used my Chanku skills to read your thoughts. Mason may have told you I was a wizard long before I was even aware of my Chanku heritage. The skills I learned studying the magical arts give me a certain edge, something I hope will come in handy when we rescue your mentor."

"Amazing." Luc took a sip of his brandy. He should have felt violated by the intrusion, but curiosity and respect won out. He felt as if their odds of a successful rescue had just gone up a few notches, now that they had Cheval helping. "When can we get started? Do you have any ideas where to begin? We've not had any contact with Mason's kidnappers, other than the note saying when they'd contact us. You're our only hope at this point."

Cheval held up one hand. "Obviously, you're in a hurry to find your alpha. I would propose, however, that before we begin, we consider two things. One, there's not much we can do until the kidnappers make contact with your pack mates. They could have Mason anywhere, and we can be assured they *will* call. I can't imagine anyone going to the trouble of kidnapping your leader and then not asking for something. Two, we shift and run. As Chanku, many of the clues you've gathered will make more sense than what we perceive when human. Nuances our human minds are unable to process will become clear as Chanku. Plus, one avenue I am considering is a tight mental bond among all of us. It's only effective if we're truly at ease with one another, something that occurs much easier in our feral state. Are you willing?" In what obviously was meant to sound as an afterthought, Cheval added, "The women will remain behind." Then he smiled, an expression that changed his entire presence. "They might prove a distraction we don't need."

Luc returned his grin. Like Cheval, he'd noticed the way Tinker had watched both women, but especially Anton's mate. With a quick glance at Tinker, he agreed. "I think that's an excellent idea." Luc set down his brandy and stood at the same time as Cheval. Sending a quick mental message to Tia, so she'd know where they'd gone, Luc followed the others back out to the deck.

They disrobed quickly and shifted, four powerful wolves slipping free of their human shells in a heartbeat. Luc shouldn't have been surprised at the instinctual posturing that followed. The four stalked in tight circles, bodies tense, legs stiff, sniffing one another, testing the inherent threat between unfamiliar wild creatures.

Without hesitation, Luc deferred to Cheval as the leader—for now. Once leadership was established, Cheval took off. Luc followed Anton Cheval as the huge wolf—powerful and agile here in his element—leapt over the deck railing and sped into the dark forest.

Racing through unfamiliar woods, Tinker at his shoulder, Luc felt his tension ebb with each stretch of his legs. His mind felt sharper, his thoughts more cohesive. Cheval had been right. They needed to return to their Chanku roots, look deep within their minds with the ability to focus at a cellular level on the few sensory clues they had.

Cheval led; Aragat brought up the rear. Without any rancor or pretense, they quickly found a speed and rhythm, found a perfect synchronicity that allowed them to share their thoughts, their ideas, their individual theories about Ulrich Mason's disappearance.

Yet, while Luc felt a bond with the two from Montana, a sense of family only those of the same species might share, he recognized the generosity of the Montana pack . . . and its limits. Though they were more than willing to share their expertise and their strength, there would most definitely be no sharing of mates.

Outnumbered, should AJ, Mik, and even Jake eventually join the search, Cheval and Aragat had still willingly accepted a plea for help, though it meant risking the stability of their own closed pack.

Grinning to himself, accepting how close to the beast each man truly was, Luc turned his thoughts to the communal discussion. Ulrich Mason's life was at risk . . . as was Luc's future with Tia.

With the combined force of the Montana pack and the men from Pack Dynamics, Luc had no doubt his mentor would soon be free.

He wished he could feel as certain about the woman he already loved.

Tia waited impatiently with Keisha and Alexandria—Xandi—for the men to return. It was well past three in the morning, her eyes felt as if they were filled with broken glass, and she'd forgotten what sleep felt like.

Keisha covered Tia's hand with hers. "When Anton has a problem, he runs. It clears his head, helps him think."

Xandi nodded in agreement. "He and Stefan are like two halves of a whole. They work well together because they love one another. Are your men lovers as well as pack mates?"

Tia nodded. "We all are, but things are messed up right

now. Luc and I are not . . . well." She shrugged. "Sexually we're fine. There's a lot of other stuff we need to work on. I'm wondering what will happen when they return." Tia flashed a tired grin at the other women. "I imagine all Chanku return from a run with their libidos in high gear."

"Oh, yeah." Keisha waggled her eyebrows. "Don't you love it? I hate to disappoint you, though, but in this case I imagine Anton intends to take that sexual energy and channel it."

"Channel it? I don't understand." Tia set down her empty wineglass and frowned at Keisha.

"Anton is a wizard with powers well beyond those of the typical Chanku. He's learned to tap into the energy of others in order to boost his own abilities. That's what he hopes to do tonight."

"They'll all have to link," Xandi added. "It's a total subjugation of self. Simple enough within a single united pack, but it may be difficult for your men to link with ours. From what Stefan said, it can be very frightening and requires a lot of trust. They don't all know each other that well, though the run should help."

"I linked with you and Keisha." Tia looked from one woman to the other. It had been such a simple thing, the sharing of comfort through a three-way link. She'd never once thought of it as invasive or uncomfortable. Just the opposite, with the added benefit of being able to catch up on years of separation from her cousin in a very short time.

She realized, though, that she'd kept Luc's secret to herself, the bit of knowledge she'd gleaned about her mother's death locked away where Keisha would never find it. At least not yet. Until Tia knew more. . . .

Keisha laughed. "We're female. We think with our brains, not our balls. Act on our need to nurture, not fight. Hopefully, they'll work out a lot of that necessary my-dick's-bigger-than-yours stuff before they get home."

Xandi turned to Tia. "Trust me, we know what we're talking about. You should have seen Stefan and Anton when they first got together."

She shared a mental image with Tia, a visual that could only be described as a violent, bestial rape of one wolf over the other.

"Oh, my." Tia blinked. She cleared the image from her mind and noticed that both women were grinning. "May I ask who was on top?"

Keisha snorted. "Depends. According to Xandi, they took turns until she finally convinced them they didn't need the excuse of establishing dominance to fuck one another. Like I said, women think with their brains, not their gonads."

They shared a quiet laugh. Tia leaned forward on the deck railing and sighed. "I just wish they would hurry. I'm worried about my father, and they're taking so long."

Xandi slipped an arm around Tia's waist. "I know it's hard to wait, but it's necessary. They'll either learn to work together, or they won't. Hopefully, they'll be able to. It'll make Anton's attempts to contact your father that much more effective."

Tia's head snapped up. "Contact him? Not mentally. . . . We have no idea where in the world he's being held. He could be hundreds, even thousands of miles away by now. It's impossible!"

Keisha and Xandi both smiled. "Just be patient," Keisha said. "Anton is a man with many skills."

From the look that passed between the two women, Tia could only assume those skills translated into the bedroom as well. She might have pursued with questions at another time. Not now. Anxious, exhausted, she turned away and stared at the dark wall of forest, waiting impatiently for the men to return.

Chapter 15

Dawn had barely broken over the towering peaks when four wolves came plodding slowly into the yard. Tia waited. She'd dozed off and on for the past few hours, wrapped in a heavy quilt Keisha had given her, curled up in the shadows on one of the comfortable deck chairs.

She watched the once sleek bodies, now covered in mud and burrs, as they trotted slowly into the grassy area just below the deck. Their tongues and tails were hanging, and she knew they'd run hard and fast through the night. Tia recognized Luc and Tinker at once. It took her a moment to figure out that Stefan was the wolf with silver-tipped fur, Anton the larger, darker one. As large as he was, as commanding, he still lacked Tinker's bulk or Luc's beauty.

Anton Cheval shifted first, his lean, muscular body morphing so quickly from wolf to man, Tia would have missed it if she'd blinked. Black hair covered his chest and arrowed down over his washboard belly. Mud, twigs, and burrs fell away, leaving smooth olive skin bathed in a light sheen of sweat. His erect cock jutted proudly out of the thick tangle of dark hair covering his groin.

Stefan Aragat shifted at the same time as Tinker and Luc. He rose gracefully erect, revealing a lean, muscular chest covered in silver-tipped hair, a perfect match to the long, black and silver hair that hung past his shoulders. Like Tinker, Luc, and Anton, Stefan was beautifully, massively aroused, his long, thick cock standing hard against his taut belly.

Tia's mouth went dry and her hands curled into tightly clenched fists. Desire lanced, sharp and furious through her body. She felt a thick rush of cream between her legs as her vaginal muscles tightened, the response as automatic as breathing . . . except, for one heart-stopping moment, she seemed to have forgotten how to breath.

What a view to start her morning! Four of the sexiest men she'd ever seen in her life, standing mere yards away, their bodies gleaming beneath pale sunlight, their cocks standing hard and proud and so inviting Tia's mouth actually watered. It felt terribly illicit and doubly arousing, sitting here in the shadows, staring at Stefan and Anton, reacting so powerfully to their nudity. She felt wonderfully wicked, as if she were cheating and getting away with it. Tia knew she would never consider acting on her desire, but it was fun to look and so overwhelmingly exciting, all the same.

Especially when none of them knew she watched.

As if he'd heard her thought, Anton's head jerked around. Tia didn't even breath, but she knew he saw her. She wanted to crawl into a hole. She'd thought herself well hidden, never dreamed any of them could see her, but it was even more embarrassing to be caught by the Montana alpha.

Their gazes locked for a brief moment. Tia felt as if he saw through her, saw her soul, her misery, her horrifying need, but Anton merely dipped his head in acknowledgment and grinned and then turned back to the other three. Tia breathed a long sigh of relief.

Relief colored by sorrow.

Luc hadn't noticed her. Only Anton. Somehow the sexy alpha had sensed she was close by, but he didn't seem to mind at all that she watched. His acceptance emphasized Tia's sense of isolation, of loneliness. Keisha and Xandi had gone off to bed . . . together. Anton had looked and then turned away. With him being engaged now in deep conversation with the other three men, it was as if Tia didn't exist. None of the others even knew she was there, just a few feet away, watching, wondering what it felt like to belong.

It might have been funny, under other circumstances, sitting silently in the shadows, staring at four beautiful, buck-naked men carrying on what must be a serious conversation in the front yard, each with his erect cock hard. Should have been worth a smile, at least, but right now it made Tia unutterably sad.

She stared at her toes peeking out from beneath the old quilt, focused on the chipped nails bare of polish and let her thoughts wander. Time was passing. Her father had not been found, but they couldn't act until Anton was ready. When that time came, Luc and Tinker would have a job to do, a role to play. They had their friendship with each other, their commitment to Pack Dynamics, their new relationship with the Montana pack.

Tia had nothing. No one.

Granted, she'd found her cousin, a part of her family long believed lost, but Keisha and Xandi were, even now, probably making love with one another somewhere inside the house. They'd made jokes about how they would have to settle with each other this night, when the men ran without women.

Before going off together, they'd teased Tia about her status within the San Francisco pack, as the only female with five lusty men. Tia hadn't mentioned Jake's treachery or the fact that Luc was shutting her out of both his mind and his heart. It was easier to let Keisha and Xandi imagine everything was fine.

Lost in her own private misery, almost enjoying this

self-indulgent wallow in her own little pity party, Tia didn't hear footsteps on the deck until she realized there were four sets of very masculine feet ringed about her chair. Startled, she raised her head and looked directly into Luc's solemn stare. Tinker, Anton, and Stefan stood beside him.

Was that a look of censure on Anton's face? Tia frowned and then jerked back around to look at Luc when she heard his quiet voice.

"Anton thought you and I were mated. I had to tell him we weren't. We need you as part of our link, the strength of your genetic identity with your father, in order to find him and lock on to his thoughts. The problem is, Tia, you and I have never fully linked, never bonded as deeply as Anton needs for us to do." Luc's gaze shifted to his left, to the others. His eyes narrowed. "Give us a minute, okay?"

"No problem. I'm headed for the shower." Anton smiled at Tia and then ambled into the house. Tinker and Stefan followed, but Tia caught Tinker's silent good wishes before he went inside. She watched the men until they went through the door and disappeared from her line of view.

Tia turned her attention from three sets of perfect buns to Luc's beloved face. How could she feel so much anger at this man, and yet love him more than anyone else on the planet?

He knelt down in front of her and grabbed her cold hands in his warm ones. There was something amazingly comforting about his strong fingers wrapped around hers. Tia smelled the forest on him, the rich, musky scent of autumn grasses and evergreens, fresh loam and aroused male.

Luc gazed at her with his heart in his eyes. "What it comes down to, Tianna Mason, is that *I* need you. Not to save your father. To save me. I love you. This separation is killing me. I closed you out to hide my terrible secret about your mother. I didn't want to hurt you, and I was too big a coward to tell you the truth. To show you what happened that night."

He shook his head, as if denying history. "I wish it could be any other way, but your father needs our help, and that's going to require a complete mental link . . . all of us. You'll know everything about me, just as I'll know you. You'll see my memories as if they were your own. I don't want you to witness your mother's death for the first time under those circumstances. It's going to be so damned hard for you, and I wish there were another way, but I can't just tell you what happened. I have to show you."

He stood up, still holding her hands. Pulled Tia to her feet without effort. Leaned close and kissed her briefly, chastely, on the mouth. "Shift. Come with me. Whether you choose to join me as my mate or not is up to you, but it's time you know the truth."

Tia left her exhaustion behind. Exhilarated, apprehensive, she threw aside the quilt, shifted smoothly, and followed Luc back into the forest. Stretching out her legs, she ran hard and fast, her paws making a muted tattoo in the thick layer of pine needles littering the forest floor. Occasional bursts of sunlight broke through the dense trees in tiny spatters of molten gold, but, for the most part, the trail was dark, the air still and cool.

Luc led Tia to a tiny meadow bordered on one side by a wall of granite, on the other by a narrow stream of clear water. The grass was thick and spongy, the bracken turning deep gold along the borders. They both drank deeply and then lay together in a shaft of sunlight, panting quietly. For the first time in days, Tia felt at peace, as though her Chanku self had finally adjusted and reconciled with the human side.

She was Chanku, as much wolf as woman. She loved the man beside her with all her heart, understood why her anger with him was so much more intense than it might have been if she hadn't cared for him.

Love made her vulnerable in ways she'd never expected, but it gave her new strengths as well. She saw it now, with the clarity of her Chanku mind, how she suffered as much if not more than Luc. She'd pushed him away, but Luc still had his packmates. Tia had no one. Not only had she been a coward, she'd been a fool. A frightened, lonely fool.

Now Luc rested his muzzle comfortably, protectively across Tia's furred shoulders. Tia shivered, afraid now that the moment had come to learn the truth of her mother's death. Afraid to discover what role Luc had played.

Wondered if and how it might affect the feelings growing between them, feelings still new and untested.

She opened her mind, searched, and found Luc's thoughts. For once the barriers were down, the pathway to his memories open, if not actually inviting. She immediately sensed reluctance, his apprehension and fear, his soul-deep dread of Tia's reaction to what she would discover.

A low whine escaped her throat. A shiver coursed along her Chanku spine as she took herself, through Luc's memories, through his eyes and ears, back to Golden Gate Park more than twenty years ago.

The first thing Tia noticed was the brilliant sunlight streaming through the windows of Luc's police cruiser. She recognized the buildings. They'd not changed much in this part of the city. He was driving somewhere north of the park, near the Presidio. The radio crackled, and Tia caught the dispatcher's words warning of a wolf sighting, as if Tia were the one driving, the one following Luc's destined path.

Everything from that moment on unfolded with stark, unrelenting clarity. One part of Tia's mind stepped back and observed, understanding how and why Luc reacted as he did. Privy to his thoughts, she heard the screaming children in the distance and worried about their safety. She observed the wolf through Luc's eyes with awe and disbelief, felt the weight of the gun in her hand, saw the look of intelligence and understanding in the wolf's eyes.

Hesitated a bare moment until the screams of children growing closer forced a decision.

The report of the gunshot seemed to echo on and on and on.

Tia watched in horror as the light went out of those beautiful amber eyes, and Camille Mason, the most exquisite wolf to ever walk the earth, tumbled lifeless to the ground.

Tia took each step with Luc, one foot after the other, bringing her closer to the body lying lifeless in the soft, green grass. Felt Luc's horror to see not a wolf but a lovely young woman with skin the color of dark chocolate and long, black hair tumbled wildly about her head. Thankfully, her eyes were closed, but Tia knew that the small wound in her chest belied the horrible exit wound that had shattered her heart, torn through her back.

For what seemed an eternity, Tia stared at her mother. The children kept screaming. Their voices rising louder, coalescing into a single voice, a single cry of unrelenting pain. The sound overwhelmed every sense until there was no color, no light, no scent.

Only sound.

No awareness of anything or anyone beyond that one child, the lonely little girl Tia kept locked inside, screaming harsh, bone-chilling screams that went on and on, screams that tore at her throat, burned her lungs. Only Luc's hands, his wonderful human hands and strong arms embracing Tia's human self kept her tethered to reality, kept her trembling body in the here and now, out of the clutching memories of death.

Tia didn't realize she'd shifted, had no idea when Luc had grabbed her to hold her crosswise in his lap, kissing her tears, crying with her, sobbing into her tangled hair as if his own heart were breaking.

The screams faded away until the only sound was Tia's

harsh, ragged breathing, each breath punctuated by Luc's rough and weary voice. As if from a great distance, she heard him repeating over and over again, "I'm sorry. So sorry."

He swept her hair back from her face, his broad palm lingering to cup the side of her head. His lips found her forehead and brushed a tender kiss against her cold skin. Ever so slowly, Tia became more aware of her surroundings, of herself.

She blinked the tears away from her eyes and sniffed. She wiped her streaming nose with the back of her hand, realized she was naked and had no tissue, and then wiped her wet hand on the grass.

Luc's short bark of laughter caught her by surprise. Tia saw him looking at her hand, she realized what a yucky thing she'd done, and flushed hot and cold with embarrassment. She flashed him a wobbly smile through her tears. "Miss Manners would never approve."

"I would offer you a handkerchief, but it's in my pants."

Tia looped her arms loosely around Luc's neck and pressed her forehead against his. "Good God." She barely got out the words. Turned her head away, coughed, cleared her throat, took a deep, calming breath. "How horrible for you, to shoot at a wolf, thinking you were protecting the children, and then to find a woman lying there." She shuddered. "To find my mother. Luc, I had no idea."

Luc kissed her, his lips warm, the pressure soft and reassuring. "I've had nightmares about that day since it happened. I've had to remind myself that I would never have met your father, never would have known you, never would have learned who I was, if not for that terrible day, but it's not enough to get me past it."

Tia ran her fingers along his face, wiping aside Luc's tears. "You have to, you know. Get past it. We both do. My mother had to have known the risk she was taking, to run during the day in a public park, just as I have to realize you were doing your job. Thank you. For showing me when we were alone. For opening yourself up to such a terrible memory. I understand now why Tinker said it was just a horrible accident. He was right. It doesn't make the pain any less, but I know in my heart I can't blame you." She felt the tears flowing again. "Luc, I've missed you so much."

Luc kissed her wet cheeks and then pressed his lips against her mouth. Barely breaking the kiss, he spoke against her lips. "I didn't block you out because I was angry. When you said you couldn't mate with me until you discovered what happened to your mother, I realized I couldn't let you into my mind. I couldn't risk it. Once I tried to bury the memories of your mom's death, they became the proverbial elephant in the parlor. I couldn't *not* think of it. I had no idea how to tell you the truth."

Tia shook her head. "Since I discovered the story in Tinker's memory, I've been as angry with my father as I've been with you, but knowing what happened, there's no way he could have told that story to a child. I can see that now. We need to get him back, Luc."

"We will."

"I know. You'll make certain we do. Make love to me?" Tia kissed him full on the mouth and then pulled away.

Luc blinked, as though her suggestion had caught him totally by surprise. "Here? Now?"

Tia nodded, pulled away from Luc's embrace, and shifted. Turning her back to Luc, she waved her great plume of a tail in blatant invitation and then headed down the sun-dappled trail at a full run.

Luc never in his wildest fantasies expected Tia to want him after sharing the details of her mother's death. Now, though, she raced ahead, her tail waving, her scent calling him, and he felt as if his heart would burst.

Leaping fallen logs, skirting tangled brambles, and

crashing through thick undergrowth, Luc slowly gained on Tia. It was her race to lose, not his to win. Her decision as to the time and place when Luc would finally catch her, would mount her as they were meant to, one wolf covering the other, mentally linking as Chanku, completing the bond for all time.

She'd brought him full circle, he noticed, slowing enough that he caught her near the same spot where she'd cried. Where he'd cried as well, purging himself of the years of self-recrimination, of the anguish and pain that had dogged him since that fateful day so many long years ago.

He'd prayed for forgiveness, hoped for some sort of reconciliation, but never had Luc imagined Tia's flirtatious posturing, her bright eyes and beautiful wolven body inviting him to mount her.

It was such a simple act, devoid of the involved foreplay of humans, free of the mating games and nuances of men and women. Instincts long buried drove him as Luc raised up on his hind legs and mounted her strong back, raking his long claws across the rough fur at her shoulders, nipping her ear and then the side of her throat in an instinctive display of male dominance.

She turned her head to watch him, accepted him with a soft grunt, a low growl deep in her throat. Tilted her throat to him in submission as Luc drove his long wolven cock deep to penetrate her hot channel. Luc felt the change in position when Tia braced herself to take his full weight, and he growled low in his throat as he thrust hard and fast inside her.

Tia's mind opened to Luc's and she shared this unique and intimate moment, this mating that would tie them forever as a pair. He felt the large knot forming in his cock, slipping deep inside her heat, despite Tia's tightly contracting muscles.

Her climax radiated back to include Luc. Locked in

place, tied tightly together while his cock pulsed and her muscles squeezed, he'd never felt closer to any single soul in all his days. Memories, thoughts, old dreams, and past mistakes. All of it shared, understood—when necessary, forgotten.

This link went beyond anything he'd ever experienced, any connection Luc had ever made with his packmates. This was a joining of selves on a level beyond conscious thought.

It came to him then, why Anton had felt this bonding would be so important if Tia were to assist in the search for her father. Luc finally understood things about Tia she was only now learning herself, her physiology as a Chanku bitch. How she controlled her breeding, releasing an egg with a specific, conscious effort on her part. How the shift would affect her unborn child, should she become pregnant.

How very much she loved him . . . and how much Luc loved her in return. How much she trusted him to save her father. It humbled him, to have knowledge such as this.

Humbled him yet gave him strength.

Tia flopped to the ground, taking Luc with her. Panting, she twisted her upper body and licked his muzzle. He felt the change in her, sensed her need to hold him just as he needed to embrace Tia. They shifted at the same time, turning their bodies so that Luc supported himself over Tia, his human cock buried deep in her tightly clenched pussy.

She grinned at him, teasing, flirtatious. Her hair tumbled about her shoulders, spreading in a dark blond nimbus over the green grass. The tight curls had gone looser each time she shifted, the texture smoother, so that it flowed softly away from her face. Her lips parted, her eyes sparkled. "Hmmm . . . I miss that thing you do. . . . Tying us together that way is something else."

Resting his weight on his elbows, Luc tapped her nose

with the tip of his finger. "True, but you have more eroge-
nous zones as a woman." He proved his point by leaning
close, dipping his chin, and taking one taut nipple between
his teeth.

Tia moaned, bent her knees, and arched her back, driving
his hard cock deep inside. Luc nipped at her other breast,
caught the taut peak with his lips, and sucked and tongued
the tender flesh while Tia writhed beneath him.

Her legs wrapped tightly around his waist, joining them
even closer.

Slowly, surely, Luc brought her to another crest, angling
his cock against her swollen, sensitive clitoris. Trading back
and forth from one breast to the other, licking, nipping,
sucking at her nipples, Luc wound his fingers into her thick
mass of hair and drove deep and hard into her creamy heat.

The crown of his cock connected with the mouth of
Tia's womb on each downward thrust, his balls pressed
against her perineum. She opened her mind fully, bringing
him with her as her climax built.

He felt the clenching muscles deep in her belly perfectly
aligned with the muscles in her cunt, the way his cock
stuffed her so full on each stroke, then dragged the clasping tissues back when he withdrew. He discovered she
liked how his balls slapped against her butt and the hard
press of his cock sliding over her clit.

When he sucked hard on Tia's nipple, he felt the shock
all the way to her pussy, so he bit down on each one in
turn and then gently tongued the hurt, building the sensation into an intense rhythm of pain and pleasure—hot, wet
mouth, sharp teeth, rough tongue, chill of the autumn air.

Suddenly Tia's body arched higher and went stiff beneath him. Her legs tightened around his waist and she
threw her head back with a long, low, keening wail as orgasm claimed her.

Tight spasms rippled through her creamy cunt, her muscles clamped down on his cock, and, with a long, deep-throated groan, Luc followed her over the edge.

Gasping for air, heart thudding in his chest, Luc slowly lowered himself to lie partially atop Tia in the damp grass. Her legs flopped loosely to the ground on either side of him; her breath sounded as loud as his in the quiet forest, but when he looked at her, she was smiling.

"No secrets, Luc?"

He shook his head. "None. Not anymore. You've been inside my head, seen everything I've done. If you can still love me after all that . . ."

"Forever, Lucien Stone. For the rest of our lives." Tia reached up and cupped the side of his face in her hand. He turned slightly, planted a kiss on her smooth palm. She drew him down, found his mouth with hers, and kissed him. Slowly, deeply, with so much love Luc ached with the power of it.

They lay there in the cool grass with the autumn sun beating down on their naked bodies. Hearts thudding in a synchronized rhythm, thoughts and memories building an even stronger link between the two of them, as breathing slowly found its cadence, as their hearts returned to normal. Luc wondered if anything, anywhere, could get any better than this amazing moment, this time of total sharing with the woman who had agreed to be his mate for a lifetime.

Tia sighed, ran her fingers across his chest, and circled one flat nipple. The tiny nub rose to immediate attention. Luc felt his cock twitch, wondered if Tia might be willing to take him inside once more.

As if in answer, Tia's fingers found the nipple over his heart, raised it to a taut peak to match its mate. Luc's cock swelled, loath to be left out of the fun. Luc rolled close to taste Tia's exquisite lips once more.

Anton's mental voice blew into their minds like an unwelcome storm. *Wherever you guys are, come back now. AJ called. They've heard from the kidnappers. They don't want money. They want to trade. They'll give us Mason— for Tia.*

Chapter 16

"No way in hell are they getting Tia." The words burst out of his mouth the moment after Luc shifted. Anton, who waited alone for them on the deck, merely nodded and smiled at Tia and then spoke calmly to Luc.

"There is a plan. It's a good one. I want you both to freshen up and meet us in the dining room. Relax. We've got everything under control."

He turned and walked back inside. Luc stared at Tia, and she burst into laughter. "The man walks like he has an entourage."

Luc shook his head, grinning. "Yeah, but don't worry about a thing. He has a plan."

Tia grabbed Luc's hand and dragged him inside. "Yep. Relax. He says it's a good one. Everything's under control."

"Bullshit." Still shaking his head, Luc followed Tia into the house. "I sure hope he knows what he's talking about."

Freshly showered, Tia and Luc met the others at the dining table in the main room of the home. Tinker raised his eyes and smiled; Keisha and Xandi both waved. Anton glanced up as Tia poured two cups of coffee from the sideboard. "I've taken the liberty of asking AJ and Mik to meet us here. They're already in the air. Mik said to tell you Jake was at Mason's home and would remain behind. He didn't say why."

Luc nodded. "At least I know he got back safely. Thanks."

Jake. Tia had put him out of her mind completely. Part of her felt relieved not to have to face him right at this time. The other part of her wanted to talk with him and get past his behavior. Since bonding with Luc, she had a better feeling for what had motivated Jake, a better understanding of the male Chanku mind. Driven by instinct and powerful sexuality, Jake had been a slave to his feral instincts, not acting at all with his human thought processes.

Still wondering about Jake, Tia followed Luc to the long buffet loaded with a selection to rival most hotel brunches. They'd not eaten for hours, and she filled her plate. Luc did the same and then followed her to the table.

They took seats together, across from Xandi and Keisha. Once again Anton took the lead. "Congratulations are in order, I see."

Luc's head came up. "Congratulations? Yeah. I guess so. Thank you." He glanced at Tia and grinned. She felt her skin go hot and then cold and then hot again. She couldn't control the blush that swept over her body.

Nor could she control the dopey grin on her face. "Thank you. I think." Flustered, she took a moment to unfold her napkin and put it in her lap. "Please. I need to know what you've learned about my father."

"Stefan took the call." Anton wiped his face with a snowy-white linen napkin, and then set it aside as he deferred to his packmate.

Stefan set down his fork and placed his hands on the table. "First of all, Tinker has set everything up so that calls made to Mason's line are directed here for now. AJ said the caller disguised his voice by mechanical means, but he's bringing the recorded copy with him in case we need it. Instructions were very simple. Tia is to fly to Dulles alone.

She will be met by a man carrying a sign with her name on it. She's to go with him. Her father will be waiting in a car in the parking lot. She'll get in. Mason will get out."

"Absolutely not." Luc threw his napkin on the table and stood up. "No way in hell is Tia trading her life for her father's. What do they want with her anyway?"

Anton raised his hand. "That's what we're going to find out. Finish your meal and then I intend to ask Mason what's going on."

Ask Mason? Impossible. He's half a world away! Luc's thoughts blasted directly into Tia's mind.

She directed her answer to Luc alone. *Keisha and Xandi think Anton can reach Dad. I don't know. It sounds. . . .*

But Anton was the one who answered. *Trust me. With our combined strength, we'll be able to reach your father. Our chances are even better, now that you and Luc have bonded.*

Incredulous, Tia stared at Anton. "How the hell did you do that?"

He dipped his head in a modest nod. "Remember, I was a wizard long before I was Chanku."

Keisha laughed. "No one keeps secrets from Anton. He heard Xandi when she needed help. Anton and Stefan were in Boston, and Xandi and I were in San Francisco when she got snatched. Trust me, sweetie. He'll be able to talk to your father."

Xandi held up her hand for attention. "If you'll recall, he and Stefan both heard me, and they got their boost from a shared orgasm. It's not like he can do it every day of the week." She waggled her eyebrows at Anton. "Do we need group sex to make this work?"

He smiled very gently at Tia, but his words were for all of them. "No, we don't need group sex, especially with this particular group. I intend to work off your desire for sex, which is always high and carries a lot of power." He gestured toward Tia. "Now that you and your mate have discovered the powerful bond that comes from a Chanku mating, I am going to ask you to try to establish that same bond with the rest of us. It must come from you, Tia, to utilize the familial connection between you and your father. Do you think you can do it? It requires total subjugation of self, complete trust. Can you trust us to help you?"

Tia nodded. "I believe I can, but it depends on Luc as well. His memories are a part of mine now. If I choose to share with all of you, I'm sharing Luc's private thoughts and memories as well as my own."

Luc's hand found Tia's. He squeezed her fingers. "I have no secrets. Not anymore. Whatever it takes to keep you safe and get Ulrich back . . . I'm willing."

Anton glanced at Tinker, who looked decidedly uncomfortable, and grinned. "Don't worry. Your secrets are safe. It's Tia who becomes an open book when I focus our energy through her."

Tinker laughed, his relief obvious. "That's good to know. I would hate to have the rest of you guys come after me, what with all I've been thinking about the gorgeous women in this room."

As they headed for the more comfortable chairs near the big picture window, Tia overheard Anton. He leaned close to Tinker and whispered, "I do know what you've been thinking. Act on any of those thoughts and you're carrion."

Tinker's eyes went wide and he took a step back. Anton smiled and continued across the room. Grinning, Tia caught Tinker's eye and shook her head. The big guy just sighed and followed after the rest of the group.

Anton had all of them pull their chairs into a tight semi-circle, leaving an opening wide enough for one more. Tia sat next to the open space. Luc was next to Tia, on her left, and then Xandi, Stefan, Keisha, and Tinker across the gap from Tia.

Anton closed the window blinds and heavy curtains,

walking around the large room until he'd achieved almost total darkness. He returned to the combined pack, lit a single candle that he placed on a table behind himself, and closed the gap between the chairs with his body.

The small candle glittering behind him lit Anton's face in silhouette, softening the harsh lines of his cheeks, the sharp blade of his nose. When he spoke, Tia perceived the latent power behind his voice, power well beyond his actual words.

"First of all, Tia, I want you to know we are all aware of Luc's role in your mother's death. We agree with Tinker that it was a horrible accident and we're all terribly sorry for your loss, as well as Keisha's. She loved her aunt very much. What happened in that park twenty years ago will not affect our ability to work together, nor our friendship with any of you. I know this has been a concern of your mate's. Don't let it be. Events occur for a reason, and our destiny is not easily changed."

Blinking back tears, Tia nodded her thanks. Luc squeezed her hand. Anton lowered his head and closed his eyes for a moment and then looked up and opened them. Tia could have sworn there was a glow in his eyes that came from within. It wasn't a reflection from the candle.

Anton gave her a quick smile, as though he'd heard her thoughts, and then he continued. "What I intend to do is mix our Chanku mental powers with very old magic. The Chanku are an ancient race. Who's to say our ability to shift wasn't born in magic? I for one can't explain what occurs at the point of change, when human becomes wolf, when wolf reverts to human. I know that when we die, if we are wolf, we become human at the moment of death. The opposite doesn't happen." He nodded in Tia's direction. "Your mother died as a wolf. She became human. Keisha's mother was killed as a human. She did not shift to wolf. That tells me our primary source of being is human, though the wolf within us is very powerful, very old, and filled with ancient magic. That is the creature whose strength we will draw on today."

Anton grabbed a chair and slid it into the circle, closing the gap, and then reached out and took Tinker's big hand in his right, Tia's in his left. He nodded in approval when everyone in the circle linked hands, and then he smiled. "You'll enjoy this part. I want each of you to imagine sex with the person on your right." He grinned at Tinker. "That's correct. I am giving you permission to let your fantasies go wild over my mate. Just as Keisha will imagine sex with Stefan, which isn't all that difficult since they fuck like bunnies almost nightly."

They all laughed, but there was already a speculative gleam in Tinker's eyes. Anton turned to Xandi. "While Stefan is leering at you, I expect you to be paying close attention to Luc. Let your fantasies run wild."

Anton raised an eyebrow at Stefan's scowl. "Stefan, there's no need for jealousy, as nothing will come of this. It's an exercise in mental frustration. I want you all so sexually aroused, you're ready to blow. Luc, you will be thinking of your lovely mate, but be aware she will be thinking of me. Consider it an exercise in storing sexual energy. Do not release your grip on your partners' hands."

Tinker cast a sideways glance at Anton. "I suppose you're going to have your way with me, right?"

Anton grinned. "Absolutely.

Tinker grunted, glanced morosely at their clasped hands, and then turned his attention to Keisha. Still smiling, Anton sat back in his chair and closed his eyes. Tia studied his strong profile, the length of his nose, the aristocratic line of his jaw. Dressed casually—for Anton, at least—he wore dark slacks and a soft, black sweater with a V-neck. Dark chest hair peeked out at the base of his throat, and though the room was dark, Tia could see his pulse beating.

She let herself go with the rhythm of his pulse, felt the tempo like drums beating in her head. Imagined licking the steady pulse, swirling her tongue over the artery, tasting a man other than Luc or the members of her own pack.

A slight smile curved Anton's mouth. She wondered what he imagined doing with Tinker. Would Anton suck her packmate's cock or would Tinker be kneeling in front of Anton, his head tilted back, Anton's beautiful cock sliding down his throat?

Maybe he thought of anal sex. Tia pictured Tinker's dark body kneeling behind Anton, saw that huge cock the color of dark chocolate slipping deep inside the wizard. Pictured herself lying down beneath Anton, taking his cock in her mouth, sucking hard and deep, with her cheeks hollowing out, as she drew him down, swallowing him until his full length slipped down her throat.

Letting her imagination run free, Tia saw herself still lying beneath a kneeling Anton, though in the opposite direction. His cock was in her mouth, his mouth between her legs. Tinker knelt behind Anton, his cock sliding slowly in and out of Anton's ass. Even with her mouth stuffed full of cock, Tia pictured herself reaching up and cupping both men's testicles in her palms. Practically felt the solid balls nestled within their sacs and rolled them gently between her fingers.

Tia grinned when she realized she was squirming in her seat, that the back of her long skirt was probably damp from her fluids. Ignoring her rising sense of arousal, she brought the mental image of Tinker and Anton back to the forefront of her mind.

She really loved the image she'd conjured. Loved having Anton's cock in her mouth, his balls and Tinker's cupped in her hands. Even more, she really loved the feel of Anton's long and talented tongue licking away her fluids, cleaning up the cream that spilled from her pussy. He suckled her thick labial lips, dipped his tongue into her cunt and lapped up the moisture.

She heard his soft moan and sucked Anton's cock deeper, Heard another moan and then a strangled whimper. Blinking herself away from the image, Tia looked around the circle and realized they were all breathing hard, each one of them totally immersed in their personal fantasies.

She looked to her right and caught Anton grinning at her with almost evil delight.

I think I enjoyed your fantasy even more than my own. Thank you.

Blushing, Tia bit back a snort of laughter. Her pussy clenched in reaction to Anton's blatant perusal of her mind. She licked her lips and stuck out her tongue.

Anton's snort of laughter was for her ears only.

Then, to everyone, *I think we're ready.*

Everyone looked toward Anton. Luc squeezed Tia's hand and shifted uncomfortably in his seat. *More than ready, if sexual frustration is what you're looking for.*

It's exactly what I'm looking for. You've done well. Here's how we're going to use all this energy. Close your eyes. Concentrate. We've all communicated, at one time or another, with Mason. Concentrate on him. I want you to imagine his mental signal, how you would find him in the city when there are others around. When it's time, follow my lead. Focus your thoughts on Ulrich Mason. Think of your searching thoughts as threads of energy. I will gather them up, like threads to a spinning wheel. Do you see it? Do you see me gathering each thread? Every one is as strong as woven steel. I'm binding them together into a cable that will stretch around the earth, into infinity, if so needed.

Anton's hypnotic voice carried Tia along with his words. She saw the cable, a shining bundle of brilliant fibers of thought, wound together from their collective search for her father.

The cable twisted and writhed like a live thing, slowly

morphing into a pathway, a ribbon of light stretching into infinity, just as Anton had promised. Luc stood beside her, Anton just ahead. There was darkness all about them, illuminated only by the shining pathway. Anton held out his hand, and Tia took it, holding tightly to Luc at the same time. When Tia looked back, she saw the others, all hand in hand along the shining path.

The shimmering visual made Tia think of paper dolls, connected cutouts, joined forever hand to hand.

Follow the path. It should lead us to your father. Don't let go. Keep your mind on your father.

Tia surged ahead, pulling Anton, Luc, and all the rest along behind her. She recognized a vague sense of her father in the distance. Tia felt as if she walked for miles, traveled for hours, but time had no meaning here. She was weightless, free, her body mere thistledown attached to her packmates by love and a sense of unity such as she'd never experienced.

The light grew brighter, the sense of her father stronger. She felt him, sensed him, his familiar scents, the sound of his breathing.

Daddy? Can you hear me?

Startled, Ulrich sat up in the bed in which he'd been sleeping. The chains holding him to the wall rattled and banged. He must be dreaming. No way in hell could that be Tia—she was still in San Francisco, wasn't she? Why did she feel so close?

Definitely Tia. Damn. Ulrich hoped she wasn't nearby. How could he protect her?

For one thing, he'd better not act like he was communicating with anyone. Ulrich was certain the room was monitored. He stretched his arms, as if he'd just awakened from a bad dream.

Tia? Is that you? Where are you? Be very careful. You're at great risk.

Her mental voice came through, loud and clear. *I'm with Anton Cheval. Luc and Tinker and the Montana pack are all with me. Where are you? We have no idea where they've hidden you.*

How the hell can you be mindtalking if you don't know where I am?

I'll explain later. Let me into your mind. I need to see what you see.

Not a damned thing. They've kept me blindfolded, wearing nothing but my skivvies, and I'm chained to a bed. From the accents I'm hearing, I think I must be somewhere on the East Coast, but I'm not sure.

We think you might be in Virginia. Daddy, Anton asked if you can hear birds singing?

Birds? What the fuck do you—

Daddy? You're not in charge here. Do you hear any birds?

Damn. He knew it was Tia's voice, but she sounded as if she'd developed a little more backbone since the last time he'd seen her. She sounded so much like Camille, it made him ache. Grinning to himself, Ulrich did as he was told and listened.

A crow called from somewhere nearby. Ulrich gave the information to Tia.

After a moment, she responded. *Concentrate on the sound. Focus on it as if you were trying to talk to the crow. Can you do that?*

Ulrich focused. The crow seemed closer, the cawing louder. He felt something unexplainable, a physical sensation of something crawling through him, over his shoulders, and away. The crow called again and pecked at the window. Three sharp taps. Then it was gone.

What the fuck was that?

That was Anton Cheval, Daddy. He's in the crow, controlling its mind. He's outside now, checking on your location. Be patient. What happened? How did they get you?

His mind reeling with so many surprises, Ulrich concentrated on what he could understand. His daughter's
voice was a link to life, to freedom. He reported all he
knew and kept to the basics. *I was asleep. Four men.
Professionals. Military, I think. Had me tied up and bun-
dled out of there too fast to think clearly. Glad you called
Cheval. I was sure he could help.*

Ulrich could have sworn he heard Luc's laughter. *You
there, too, Stone?*

Yes, sir. Are you okay? Injured at all?

*Just my pride. Have they ransomed me? I have no idea
why they took me.*

*We've got some ideas, nothing concrete. We'll get you
out of there as soon as we can. Be patient. Try to watch
for our contact. We may arrive in some unusual form, if
Cheval has anything to do with it. I'm not sure how long
we can keep this link open.*

Where the hell are you?

We're in Montana, Daddy. At Anton Cheval's home.

Impossible. No way in hell could they cover that much
distance with mental speech. They talked about a link as if
it were a damned phone line, not the nebulous power of
one mind communicating with another.

Ulrich heard the crow again, the series of taps at the
window. He sent a thought in the direction of the unseen
bird.

Anton Cheval answered him.

*Mason? You are about an hour west of Reston, Virginia,
far enough from the city that it's fairly rural. You should
know this: your kidnappers have asked for an exchange.
Tia's life for yours.*

Ulrich sputtered in outrage. *Goddamned bastards.*

*Quiet. I can't maintain this form for long. We intend to
free you before any such exchange takes place, but we
must let the kidnappers believe their plan is working, especially if we want to find out who is behind this. We'll try to*

maintain communication, but if we can't, remember we are going to get you out. Wait for our contact. For now, concentrate on the crow.

Ulrich did as he was told, feeling utterly ridiculous and totally helpless. Blindfolded, chained to a bed in his fucking underwear, thinking about a goddamned bird. . . . He was as worthless as an old lady.

An old lady with a mouse running across his spine. He shuddered at the odd sensation that lasted only a heartbeat.

Thank you. I would not have wanted to remain a crow forever. However, it was the perfect form to scout your area.

Cheval, when I get out of here, you and I need to talk.

He heard laughter in his mind. Cheval's laughter. *Be patient, my friend. I'm glad you've not shifted to escape your chains. The room is filled with cameras. I saw them from my perch at the window.*

I suspected as much. Take care. Tia, I love you. No matter what happens.

Nothing's going to happen, Daddy. Except the fact that we're coming to get you out.

He felt the link slip away like a live thing that had somehow attached to his mind. Ulrich lay back on the hard mattress, adjusted his shackles, and thought about what had just occurred. Obviously, there was a lot more to Anton Cheval than his Chanku heritage. Whatever it was, Ulrich was thankful Cheval was on his side.

He missed his pack, especially Tia. And Luc. Damn his hide, but Ulrich was almost certain he'd sensed something in Tia he'd not known before. She'd bonded with Stone. He was sure of it, though he wasn't certain how he felt about Luc's position in his daughter's life.

Lucien Stone could be a real hard-ass when he wanted to be, though Ulrich loved him like the son he'd never had. The man fit his name much too well. Ulrich wondered how he'd handled Tia finding out about her mother. She would have discovered everything if they'd mated as Chanku. Ulrich should have been there, damnit. A father should always protect his daughter.

Not lie to her.

He had to assume Tia knew about Camille. She would realize Ulrich had lied to her all these years. He hoped she didn't hate him. She couldn't, not if she was trying to save his ornery hide.

Ulrich's brain wouldn't quit spinning, so full of questions he felt as if he was going to explode. He wanted to shift. Wanted to run through the woods and feel the wind against his muzzle. Needed the honesty of the beast, the cleanliness of the wind.

He wanted to hunt. Hell, he really wanted to hunt the bastards who held him, who'd essentially emasculated him, chaining him up like this. Anton thought Ulrich hadn't shifted because of the cameras. There'd been a better reason not to shift in order to escape.

Ulrich tugged at the tight collar around his neck, felt the heavy chain linking him to the wall. Chanku paws might have slipped the shackles holding his human wrists and ankles, but the one around his neck was a killer.

Drugged while still in San Francisco, Ulrich was thankful he hadn't attempted a shift the moment he regained consciousness. . . . The iron band under his chin would have crushed his damned Chanku neck.

Chapter 17

AJ and Mik arrived in Montana just in time to refuel Cheval's jet and fly on to a private airport near Reston, Virginia, ahead of Tia. Tinker went along with them.

Somehow Stefan had managed to transfer the ticket that should have been waiting for Tia at San Francisco International Airport to a smaller airport in Montana, closer to their current location. The plane was due to arrive within minutes of her scheduled flight. Anyone checking would think she had flown out of SFO, according to plan.

Tia knew she should have felt nervous boarding the plane, but she had an almost preternatural calm about her. She also had plenty of backup. Luc sat several rows behind her, and Cheval was, of course, in first class with Keisha.

She grinned, trying to imagine his imperious self shoved into sardine class on the plane, and couldn't. There was something so otherworldly about the man, as if he were royal or blessed or quite possibly alien. Tia loved the way Keisha kept him grounded.

Obviously, Anton loved it, too. The man was totally besotted with his mate. Would Luc one day look at Tia with his heart in his eyes? She hoped so. For now, Tia knew he still walked on broken glass around her, still worried about every little thing.

Once this entire charade had ended, she fully expected some time to work on the two of them.

So long as it ended well.

Tia thought about Xandi and Stefan. They were on a separate flight out of another city, due to arrive about an hour before Tia and her group. All of them, perfectly normal in appearance, converging on Dulles airport around the same time.

Most of them practically strangers, yet willing to risk their lives for a man they hardly knew.

All because they were Chanku. Tia was beginning to think of it as another word for *family*.

She wished she could contact her father on her own. Wished she could tell him they were on their way, that all would be fine. Instead, she snuggled down into the seat and closed her eyes. As tired as she was, sleep was a long time coming.

Tia followed Anton Cheval and Keisha Rialto off the plane, and hoped the car they'd arranged for would be exactly where it was supposed to be. So much of Ulrich's rescue depended on luck, on all the puzzle pieces falling together exactly as planned. She glanced once over her shoulder but avoided making eye contact with Luc. Disguised as he was, though, with his baseball cap pulled down over his eyes and his dark hair trimmed short, she might have missed him if he weren't a constant presence in her mind.

Tia readjusted her handbag on her shoulder and quickly walked the length of the concourse before turning toward the escalator to the baggage-claim area. Her father should be waiting just outside, unless his captors had lied.

Which, of course, was exactly what everyone expected them to do, especially since none of them had been able to contact Ulrich mentally.

Tia kept reminding herself that Ulrich was alive, that

his mental silence might merely mean his captors had drugged him, or that he slept too soundly to hear Tia's mindtalking.

She stared out over the baggage-claim area as the escalator took her slowly down to ground level. A nondescript man dressed in a chauffeur's uniform held up a sign near the foot of the escalator. Tia read her name, nodded in his direction, and followed the man.

Anton and Luc's approval let her know she was doing okay so far, but their quiet presence in her mind didn't alleviate the butterflies that suddenly took flight. The claims area was practically empty so late at night, but Anton and Keisha managed to remain inconspicuous though still close as Tia followed the silent driver out the door toward the curb where a black Lexus waited, parked with the motor running just behind a crosswalk.

The man stopped and turned toward Tia, though it was impossible to see his eyes through his dark glasses. "Wait."

Tia nodded and stopped in her tracks while the driver walked around the back of the car and climbed into the driver's seat. The windows were tinted too heavily for her to see if anyone else was in the car. She heard a click, as though a door lock released. Tia was peripherally aware of Anton and Keisha waiting near the car's front bumper, as though checking to see if the street was safe to cross.

Tia almost blew it when Keisha stumbled and dropped her purse, but Anton leaned over and picked it up as if nothing had happened. The two of them continued across the street.

Tia glanced back toward the car in time to see the passenger door slowly swing open. A large man climbed out of the car, acknowledged Tia with a slight nod, and then reached around to open the back door.

Hoping against hope that her father might be inside, Tia couldn't hide her disappointment when the door swung open to an empty backseat. Before she had time to react, the large man grabbed her handbag off her shoulder, shoved her into the car, slammed the door, and got back inside.

Tia fell to her knees on the floorboard and then slammed back against the leather seat when the car surged forward. She grabbed for a handhold, fought the overpowering instinct to shift, to become the wolf.

A hissing noise caught her attention. As the car skidded around a corner, Tia glanced up and realized a dark glass window separated the front and back seats.

Her hand rested on a tank of some sort. A valve at one end hissed ominously. An odorless cloud slowly filled the back compartment of the Lexus.

Luc, you were right, it's a trick. Some kind of gas. . . .

Tia! Standing just inside the double doors leading out of the airport, Luc caught Tia's thoughts, and then nothing. He put aside his fears, his anger that she should be caught in this horrible mess, and then slipped into the persona that had kept him alive so many years with Pack Dynamics. *Cheval? They've gassed her. I think she's unconscious. Did Stefan get the backup bug planted? The guy grabbed her purse. I imagine they'll toss it as soon as they get away.*

Yes. Under the front bumper, and the signal is loud and clear. Meet us in front. Keisha and I are bringing the car around. She's got the trace going. Stefan and Xandi have gone on ahead. The Lexus is on the airport access road; looks like they might be heading for the Dulles Toll Road. That's my guess.

The car appeared, and Luc reached for the back door before Cheval brought the vehicle to a complete stop. "Where are they now?"

"Just leaving the airport access road." Keisha held up a small handheld device with a screen so that Luc could see it. A tiny green blip led away from the airport.

While Luc watched, another blip pulled in behind the

first, and then a third. "There's AJ, Mik, and Tinker, right on schedule." Staring at the tiny dots moving slowly across the screen, Luc realized he was sending up a prayer for Tia's safety. Thank goodness they had planned for such a contingency! Luc had grown so accustomed to Tia's constant presence in his mind, he felt totally lost without her.

Right now, though, there wasn't a damned thing he could do but wait. He hated the fact that she'd agreed to Anton's plan, hated knowing she was in danger. He sat in the backseat, his mind open and waiting for Tia's voice. A few more minutes passed, dragging like hours, before Keisha showed Luc the screen once more.

"See this third blip? That's Xandi and Stefan coming in behind us. This one is Tia. They're on the Dulles Toll Road." She flashed her mate a quick look that spoke volumes and then turned back to Luc. "Don't worry, Luc. We'll get her back."

"Not too soon, though." Anton glanced back over his shoulder and winked at Luc. "Not until we can get the bastard that set this up."

"Agreed." But he didn't have to like it. Hell, Luc was trained for operations like this! He took a deep, calming breath and slowly let go of his resentment against Cheval. Ulrich's best chance for survival lay in the wizard's hands. So did Tia's. It was time to put all the alpha posturing aside and follow Anton Cheval's lead. Luc settled back in the seat and pulled his cap over his eyes. He'd lost track of time but knew it must be well after midnight. He caught snippets of mental conversation between AJ, Mik, and Tinker, knew they must be drawing close. Sensed that Anton and Keisha were talking with one another as well.

Luc put out another mental call for Tia. Nothing. His chest ached and he felt her distance like a physical blow. She had to be safe. He would accept nothing else. With that thought uppermost in his mind, Luc willed himself to rest.

One thing he'd learned over the years of service in Pack Dynamics was to conserve his strength. Worrying accomplished nothing. Of course, he'd never cared enough about anyone to worry the way he worried about Tia.

He'd barely fallen asleep when he realized Keisha was leaning over the seat, shaking his shoulder.

"Luc, wake up. They've switched cars. AJ, Mik, and Tinker are still on them, but we've lost the bug. Try to reach Tia. See if she's awake. Let us know when you finally make contact."

Tinker checked in. They were heading west on Highway 7. Luc tried again for Tia without luck.

Whatever they'd used to knock her out had definitely done its job. He couldn't contact her. Luc fretted, wondering if she was okay, if they might have given her too much gas, but he forced his mind away from any negatives. They wouldn't help bring Tia back.

Time seemed to crawl, but Tinker continued reporting back. They'd managed to stay within sight of the vehicle, an older Cadillac that was fairly easy to track.

Luc realized the car was slowing, pulling off whatever side road they'd been following. Taillights glowed dimly in the darkness ahead.

Anton's quiet voice popped into Luc's mind.

The car is just over that rise. AJ's got night goggles. He's watching a small barn. The Caddy is parked out back. No sign of anyone yet. They're still in the vehicle. Must be waiting on something or someone. Let's move closer. I want to see for myself. No more verbal speech. Luc, see if you can reach Mason.

Luc nodded. He sent out a searching thought for Ulrich as he quietly got out of the rental car. *Hey, boss . . . you there?*

Luc? Where are you?

Just over the hill from your hotel room. I thought you had better taste than this. It's a dump. We're moving into position so we can see the layout a little better. Tia's just outside, but she's been drugged. Don't try to contact her. We don't want her to react to voices she shouldn't be hearing before she's fully awake.

Gotcha. I thought I heard some activity. Can you see all sides of the building?

No. Not yet. Luc stretched out on his belly at the top of a small rise. The only light below came from the interior dome light in the car. Knowing Tia was so close, yet still in mortal danger, scared the crap out of him.

At least now the operation belonged to Luc. Anton had easily ceded control to Luc, acknowledging his experience in situations such as this. Luc filled in Ulrich as much as needed.

We're a bit southeast of you, just over a small rise. AJ, Mik, and Tinker, Cheval and his mate. Stefan and Alexandria should be moving into position as well on another rise across from us.

Where's Jake? You haven't mentioned him.

Long story. Later. Hold tight until I get back to you.

Like I've got a choice? Ulrich's mental grumble would have made Luc smile under better circumstances.

Luc quietly followed Anton and Keisha through the brush.

Another car pulled slowly into the yard and parked next to the one holding Tia. After a few moments a man got out, moving stiffly. Luc felt his nonexistent hackles rise. *AJ? Mik? Recognize this guy?*

The rescue in Florida? That's Secretary Milton Bosworth. He's a fucking cabinet member! I don't believe it.

Believe it, Mik. That's the same bastard we pulled out of the cave.

I don't get it—what's the connection? He's supposed to be one of the good guys. What the fuck is he doing in the middle of a kidnapping? Tinker's questions were the same ones Luc wanted answered as well.

Luc heard a quiet rustling and glanced to his right. Anton and Keisha were shedding their clothes. Naked, each one shifted and headed in opposite directions. Luc knew Stefan and Alexandria would do the same thing, until the barn was surrounded by wolves.

AJ's soft voice rumbled in Luc's ear. *Mik, Tinker, and I have shifted. We're going in as close as we can. We've got a couple hours before daylight, so we're practically invisible until then. I'll bring your weapons to you on our way down.*

Thanks, I'm moving in, too, but I'll stay on two legs, as planned. Luc heard another slight rustle in the thick undergrowth, recognized the wolf slinking quietly along the down side of the ridge.

AJ carried two knives in his mouth. He dropped them in front of Luc, then turned to rejoin Mik and Tinker. Luc nodded his thanks and then tucked the eight-inch blade into his boot, the six-inch knife into his waistband.

No way could he have brought these on a commercial flight.

Someone's coming.

Stefan's warning caught Luc by surprise. Now who the hell else was showing up?

Luc's question was answered when a large rental van pulled into the yard in front of the barn. He should have guessed they'd be planning to move their prisoners. Two men climbed out of the U-Haul. Luc recognized them as special operations forces, good men he'd worked with in the past. In fact, as he looked around, Luc realized every man there was part of special ops.

What the hell was going on? They had no idea he was able to shift, but they'd covered his back on more than one operation. Luc had trusted them with his life. What were they doing in the middle of something like this? Luc opened his mind, made sure everyone was listening. *Looks like the party's ready to rumble. Everyone in position? Ulrich? You listening?*

Goddamnit, yes, I'm listening. Stone, you keep my daughter safe, you hear me?

Yes, sir. Okay, report first. What've we got?

Stefan Aragat answered. *Two in the Caddy with Tia, the muscle and the driver, two just climbing out of the U-Haul. Bosworth is standing by his car, but I think his driver's still inside. I've checked around the barn and it appears Ulrich is alone, still secured. Xandi and I will take the two holding Tia.*

AJ checked in next. *Mik, Tinker, and I are on the two from the U-Haul. We're currently about two feet behind them. Clueless bastards.*

Don't get cocky. That's when you screw up. Every one of these guys is special ops, all highly trained soldiers.

Yes, sir.

Cheval, you and Xandi stay close to the target. I want him alive.

You got it. We're at the back of his vehicle now.

Gazing out over the dark parking area, Luc couldn't see a single wolf. Their dark coats blended with the shadows, their feral instincts kept them totally silent. However, all the humans except Tia were now out of their vehicles, standing while the older man spoke in an anxious whisper.

Moving cautiously, Luc made his way closer to the back of the van. He had no idea if more forces waited inside or not, but he slipped a heavy stick through the latch, thoroughly jamming it.

Luc? Luc, where are you?

Tia! Don't move. We're nearby, we've got the area surrounded. I want them to think you're still unconscious. Are you okay?

I'm fine, other than one hell of a headache. I love you.

I love you, too. Stay down. Whatever you do, don't shift.

Okay.

Luc strode into the clearing as if he belonged there. "Hello, sir. You're looking well."

"What the fuck?" The man Luc had rescued only days before jerked around and stared. "Arrest this man. He's the one I warned you about."

The two heavily armed special-forces soldiers turned their weapons on Luc. AJ, Tinker, and Mik burst out of the darkness and soundlessly took both soldiers to the ground. Tinker stood in front of the older man, teeth bared.

At the same time, wolves burst from the shadows on either side of Luc, overpowering both drivers and the man who had aided in Tia's capture. Well-trained operatives or not, none of them was willing to do battle with an angry wolf.

It was over in seconds. Luc grabbed plastic restraints out of his back pocket and immobilized all six men. Bosworth's face looked ashen in the darkness. He stared at the seven wolves milling about snarling and growling, his eyes wide, his mouth slack and hanging open.

"Watch them." Luc's terse order hung in the quiet darkness as he went to the Caddy and opened the back door. Tia tumbled into his arms, her clothing askew, her hair a tangled mess. He'd never seen her so beautiful.

Luc caught Tia in a tight embrace, buried his face in her sweet-smelling hair. His chest ached, his hands shook, and if he wasn't careful, he'd be crying like a baby.

"Damn, baby. You feel so good."

Tia clung to him. Her body trembled, her breath exploded in sharp gasps. Luc ran his hands over her arms, her sides, touched her everywhere to assure himself she was okay. When her breathing finally settled down, Luc kissed her once more and put his arm around her waist. "C'mon, sweetie. Let's get your dad."

Tia's smile was a bit watery but definitely triumphant. Her arm went around Luc's waist. Their hips bumped when they walked.

The barn door was heavily secured, but Luc slammed it once with his shoulder and the old wood splintered. Tia raced ahead of him as Luc flipped on a light switch. They found Ulrich chained to a cot near the far wall, inside what had once been a stable. He sat on the edge of the bed, smiling.

Tia threw her arms around him and sobbed. Ulrich hugged her back as well as his restraints would allow.

"Hush, sweetie. I'm okay. Or I will be, once you find a key for this setup." He looked over Tia's shoulder and grinned at Luc. "Looks like I trained you well, son. I'd get up, but they've not given me much room to maneuver."

Luc turned and marched back outside. None of the prisoners had moved. Guarded by a phalanx of angry Chanku, there wasn't much they could do beyond holding very still. Luc held out his hand. "Mr. Secretary? The key, please."

The men with Bosworth kept their attention glued to the wolf pack surrounding them. Bosworth glared at Luc. "You'll hang for this. It's treason, you and your damned wolves. They're shapeshifters, aren't they? Not animal, not human. I've heard about them. Heard about you. You'll pay for this."

Luc squatted down in front of the older man. "Shape-shifters? Like werewolves? What kind of drivel is that? There's no such thing, Mr. Secretary. These are highly trained, intelligent animals in the service of our country. As far as treason . . . it wasn't treason when we pulled your ass out of that setup in Florida. At least, not our treason. You, on the other hand, are questionable. You were no more the prisoner of al Qaeda terrorists then than you are now. The key."

Luc's hand remained perfectly still. Secretary Bosworth continued staring at him for a moment longer and then nodded to his left. "My back pocket. On the right."

Luc fished out the key and left the wolves in charge as he went back into the barn to free Ulrich. He heard voices outside but nothing that caused any alarm.

Once the collar was off Ulrich, Luc released the other restraints. Tia found his clothes in another stall, shook them out, and gave them to her father. Luc took Tia's arm and guided her back outside.

"Anything you want to say to these guys before we leave?"

Tia stepped forward, ignoring the cabinet member, and spoke to the soldiers. "Why? My father has worked for this government for years. Why would you kidnap him, kidnap me? What have we done to deserve this?"

One of the men looked at the cabinet member. Bosworth wouldn't meet his eye. Instead, Bosworth turned his head away. That seemed to answer whatever doubts the soldier had. "Ma'am, Secretary Bosworth told us you were all part of a secret government force that had gone rogue. He said you'd started working against the government. We believed him and he's our superior. You were our first target, but we settled for your father when our attempts on you were unsuccessful."

Tinker's mental voice intruded. *I recognize the scent of the guy on the ground next to him, sweetie. He's the one who was nosing around your apartment.*

Ulrich Mason chose that moment to walk out of the barn. "Settled for me, eh?" He shook his head and then came to a halt in front of Secretary Bosworth. "Milton, you damned fool. I've told you there is no such thing as a shapeshifter. Is that what this was all about? You scared the hell out of my daughter, took me away from important work, and dragged along these good men on your stupid quest because you think I'm a goddamned werewolf? Do I look like a werewolf? Do you know how stupid this makes you look?" He gestured behind him, pointing at the wolves sitting silently at guard. "They're wolves, Milton. Vicious yet well-trained wolves. Not humans who turn into wolves. You're nuttier than a fruitcake, Milt. You've got no business in a position with as much power as our President sees fit to give you. Idiot." With a look of utter disgust, Ulrich turned away from the Secretary and went to stand next to Tia.

The soldier who'd been talking dipped his head, almost touching his chin to his chest, and then looked back at Tia. "I will apologize for all of us. We were beginning to have doubts about the entire operation, but Secretary Bosworth has the power to command our unit. We're trained to follow orders." He glared at the older man for a moment. Once more, Bosworth turned away. "We won't follow any more from him, that's for sure, and I'll make certain the right people know what he's done here."

Luc pulled the knife out of his waistband, leaned over, and cut the restraints on the soldier's wrists. "We've served together in the past, and you've always been honorable. A good soldier. My group is classified, so we can't bring anyone in on this. We'll make sure our contact in D.C. knows what's happened here, but I'm putting you in charge of getting this bastard away from me before I lose my cool."

Luc handed over the knife, grinned at Ulrich, and then took Tia's hand in his and whistled. Like a pack of well-trained dogs, seven large wolves trotted after him into the darkness. Looking back from the top of the ridge, Luc paused to glance back. The light spilling from the open barn door highlighted the soldiers standing in a small group, while their leader hauled a sputtering Secretary Milton Bosworth to his feet.

When Luc turned around, seven humans were pulling on clothing where once wolves had stood. He glanced at Tia and then caught Ulrich's eye. Biting back laughter, they headed for their vehicles and drove back to the small airport where Anton's jet waited. Right now, Montana sounded every bit as inviting as home.

Chapter 18

Tia and Luc sat across the aisle from Ulrich on the flight back. Clinging tightly to Luc's arm as if she'd never turn him loose, Tia fell asleep before the plane left the runway.

Xandi and Keisha slept as well, curled up in the very back of the aircraft. Stefan and Anton, AJ and Mik sat near the front by Ulrich and Luc, all of them admittedly too wound up to relax.

Luc checked once more to make certain Tia slept soundly and then turned to her father, speaking softly. "It doesn't make sense. Why the elaborate ruse in Florida? Why take you if Tia was the target, and why the hell did Bosworth want Tia?"

Mason rubbed his eyes. "The only thing I can figure is the Florida deal was a setup to prove we existed. Bosworth got wind of Pack Dynamics through one of the scientists who helped develop the supplement, but he wanted proof. Ergo, he needed to see one of us shift."

Anton interrupted. "I've heard you mention a supplement. The nutrients?"

Mason nodded. "Yeah. Condensed into capsule form so we can take them daily, though I've gone for as long as a couple months off them without affecting my Chanku abilities. I imagine once the physiology changes from human to Chanku with the first few doses, it's going to stay changed. I've just never been willing to push the envelope."

"I'd like to get them for our group. Would that be possible?"

Laughing, Mason shook his head. "After all you've done, Cheval, you need to ask?"

Anton shrugged. "It never hurts. Thank you. We've got so much to learn about Chanku. Sharing information will help all of us, but I'll admit I'm concerned about your scientist speaking openly of our existence."

"It was purely accidental. The doctor warned me he'd talked to Bosworth—thought he was our contact. I made the mistake of discounting the risk. Bosworth's such an idiot, I never dreamed he'd be a threat."

Mason glanced back at Luc. "Turns out Bosworth had the entire cavern monitored, assuming you'd shift during the rescue, but you went in as wolf and human teams and stayed in character. Still, he was convinced there might be something to the werewolf theory."

"We are not werewolves." Anton's voice, with its usual haughty timbre, had Tinker and Luc grinning ear to ear.

"Semantics, Cheval." Mason smiled as well, but only for a moment. "I have no idea why they took me, or why Bosworth wanted Tia. We need to understand his motive before we can figure out a solution."

Anton sighed. "I can answer that. Bosworth envisions a breeding farm where he will create a cadre of werewolves. The idiot doesn't know the difference between mythical creatures and shape-shifting Chanku."

"What?" Luc glanced at Tia to make sure she still slept. "A breeding farm? That's not good. How do you know?"

"His thoughts are an open book to me. A disgusting manuscript, but quite simple to decipher. An attempt to grab Tia was actually made while she was still in Boston, but it failed. Once she arrived in San Francisco, Tinker made an excellent bodyguard. Mason was a target of opportunity. Bosworth figured, quite rightly, that Tia would do anything to save her father. He appears to know that the genetic code for Chanku is carried by the female."

"Could Tia's friend Shannon Murphy be in danger?" Luc turned to Mason, but once again Anton answered.

"If she is Chanku, yes. Bosworth is a powerful man, despite his stupidity. She should be protected."

Mason shook his head. "We merely suspect Shannon might be Chanku, but damnit, I hate to risk her safety. AJ? Can you reach Jake, have him fly to Boston immediately and keep an eye on the young lady? Her phone number and address are in the Rolodex on my desk."

"Will do." AJ stood and headed for the cockpit.

Luc grinned. "Boss, that's the perfect solution for Jake right now. I've been worried about him. Thanks."

"Tinker explained what happened. Personally, I'd like Jacob Trent as far from my daughter as we can get him. Boston sounds like an excellent destination. Something needs to be done about Bosworth, however."

Mason tapped his fingers on the armrest for a moment and then muttered, more to himself than the men around him, "Looks like I'm flying back to D.C."

Cheval turned and caught Luc's eye. *Be sure to let us know if your alpha needs assistance.*

Luc nodded and squeezed Tia's hand. She slept on, peacefully, safely, beside him.

Exhausted, the members of the Montana pack headed to their quarters as soon as they reached home. Though it was still early afternoon, AJ and Mik took one of the guest rooms. Obviously exhausted by his ordeal, Mason headed for another.

Tia paused in the kitchen to make a brief phone call and then quietly set down the phone. "Okay, Luc. I've called Shannon and told her Jake's on his way, that she might be in danger. I didn't mention Chanku, merely the fact it's tied to my father's work and her connection through me." Tia shook her head, obviously worried. "I sure hope it wasn't a mistake to send Jake."

"I think it's the best thing for Jake right now. He needs a project to take his mind off you."

Tia looked up and laughed.

Damn. Luc wondered if he'd ever hear that sound enough.

"Well, Shannon is definitely a project. She might be more than Jake can handle."

"Then it's definitely an excellent plan." Luc grabbed Tia's hand and then looked across the room and caught Tinker's eye. "Are you coming?"

Tinker set down his bags and frowned. "With you?"

It was impossible to ignore the hopeful, almost wistful sound in his voice.

Tia held out her hand. "Yeah. With us. It's a big bed."

Smiling self-consciously, Tinker followed them into the third guest room.

Tia headed straight for the shower. Luc grabbed a couple of cold beers from a small refrigerator in the room and handed one to Tinker. The two men walked outside to the shaded deck.

Luc stared off toward the dense forest, now bathed in sunlight, sipping at his beer, his mind still buzzing with all the activities of the past week. The sound of the shower in the background, the knowledge his mate was just on the other side of the room, filled him with a sense of satisfaction he'd never imagined.

Luc turned to his friend, his packmate, and held out his hand. Tinker grasped Luc's wrist in the manner of brothers. Luc held tightly to Tinker's. "I owe you, big guy. Anton said there was more than one attempt on Tia while I was gone. You never left her side, and you kept her safe."

Tinker looked away. His chest rose and fell, but he didn't release his hold on Luc. "You know I love her, don't you?

She's your mate, and I would never do anything to hurt either one of you, but I will always love your woman."

Luc nodded. He'd suspected as much. Trust, though, was an amazing thing. As was the love of the pack. "Tia loves you, too. Don't ever doubt that, but she chose to mate with me. That doesn't mean you won't always be welcome in our lives, in our bed."

Tinker slowly turned to stare at Luc. "Are you sure? Does Tia want me as well? I thought that one time . . ."

Luc shook his head. "I'm learning a lot from our hosts. A lot about love, about the power of the pack, the strength inherent in our ties to one another, sexual and otherwise. We're not meant to be alone, Tink. Look at Anton Cheval. The man seems all-powerful, almost impossibly contained, but until he met Keisha, Anton Cheval shared Xandi and Stefan's bed. He didn't want to be alone."

"Well, neither of you are sharing my bed until you're clean." Tia stood in the doorway, her hair flowing about her shoulders in damp, silky waves, and a bright yellow towel wrapped around her torso. She reached up and touched her hair. "Keisha told me it's the shifting that does this, takes the kink out of hair. Amazing, isn't it?" She took Tinker's beer out of his hand and shooed him toward the shower.

The big man left with a bemused expression on his face. Tia grabbed his chair and sat, took a sip of Tinker's beer, and turned her beautiful eyes toward Luc. "I know Bosworth is still out there, still a threat, but I want you to know I've never felt happier or more complete in my entire life. I love you."

Luc could only smile at her. There were no words to express his feelings, no containing the emotions that threatened to boil over and turn him into a complete idiot. *I can't even express how much, how . . .* He blinked, shook his head, and grabbed Tia's hand. Her love humbled him.

Made him vulnerable in a way he'd never experienced in his life.

Made him strong. "I love you, too. So much it scares me."

She rolled his callused fingers in hers and kissed his knuckles. "Go take a shower. I want to make love with you. With both of you."

Tia waited in the bed, anticipation growing by the second. She caught back a giggle when it suddenly dawned on her that she had her first classes to teach in a couple of days. Thank goodness the classroom and lesson plans were ready. She certainly didn't feel much like an elementary school teacher, not in this particular pose.

Tia had placed herself smack dab in the middle of the big bed, as if either Tinker or Luc needed a hint. Tired as she felt, way too much adrenaline still coursed through her system to allow her to fall asleep.

Her body tingled with awareness; her head absolutely buzzed with all that had happened over the past two weeks. The shower hadn't relaxed her a bit. So far as Tia was concerned, it merely made her body more sensitive, her needs more pronounced.

Absentmindedly, Tia ran her hands along her sides and felt her skin tingle. Even the silky sheets left her feeling sexy and aroused.

Tinker walked into the room, dark and glistening in the afternoon light. His eyes glowed with feral intensity, his attention focused entirely on Tia.

Lord, but the man was beautiful, his silky skin an all-over dark chocolate, his thick cock standing straight and strong, the taut, blood-filled head darker than the rest of him. A tiny white bead of fluid decorated the tip.

Tia's mouth watered; her nipples puckered in anticipation. Tinker stopped beside the bed and stared at her. Tia had a feeling he was cataloging all the things he'd like to do, the parts of her body he wanted to touch. Tia tested his thoughts, found Tinker's mind so filled with sexual fantasies beyond her own active imagination, she blushed.

I told you not to go looking in my head without permission, little girl.

Self defense. Tia grinned and palmed her right breast. The nipple puckered beneath her hand, and she felt an immediate connection between her legs. *A girl likes to know what's coming next.*

Tinker glanced over his shoulder, grinning broadly as Luc wandered out of the bathroom, toweling his dark hair trimmed short. *She wants to know what we've got planned. You wanna tell her, or should I?*

How about we just show her?

Luc slipped into the bed on her left, Tinker on the right. Tia sighed. That night in the Sierras seemed years behind her, the incidents in between like something out of a prolonged dream.

Not so many days ago she'd been flying into San Francisco, wondering what her future would bring. The most excitement in her life consisted of sexual dreams and fantasies revolving around a beautiful black wolf with a long, pink tongue. Now she lay between her bonded mate and their lover, and all of them had the ability to turn into wolves.

Sometimes reality put fantasies all to shame. Biting her lips to stop the giggles that threatened, Tia glanced first at Luc and then at Tinker.

Luc made the first move, running his hand slowly along her left thigh. Tinker followed suit, leaning over to gently suck her right nipple into his mouth.

Not to be outdone, Luc found her left breast and pressed the nipple lightly between his tongue and the roof of his mouth. He feathered the very tip, teasing, tickling.

Barriers down, thoughts open, each man kept the pressure light and teasing. Tia groaned and arched her back. Her body quivered, wanting, needing more.

Luc released her nipple and blew cool air over the tip. Tinker did the same and then licked the puckered flesh, nipped it lightly between his teeth and blew against it again.

Tia moaned. Shivers raced the length of her torso as two hands softly brushed at her inner thighs and then moved onward. Luc's fingers teased the entrance to her pussy, tugged lightly at her labia and circled her sensitive clit without touching the center, while Tinker's broad fingertip traced a line over the top of her thigh, around to her buttock. He brushed her tightly puckered anus, pressing lightly, retreating.

Setting her on fire. Tia arched her back and groaned. She twisted her hips, but the men kept their touches much too light, barely feathering her needy flesh. "Damnit," she said, laughing between whimpers, "don't tease me. I can't stand it! Fuck me, damnit!"

Tinker sat back, both hands on his broad thighs, his erect cock bobbing upright. "Bossy, isn't she?"

Luc shook his head, grinning. "You're not kidding. Hang on to her, would you, Tink? And find something to shut her up?"

"I've got just the thing." Tinker threw a leg over Tia and grabbed her wrists in one big fist. With the other hand he dragged his swollen cock across her closed lips. Tia tasted the salty pre-cum that coated the broad crown. The temptation was too great. She opened her mouth.

Tinker slowly fed her his cock, careful not to choke her. Tia opened wide, taking him as deep inside her mouth as she could without swallowing. Her tongue traced the ridge around the smooth crown, found the tiny slit at the end and licked that as well.

Tinker sighed. "Damn. That was easy. A man just needs to take control."

Tia bit down, not lightly.

Tinker's eyes went as wide as his grin. "Okay. I got your message."

Chuckling softly, Luc knelt between Tia's knees and spread her legs wide. At the first brush of his tongue against her clit, she whimpered, sucking harder on Tinker. Trapped by Tink's strong thighs and the iron grip of his hands, her mouth stuffed full of more cock than she'd ever tasted, Tia couldn't move to escape Luc's thorough assault on her pussy.

He sucked her labia between his lips, licked and nipped at her inner thighs, teased her needy clit, the pressure so light and teasing, Tia writhed and twisted and took her frustration out on Tinker's willing body.

Sucking hard, her cheeks hollowing with the pressure, using her tongue and lips and teeth, Tia poured everything she had into Tinker's pleasure . . . and he poured his thoughts into Tia.

She felt her lips tightening around his cock as if the engorged penis in her mouth was her own. Raked her teeth across the velvety crown and groaned with the combination of pleasure and pain. Tongued the tiny slit at the end and jerked with the electrical shock coursing through *her* body.

Tia's pussy clenched, not so much from Luc's thorough suckling and licking but from her sharing of Tinker's impending orgasm. Tia felt him stiffen, sensed his plan to pull free, and tightened her mouth around his pulsing cock, sucking even harder.

Tinker's hips thrust forward, his grip on her hands loosening as he supported his weight over her face. Tia snaked her hands under Tinker's thighs to capture his testicles at the point of climax, tenderly kneading and massaging them until the big man cried out and jerked his hips once more.

Tia tasted him, his hot, salty ejaculate filling her mouth

as she continued massaging him with her hands and working him with her lips and tongue. Moaning, legs quivering, still sharing every bit of his pleasure, Tinker gently pulled away from Tia and rolled to one side.

He lay still for a moment, his chest heaving, and then turned and grinned at Tia. "Damn. You win."

Luc raised up from between her thighs. "Not yet, she doesn't." Then, without any warning, Luc shifted.

The fantasy that had bedeviled her for years, the image she'd both welcomed and feared, the one that had left her shivering with need and aroused beyond measure, materialized between her trembling thighs.

Amber eyes alight with humor and love, the black wolf, her mate for life, wrapped his long pink tongue around his muzzle, lay back down, and began to feast on Tia's swollen cunt.

Tinker held her hands, kneeling behind her head while Luc ran his long, pink tongue across her belly, along the crease between her thigh and groin.

Whimpering, Tia jerked with each pass of Luc's rough tongue over her flesh and then cried out when he licked and swirled deep inside her pussy, finding her distended clitoris on the outward sweep. Lapping, licking, nibbling with sharp lupine teeth, he took her to the edge and back, over and over again.

Writhing beneath a sensual assault beyond anything she'd ever imagined, Tia let the fantasy fly. Luc's thoughts flowed into her mind in sharp relief, tender and loving, sharing her flavors, her textures and tastes as his Chanku body experienced each one.

Higher, her mind and spirit flying, her body aroused beyond comprehension, Tia hung on to Tinker's strong hands, his gentle but firm grasp anchoring her to reality. She hardly knew when Luc shifted once more and entered her, his human cock hard and powerful, filling her, taking her beyond orgasm, beyond the mere physical experience of two people making love.

Tinker's big hands still held her, Luc's body loved her, the minds of both men melded with Tia's as she arched her back, cried out, felt the hot rush of Luc's release joining with her own.

Body tingling, legs quivering, pussy clenching and squeezing Luc's softening cock, Tia freed her hands from Tinker's gentle grasp. She reached for Luc when he lowered himself onto her chest and held him close when he tried to roll to one side.

Tinker lay down beside them both, his broad palm brushing back the tangled hair from Tia's face, his eyes almost closed in sleep. Luc nuzzled her neck. Then he nipped at the same spot beneath her left ear, the place where his mark was finally beginning to fade.

She felt his lips there, felt the sharp nip of his teeth, the hot suction from his lips, and smiled. *There's no need for you to mark me, you know? I'm yours. I have been, since the beginning.*

Luc rubbed his beard-roughened chin against her throat and licked the spot he'd just bitten. *Humor me, okay? I'm insecure. Get used to it.*

You can say that, with Tinker sharing our bed?

Tinker chose that moment to roll over on his back, snoring. Luc slipped off Tia to lie close to her other side. He leaned over and kissed her full on the mouth. *Good point. Get some sleep. Tonight we run with the wolves.*

Epilogue

Wearing his favorite red velour bathrobe and comfortable slippers, Secretary of Homeland Security Milton Bosworth stepped out the front door before dawn and reached for the morning paper.

He certainly didn't expect to see Ulrich Mason on his front porch.

Bare-ass and buck naked.

Bosworth jerked to a halt, staring stupidly at the man he'd kept chained in a barn for days. For some reason the only thought that came to mind was the fact that he'd let Mason keep his skivvies on.

All those cameras, and not once had the man shifted.

Now, not a camera in sight, Ulrich Mason suddenly faded before Bosworth's eyes, sort of melted in on himself, dropped his front feet to the ground, and growled.

Bosworth blinked. This was no ordinary wolf. No, this wolf was huge, its ivory-colored teeth shaped like sabers, the eyes feral yet imbued with the intelligence of a human killer.

It leaped, front paws reaching, teeth glimmering in the morning light, all fangs and mouth and strange, intelligent amber eyes.

Bosworth wasn't sure if the wolf bit him or not. In the

scheme of things, he guessed it really didn't matter. There was an amazing pain in his head, a sense of numbness, of unreality. His only thought before the pale morning disappeared was that the doctor had gotten it dead wrong.

It wasn't his heart at all, he thought. No, it was a fucking blood vessel in his brain waiting to kill him.

Ulrich Mason leaned back in his metal chair in front of the small café, sipped his coffee, and watched the crowds pass by along the sidewalk. His back hurt, and he'd pulled something in his left thigh, but still, it had been a good feeling, getting back in the field again.

Especially this job, since it well might be his last. Sometimes he missed the excitement of D.C., the secrets, the power, the rush of skirting the edge, but lately he'd been thinking of retirement more often than not. Luc was ready to take over. Under his leadership, Pack Dynamics would continue to thrive, doing the jobs no one wanted, saving some lives, ending others.

Mason glanced at the paper on the small table in front of him. It seemed fitting that Bosworth's death didn't rate so much as a half column above the fold, but it was obvious he'd been losing his hold on power in this politically incestuous community.

Bosworth's personal vendetta against Ulrich Mason, the absurd plans for a werewolf army, had been the final straw. Too bad about the stroke. Of course, his health had been failing for quite some time.

Mason folded the paper, stood up, stretched. He had a plane to catch, a new son-in-law to harass, a daughter to hug.

Maybe, before he grew too old to enjoy them, grandchildren.

Damn, if only Camille had lived to enjoy this. She would have been so proud of Tianna, of the wonderful young woman she'd become . . . but then again, Camille's death had been the catalyst, the beginning of so very much that was good.

As well as so much pain. . . . Ah, but Camille had always insisted on doing things her own way. Mason couldn't help but wonder if the risks were worth it.

Glancing up at the lazy white clouds overhead, Mason sent a thought winging skyward. *It's all good, Camille. In fact, sweetheart, it's almost fucking perfect.*

Take a sneak peek at PURE SEX, starring three hot new authors of contemporary erotica: Lucinda Betts, Bonnie Edwards, and Sasha White. Available in July 2006 from Aphrodisia . . .

Alone below, Teri took in how sumptuous the boat was. The Web site hadn't done it justice. Pleased, she noted an extra-long cream-colored leather sofa along one side. A couple of armchairs completed the furnishings while a plasma screen television was set on the wall. Light wood cabinets kept the cooking area from being dark. She marveled at the ingenious use of space and opened every cupboard she saw.

The bathroom off the master cabin was small but well appointed with a shower set in a tiny tub. She opened the medicine chest over the sink to check out what it was that Jared had put away. A variety pack of condoms: glow in the dark, flavored and ribbed for her pleasure.

Extra large.

She snorted. Philip should be so lucky.

Back in the master cabin she checked out the drawer in the night table. The DVDs Jared had put away were X-rated. She popped one into the player, propped herself on the bed and skipped through the beginning to find couples enjoying strong, healthy, powerful sex. Great sex. Friendly sex. Even affectionate sex.

Philip's pious expression when he'd explained the concept of revirginizing swam in front of her mind's screen. He wanted them to remember their wedding night as special, he'd said. She'd been amazingly agreeable. It had been so easy to give up sleeping with him; she should have seen the signs of a dying relationship.

But by then the wedding had taken on a life of its own, a juggernaut, there was no stopping it. His mother, her mother, the caterer, the church, the dress!

None of the energetic sex she saw on the portable bedroom television had ever happened with Philip. She sighed, wandered out to the little kitchen, retrieved the champagne from the fridge, opened it and poured herself a tumbler full. She considered digging out the flutes Jared had put away but the tumbler held more. And Teri wanted lots.

When she settled back onto the bed a couple onscreen was enjoying a fabulously decadent soixante-neuf. The actor's tongue work looked enthusiastic. The actress looked happy.

Teri watched closely, amused at first. The moaning and sex talk were obviously dubbed in afterward. No one really said things like that, no one felt things as strongly as the actors pretended.

She changed positions on the bed, lying on her belly with her head at the foot so she could see the action up close. And up close was what she got.

The camera closed in on his tongue so Teri could see the moisture, the red, full clit he was licking and sucking gently between his lips.

Her own body reacted to the visual stimulus and moistened as the actress widened her legs and the actor slid his tongue deep into her. She thrashed on the bed in a stunning display of sexual hysteria that had never, ever overcome her.

Teri was jealous. Did people react this strongly to oral sex? She never had. But, then, Philip was so fastidious she doubted he'd ever been as deeply involved as the actor was. Even an actor who was being paid to fake it was more turned on that Philip had been the few times she'd insisted.

Teri knew what she wanted, knew what she liked, knew what would get her off like a rocket, but Philip had issues.

She'd always hoped he'd warm up more. Get hotter, get horny. For her. But he hadn't. Wouldn't. Not ever.

The onscreen couple switched positions and the actress performed fellatio until the man bucked and howled with his orgasm. The couple tumbled onto the sofa, sated.

Teri clicked off the TV, took another long drink, and rolled onto her back. Her legs slid open and she felt herself, moist and heavy with need.

The bedroom door was open and from here she could see through the living area and up the stairs to one small rectangular patch of sky. She wondered what would happen if Jared were to peer down the hatch and see her here with her legs splayed and her hand on her wet slit.

Would the pirate on the deck come down to the master cabin and grab her ankles like the actor had? She closed her eyes and let her fantasy play out. It was better than any porn flick because she could control every movement, every word, and all of her responses. She could tell Jared what to do and he'd do it.

She could tell him to lick her breasts and lift her hips to bring her closer to his mouth. He could trail his scratchy chin delicately along her inner thigh until he got close enough that she could feel his hot breath on her hotter pussy. She slid her other hand to a nipple and plucked it while she opened to her questing fingertip.

She would tell him to linger there, just far enough away from her that he'd be able to see her wet lips, smell her aroused flesh, feel her need. Sliding a fingertip into herself, familiar tension built while she worked to bring herself to orgasm. He would kiss her there where she was hottest, moist and achy. He'd do whatever she told him to and like it.

She wasn't wired for abstinence, hadn't wanted to go along with Philip's crazy idea, but—oh, yes, it was building to a peak now and soon she'd be over the—on a weak sigh, her orgasm pulsed through her lower body in a poor imitation of what she'd witnessed onscreen.

She opened her eyes on the wish that Jared had seen her, that he was right now on his way to ravish her like the pirate he was. But no, he'd been a gentleman and left her to herself.

Her unsatisfied self.

She'd taken the edge off, but it had been far too long since she'd had a truly good orgasm. And she deserved one. Or three.

Or a week full of them. She smiled and rose to wash her hands. In the mirror, she faced herself.

Philip was gone. She was here. Jared was here.

And Jared was hot, hot, hot.

She decided to unpack her lingerie after all.

Her carry-on bag sat on the floor beside the bed, tagged and zipped and bulging. A couple of sharp points threatened to poke holes through the sides, but still, she couldn't bring herself to open it.

She took another drink of champagne instead.

The bag was full of shoes. Stilettos, each and every pair. Toes pointed enough to cripple, Philip always wanted her to wear them. If he'd wanted a tall, lanky, long-limbed wife why had he asked her out in the first place? She would never have that look, no matter how high her heels were. She was lean, yes, but her muscle tone was obvious.

Some men liked her athletic build. The pirate above deck for one, she realized as she poured and drank another tumbler of champagne. She sat on the edge of the bed, one toe on the floor for balance, the other heel tucked into her crotch. She bent over toward the night table to grab the bottle again, but nearly fell off the bed.

She was tipsy. Well and truly feeling no pain. She giggled.

Oh, hell, who cared? There was no one here to judge her. No one to tell her she'd had too much and had to mind herself.

No one to tell her to keep her hands to herself and off Jared MacKay.

"Step away from the pirate," she intoned in a dramatic imitation of Philip's most commanding tone. Then she laughed harder.

Philip had no say in anything she did anymore. He'd given up the right to chastise her, instruct her, or humiliate her when he'd dashed out of the church this morning.

She stood, still laughing, curiously aware of an incredible sense of freedom. She set aside her carry-on bag. She'd open it later. Right now she wanted her bathing suit and sarong.

There was a sunset waiting for her.

A sunset and a pirate who needed taming.